ABOUT TH

Julian Ruck was born in Swansea, South Wales. He trained as a lawyer in London before spending some time in both Denmark and Israel. On his return, he entered the world of Academia, lecturing law. He is now retired and writes full time.

Also by the same author:

Ragged Cliffs

". . . an incredible twist in this gripping read."
— *Western Mail*

Inheritance Lost

Julian Ruck

Isis Publishing
(Wales)

Published in 2008 by
Isis Publishing
isispublishing@yahoo.co.uk

Distributors:
Welsh Books Council, Glanyrafon Enterprise Park
Aberystwyth, Ceredigion, SY23 3AQ
Telephone: (01970) 624455
www.gwales.com

The author would like to stress that
this is a work of fiction and no resemblance
to any actual individual or institution
is intended or implied.

A catalogue record for this book
is available from The British Library.

ISBN: 978-0-9552658-1-5

Cover illustration: Jeff Kirkhouse

Printed in Wales by Dinefwr Press
Rawlings Road, Llandybie, Carmarthenshire, SA18 3YD

For my father,
who instilled in me a love and passion
for books and literature.

INTRODUCTION

May 1982

Falkland Islands, South Atlantic

Two hundred metres from the landing point the engines of the two Geminis were cut and the propeller shafts lifted. This was done to prevent any entanglement of the propeller with the steaming slicks of green kelp that stuck to the shore and oozed onto the shingle in order to confound any hostile footsteps. The engines were also cut in order to keep noise to a minimum. After this point, oars alone were relied on for propulsion. This was the most dangerous position for the men to be in; they were exposed and vulnerable.

One of the Geminis drifted into the stand-off position to cover the other going in to deposit the men. This would act as a firm fire base should any trouble arise.

The four man team beached without incident.

A Gemini engine started up.

"The bloody fool! Get down!" Treharne ordered. The team dissolved into the shingle and carried on cursing where Treharne had left off. The cox would be dealt with later; he could have blown the whole mission. Anger soon waned however as the fading Gemini engine reminded the team that they were now alone. Isolated.

As they prepared to set off an inconsiderate moon decided to make an unannounced appearance. This was not supposed to happen. Another balls-up. The military was full of them. Treharne stuck two fingers up at the white face that sneered its treachery and allegiance to the enemy within.

When they were one hour away from the target they stopped. Weapons and kit were checked. With Treharne leading, the team set off again. They were confident, strong. They were about to reach their target when the ground erupted as an explosion ripped and tore into the team, bringing the secret mission to an abrupt end.

Captain Kristian Treharne, Special Boat Service, formerly of 42nd Commando Royal Marines, flew through the cold night air unaware of the firework display that had sent him on his wingless flight. The bloody debris of an arrogant Argentinian anti-personnel mine had neutralized the puny efforts of the four-man team to wreak havoc upon its sovereign territory.

PART I

March 1983

CHAPTER 1

Richmond, Surrey

Treharne's eyes struggled to open. He wanted to run away from the ache. He didn't want to look at it. His fingers reached down and prodded at bed sheets soaked with perspiration. His eyelids pushed upwards and for a few moments he examined the darkness as he tried to adjust. He was alive after all. He prodded again just to make sure and confirmed for the millionth time that below his left knee there was no leg or foot. Both items had been thrown around the Falklands by an enemy conscripted to fight face to face. He remembered again, for the millionth time.

He sat up and reached for a crutch at the side of the bed. To hell with the prosthesis, where was he going at 3.30 in the morning? One year, his mind moaned, give or take a month or two, of phantom pain and artificial limb – nothing beat the real thing, not even Wood's 100% rum and Coca Cola. He stretched, threw the crutch and cursed. Another sound of broken glass. He cursed again; he should be used to the sound by now. He hopped through to his sitting room, sat down and lit a cigarette – at least there was no chance of his left leg being amputated from smoking too much! Mind you there was still a bit of it left, who knows? He had learnt all about unpredictability – the hard way!

Captain Kristian Treharne (also known as 'Guts', both for his courage and his capacity to swallow bottles of rum and remain upright when all those around him lost their heads and disintegrated) was a thirty-six-year-old adopted Welshman, although his grandmother had been Welsh and his mother half Welsh, so there was plenty of genuine Celtic fury and passion in his blood. In spite of the other three-quarters of his blood being Danish he had never considered himself anything other than Welsh. He had no recollection of his country of birth, Denmark, neither did he desire any. His mother had left Denmark and brought him to Swansea, South Wales when he had only been two years old and this is where he had grown up. His Danish father was still an unknown quantity and he wanted to keep it that way. Besides who could ever replace William Treharne in his heart, his mother's late husband and his adopted father?

Treharne had fought his way through prep and public school. The fighting had continued into adulthood and had become a way of life. He survived. He had never been a bully; indeed in his younger days he could often be seen using his fists to protect the weak. He believed with unwavering conviction that the strong should always protect the weak. Oxford had given him a degree in philosophy and a love of literature. In war he was the consummate soldier, a missile with a mind and compassion, a worthy adversary who broke all the rules but still got there in the end – his last mission notwithstanding. In peacetime he was an outspoken nuisance who refused to comply and who caused many a sleepless night for his exasperated superiors. He was an intellectual warrior, the best of all warriors in time of war but utterly dysfunctional in times of peace. Treharne wore his personality with ease and damned all those who didn't like it. He was an individual, his own man.

Removing the cigarette from his mouth he reached down for the stump. It was so damned irresistible. His foot itched or at least the air around it did. One year on and he was still trying to come to terms with his one-legged condition. Hell, he had only gone to the shop to buy a pair of shoes and look what had happened! Now he was scared stiff of going to the barbers for a haircut! He smiled at the darkness. Even death and mutilation had its funny side and thank God he hadn't lost his sense of humour.

He stood up and hovered. The gaping air below his left knee wobbled and laughed. He was a tall man, 6ft 2in and slim.

Excess weight, particularly now, would have caused him further inconvenience. He switched on a table lamp and retrieved the wooden object that never stopped reminding him of his disability. 4 a.m. Nothing to do. During the past year he had read his brain into a coma. He had revisited all the classics and now as far as he was concerned Thackeray, Proust, Jane Austen and Dickens could all go to hell in a handcart.

He looked in a mirror. Bright, uncompromising blue eyes stared back. At least his moustache had not been blown off, neither had his hair; in fact he had let it grow way beyond the military standard issue and grey hadn't yet intruded to fade the yellow glow of his Nordic past. His mother's Viking blood ran through him, fierce and bold.

He had inherited his mother's striking looks but not her reserve. War and terror had brought him into the world. His mother had been raped by her own countrymen and Kristian had been the result. Father unknown. War was in his blood. The malicious and criminal violation of another human being was not.

Trcharne was a handsome man whose deep voice still caused knees to buckle and vocal chords to simmer. It was often said by the female of the species that his voice alone could give multiple orgasms, with or without the foreplay. He looked in the mirror long enough to confirm that his thirty-six-year-old wrinkles had been retarded by his refusal to suffer wives and children. For the briefest of moments he wondered if this had been a mistake. Particularly now. His life was empty. Meaningless. His days were spent trawling the pubs of Richmond, reading every word of *The Times* and predicting social disaster under the harridan Thatcher. What was he going to do with the rest of his one-legged life? Self-indulgence was not his style, neither was wallowing in self-pity, but boredom and inactivity were becoming problems that he was encountering every day. He had to move his handsome arse soon – otherwise he would die. There must be something out there that would hold and interest him.

There must be. A woman might distract him for a while but then this probably wouldn't last long. His intellectual barbarism, clever wit and easy looks, attracted plenty of women but not one of substance and Treharne demanded substance – and challenge. Sex was fine but he needed some communication after all the work had been done. Some intelligent discourse.

He took a sleeping tablet out of a brown bottle and put it on the coffee table. He looked at it. He hated taking pills of any description but the sleepless nights were beginning to grate and dominate. No one dominated him, not even his own frustrated mind. He continued to stare at the pill. It remained a mystery to him as to how he could swallow the bastard and yet it still seemed to know where to go. It obviously had more sense than he.

Treharne lit another cigarette and looked around his sitting room. His character shouted from every wall, floor, ornament, picture and piece of furniture. There was no clutter, no fuss. Everything in the room was balanced and in its rightful place even the layers of books that lined most of the walls. Chaos was left at the front door along with media vacuity and human nonsense. Radio 4 played the role of constant companion and as yet had never been betrayed by televised garbage. In daylight the room, with its olive green and ivory cream walls, its long-boat settee, its tumescent figurines from Egypt to South America, its framed prints of Victorian erotica and the occasional Chippendale chair all told of a man with a sense of humour, bold taste and a contempt for the conventional.

Kristian stubbed out his cigarette and decided to give sleep another chance. He went back to bed and hoped. Sleep had to call sooner or later. It had to. As he fought the lack of activity and challenge, he knew that he would have to go home soon. His mother was already starting to fret and his little sister, Charlotte, was throwing tantrums. Well, his sister wasn't so 'little' these days. She was twenty-two now and full of hell – it ran in the family. He would have to go home soon. The Cliffs was an impatient mistress. Besides he missed the drama and turbulence of the Gower Peninsula, its anger and its calm. Before he finally dropped off to sleep, the past decided to make an unannounced visit. A past that in the morning he would be unable to resist.

CHAPTER 2

"How are you Captain? It's been a long time. Come in." Kristian looked at the blond cropped hair and tattooed stump of hard flesh that stood in the doorway. Kristian wore a navy blue Savile Row suite, without a tie and without any cufflinks to stop his double cuffs flopping around his wrists. He had been too lazy to shave that morning but even so the contrast between privileged background and council-estate poverty was obvious to anyone taking the time to look. In spite of their different upbringings the men had two things in common. The Royal Marines and courage.

"Fine Spiv, how are you?"

"Oh you know me, might be back in civvy street but the duckin' and divin' still goes on. More opportunities out 'ere for entrepreneurs like me, if you know wha' I mean. Marines was a bit limited."

"I can see that," Kristian replied. From the hallway to the sitting room and no doubt beyond were boxes of all the latest electrical appliances. From microwaves to the latest energy saving fridges and super-powered dildos. Spiv had been an RSM and a good one until his extra-curricular activities were discovered. He had cost the military a fortune in 'lost' kit. It was rumoured that at one time he had even tried to sell some African dictator a Centurion tank! They had spent some good times together, both in peacetime and in war.

"Joined a Zulu war party now have you, Spiv?"

"What?"

"Good God Spiv, you've more ear-rings dangling from your skin than Shepherd's Market on a rampant Saturday night!" Kristian looked at his erstwhile RSM in despair.

"Don't knock it Captain, the fillies like 'em, particularly the one down below."

"What! My God, civvy street really has gone to your head. Now . . ."

Spiv pointed to a settee. "There it is. Polished, cleaned, oiled and always treated with tender lovin' care."

"I don't doubt it. Thanks for looking after it."

"No problem. It's been a privilege, it's a beautiful piece. Deserves respect like all firearms, but a lot more than most." Kristian sat next to the hide leather gun case. The shotgun it contained had been made to order by one of London's finest gunsmiths, Holland & Holland. He remembered the long discussions about bore requirements, chokes, chamber lengths, weight and triggers. He had examined engraving pattern books and had finally settled on a simple country scene. It was to be a working gun not an object to be stored in a glass case and looked at whenever the owner felt like it. It was the perfect English gun, a masterpiece. It had also cost Kristian a fortune. Not that he was short of money; his adopted father, William, had seen to that. He should have bought a proper house his mother would have moaned, but then he wouldn't have loved a house as much.

He unclasped the case and looked. It had been a long time. There had been nowhere safe to keep it as his mother wouldn't allow guns anywhere near their home and his own flat wasn't secure enough, thus its deposit with Spiv. The man would guard it with his life, which Kristian had once saved. It had never been forgotten. He touched the barrels, the stock. The gun demanded gentleness until it was it was brought out to do its work. All was in order, even the license which he had only obtained that morning, another reason for leaving the shotgun with Spiv.

"Off somewhere nice, Captain?"

"Nowhere where there is going to be any action, if that's what you are thinking."

"Perish the thought! Me, I'm retired."

"That's not what I've heard."

"Gossip, Captain, idle gossip." Kristian doubted it. A lot of ex-servicemen, particularly of Spiv's calibre, undertook work in the private sector. It was much better paid apart from anything else. "Anyway, what are you up to these days, Captain?"

"Not a lot."

Spiv thought for a few moments. "Look Captain, there could be some work that might be of interest to you." Spiv had always liked Treharne. As 'Ruperts' went they didn't come much better. Treharne was an officer who knew what he was doing in a firefight and knew how to look after his men. Spiv wanted to help. His ex-commanding officer must be struggling; he knew that Civvy Street was not an easy place for a man like Treharne. God knows he had found it hard enough himself. He understood. He also knew that the Captain would never admit it. He was a proud man.

"Come off it now, Spiv, will you? I've only got one leg you stupid sod!"

"I know that, but good planners are always in demand. You were one 'ell of an officer too you know. One of the best."

"That's as maybe but you know me well enough. Being a backroom boy is not my style. Thanks for the thought though."

"Ah well, at least I've tried. You always were a stubborn bastard."

"I know. Right, I'm off and thanks again for the thought."

"Let me know if you change your mind." Spiv knew he wouldn't.

"I will. See you."

Kristian had hired an automatic car for the afternoon. He had always loathed automatics. He preferred to be in control. At least though he didn't have to worry about his left foot pumping the wrong pedal!

CHAPTER 3

The train wheezed its way up and down the mountains of Mid Wales with the panic stricken intensity of a chronic asthmatic who has lost his inhaler. The carriage was old, more youthful models being required for the chaos of urban insanity. Kristian was the only passenger. He looked out of the window and knew he was home. The green and space brought back the taste and sound of Welsh harps, thick *cawl* stews and hot-buttered Welsh cakes. The mountains sprawled across horizons that spoke in ancient languages about chieftains, myths and glory. The air was innocent and unspoilt by noise and human clutter. It was a place where one could die in peace. Part of his childhood and early adulthood had been spent in this part of Wales. Memories of wet, mud-splattered Royal Welsh Shows with their oceans of trembling umbrellas, vast reservoirs that jumped with the fly-catching antics of hungry trout and scruffy cottages that stank of fatty Welsh bacon came back to him and gave a sense of comfort. Safety. He had never left his home of dreams and peace. Of Wales. Of Myfanwy.

Kristian's blood oozed the mystery of Welsh choirs and the determination of an Imperial longboat. Sentimentality fought with his fighting spirit as the train cut through rock and laughed at sheer drops of mountainside. Kristian Treharne, the battle-scarred veteran, was also capable of intense emotion. As he looked through the window a tear spilled from his eye and he let it fall. For him a tear demanded more courage and strength than the squeezing of a trigger finger.

It had been fourteen years since his last visit. Since then he had grown and suffered. His compassion had become more refined and certain, his understanding more exact. As the train tore into the guts of yet another mountain with the precision of a well-planned act of violent sabotage, the lights in the carriage flickered for a few moments then gave up. The mountain was not going to suffer this rude intrusion without voicing some protest. Kristian welcomed the sudden blackness and obscuring of activity. The isolation. His whole being calmed and soothed for a few moments. Myfanwy again.

Night and February country cold had arrived by the time the train stopped at his destination. The small station was deserted, as expected. This part of Wales remained constant. There was no corruption. No clashes of financial might and modernity. Kristian pushed through a devastated wooden gate that was about to give up its bucolic idleness and fall apart altogether. No taxis, again as expected. Nothing had changed. The lack of transport didn't bother him, everything he wanted was within walking distance, peg-leg or not.

He walked passed a small church. As a child he had gone there many times with his parents. Why, only some God or other knew, since his parents were a couple of heathens and he had followed in their heretical footsteps. Some gravestones had tilted over a wall to hover above the road, waiting it seemed, to drop on someone's head as an act of revenge. They didn't seem to give a damn either way. The same seemed to apply to the vicar and congregation – wherever they were, they too had probably given up the Good Fight.

After a few minutes he rounded a corner and arrived at the The Llewelyn Hotel. In Mid Wales the ubiquitous Prince was everywhere. Kristian remembered that not far from the village was an upright conical stone that marked the spot where the last true Prince of Wales, Llewelyn II, was supposed to have been slaughtered by the invading hordes of the unionist English King, Edward I. As far as Kristian was concerned it was all nonsense of course but the myth helped the tills ring with enthusiasm and derision at the naiveté of English and American tourists. Owain Glyndŵr had been another 'Last Prince' of Wales but Kristian had always stuck with Llewelyn. Owain was a hybrid created from a mixture of Royal Welsh blood, so in Kristian's book he was not, like his peg-leg again, the real thing – even if he and Owain did look like one another! Apart from anything else, Owain had crowned himself like any good dictator would, and worse still, had trained to be a lawyer!

Some lights shone from the ground floor of the hotel. Everything else was covered by the blackness unique to unspoilt countryside. He walked through the front door and into a bar that remained exactly as he remembered, all oak, disgruntled wooden chairs and worn-out flagstone flooring. A column of coins was trying to touch the ceiling. When they did, the landlord would destroy the tower of mammon and count and distribute the total sum to local charities. The bar like everything else at this time of year was empty and lifeless. No fishermen, no walkers, no shooters (apart from Kristian) and no people – just as he liked it. It was off-season and off disreputable brats with deluded and obsessed parents intent on swapping roles with their offspring. The only life that could be confirmed was a fat-arsed, dribbling St Bernard who monopolized the space in front of a log fire. British Gas hadn't yet moved in on the reality of chopped wood. The dog looked at Kristian and spat some of his saliva on to a rug as it ignored the fiery missiles that crackled and sparked all over its hairy rump. The lazy brute was there for the duration. Kristian looked to see if anyone was about and was tempted to give the dopy monstrosity a kick but refrained. Cruelty to animals and all that tosh. As far as he was concerned, it was a dog's lot to receive a boot up the backside now and again, so where was the cruelty in that? His inherent good manners prevailed however.

He stood in front of the bar and waited. The till was in front of him and within easy reach but he knew that in this part of the world villainy was at a premium and rarely encountered. A brass hand-bell, polished and alert, stood on the bar amongst antique soda siphons and jars of obscene pickled eggs that looked like something out of a redundant mortuary. He gave the bell a modest shake and waited for some sign of life. Any sign of life!

Eventually a trimmed Van Dyke beard and immaculate moustache appeared in the doorway. Even that stubborn Stuart, Charles I, would have been shamed. The rest of the man's face enjoyed the healthy shine of country living. This was a face that must have been dusted and polished every day without fail. His clothes looked worn and exhausted, yet Kristian was certain that the cloth had seen more affluent days as he knew all about expensive tailors. There was a whiff of Savile Row memory and clapped-out decadence in their threadbare reduction. The man had experienced more lively times. What was he running away from? Kristian pondered Everyone these days seemed to be jumping ship including himself.

"Good evening, sir," the man smiled, "what can I get you? Sorry you had to wait but it's a bit early yet. Locals don't start coming in until later on; they usually help themselves if I'm not about."

"Hello," Kristian smiled back, "a pint of bitter please and do you have a room for a couple of nights? I know it's off season but . . ."

"No problem," – the faded hotelier was behind the bar now – "we could use the business. We are officially closed until the end of March, at least the Hotel bit is. I dare say the wife will be able to fix you up though. Enough empty rooms. I'll have a word."

"Thank you, it's appreciated."

The man handed him a warm pint of beer and disappeared. Kristian had not seen him before so the Hotel must have changed owners sometime during the past fourteen years. So some things did change. About thirty minutes later the man returned, "As I said, no problem. We'll put you in the back – less wind. If you could hang on for a bit the wife will prepare the room and light a fire in there for you. Brass-monkey weather round here at this time of year, particularly at night. We haven't got round to central heating yet. I'll take your things up to the room and give you a shout when the wife has finished. All right with you?"

"Yes, that's fine. Thank you. I only hope I haven't put you too to much trouble."

"Not at all, Mr . . .?"

"Treharne, Kristian Treharne. Please call me Kris if you prefer." The man picked up Kristian's gun case and overnight bag. The disillusioned Cavalier did not give his own name.

"Oh, before I forget the wife wants to know if you'll be wanting something to eat before she settles down for the night. I noticed you didn't come by car so you must have had to suffer that British Rail rubbish." Kristian hadn't eaten since lunchtime, but he didn't want his hunger to cause any more inconvenience.

"Well to be honest, a few sandwiches wouldn't go amiss. No need to go to a lot of trouble though."

"Oh, I think we can stretch to a bit more than sandwiches. Ham and eggs all right?"

"That will be fine," Kristian answered, glad that there was more on the menu than a couple of hopeless ham or cheese sandwiches. His memories of haute cuisine in this part of the world were not impressive. The man did another disappearing act. He returned a few minutes later along with the inevitable question.

"What brings you to these parts then? Picked the wrong time of year if you ask me, quiet as an angels fart round here at the moment."

Welsh curiosity, Kristian thought, you couldn't beat it. There was a hint of North Wales in the man's voice. Only a refined hint though, the usual nasal outrage was absent. What was a man from North Wales doing in these parts Kristian pondered again? That lot hated everything and everyone that had anything to do with the outside world. The latest example of extremism was setting fire to holiday homes owned by 'the English foreigners'. This chap didn't seem so bad though, although the log fire did look a little over-enthusiastic. He spoke educated English too and actually smiled! To a southerner at that! Those from the industrialized south, or even close to it, were considered traitors by the north – they had forsaken their heritage and their language. It was all a load of profound crap as far as Kristian was concerned. That's nationalism for you, and it had already cost him half a leg!

He decided to satisfy at least some of the man's curiosity.

"I felt like a bit of rough shooting."

"Ah, thought so. The gun case. Don't forget to get the farmers' permission. They can be a bit fussy."

"Oh, don't worry. I'm not unknown in these parts."

"Really?"

"I spent some of my childhood here. Holidays and so on. Love the place."

"Wait a minute. Treharne . . . thought the name was familiar. I've heard the locals talk about your family. How are they? They were well thought of. I've heard a bit about a son too. Bit of a lad. Would that be you?"

"It would. I'm not so sure about being a 'bit of a lad' though! As for my parents – well, the old girl is still going strong but my father died a good while back." Kristian didn't go in to the details of William's death; he hated fickle condolence and vacuous sympathy.

"Really? Sorry to hear that, not that I knew either of them personally you understand. Bit before my time." The man smiled. "Thought you were English, that's why I missed the connection and the name. You don' have a Welsh accent. Do you speak Welsh?" This question had to arise at some time or another particularly from a northerner. Kristian could speak six languages fluently but Welsh had never been one of them. Apart from not liking the harsh and guttural sound of the language, it had no application outside Wales, which was fine for the likes of those who lived north of Aberystwyth and considered themselves runners-up to the Israelites as God's Chosen People, but not for Kristian who considered himself a man of cosmopolitan taste and vision. Primitive xenophobia and critical ignorance were not for him. Apart from anything else he had been born and bred in Swansea, a town that had long ago come to its senses.

"No, not a word." Kristian nearly added 'and I've never felt like trying either, before you start and I'm damned if I will apologize for my democratic right to speak whatever language I choose', but instead he said, "I've been away a long time." Surprisingly the man didn't react with a 'For shame on you,' the usual fascistic response from the fanatics up north.

"Always good to come home, isn't it?"

Kristian didn't reply immediately but paused and looked into his pint.

"That remains to be seen," he said quietly.

"What? What was that, Kris, I didn't quite catch you?"

"Oh, nothing. Nothing at all."

"Now before I forget, you must sign the visitors' book. The wife will do her nut if you don't. Always playing hell with me about it." Kristian took the proffered pen and signed as ordered. 'The wife' had yet to make any physical announcement of her existence. Kristian was beginning to wonder if she existed at all. "Oh, and by the way my name is David Davies or 'Dai Twice' as the insolent buggers round here prefer to call me, forgot to introduce myself." They shook hands. The man had that 'beaten' look in his eyes, a look that Kristian had seen so many times before in the eyes of the defeated and those who knelt before a rifle barrel waiting to be trussed up and taken prisoner – or shot. No wonder 'the wife' stayed in the background – she did all the ordering. She was probably sitting in front of a television some- where issuing orders whilst guzzling mounds of chocolate and stroking the furry rear end of some over indulged feline monstrosity who no doubt was as fat as she was. "Right then, I'll go and see how the food is doing, shouldn't be too long now." Off he went again, to do all the work no doubt. The man's energy was impressive. He couldn't stand still. Kristian wished he could move like that. As Davies passed through the door a reflection of light caught his forehead and for the first time Kristian noticed a boot print embedded upon it.

An old man of the countryside walked into the bar and disturbed Treharne's brooding memories. A cloth cap, battered and worn out by time, covered his few strands of grey hair. An ancient pipe stuck out of his mouth and sucked in air. He looked at Kristian and ignored him. He grunted a word or two then went behind the bar and poured himself a pint of beer. As the beer flowed he mumbled, "Dai Twice buggered off again 'as he?"

"I believe so," Kristian answered, unsure whether to smile or not. The old boy didn't look the smiling type. In fact his face didn't seem to do anything except scowl.

"Beer is flat again. Typical. Ought to get that lazy cow of a missus off 'er fat arse. Never does a thing. Never see 'er. Turns up at the bar now and again to get pissed and that's it. More fool 'im." The old goblin sat down in a dark corner and continued to suck on air and argue with magical demons. He kicked the St Bernard on his way and muttered "Another lazy fuckin' lump" as he did so. Treharne said nothing, how could he? He knew neither the husband nor the wife. Or even the dog for that matter. He was quite happy for the dog to receive a kick though, not that it had any effect. He seemed content enough with the abuse. Probably used to it. He stayed put anyway.

As the evening wore on the bar began to fill up and the night got blacker. Kristian recognized some of the farmyard faces. There was a mixture of old and young, all male and all rural by looks and occupation. Wind, rain and sun had created the faces that had been left worn and noble in the plight to survive and outrun Nature's misfortune. Nobody appeared to recognize him. He enjoyed the anonymity but also knew it wouldn't last for long. It was probably all the hair that was keeping recognition at bay. Occasional glances of suspicion flew his way but no words.

A plate of ham and eggs eventually arrived. Kristian said nothing about the wait, instead he tucked in and marvelled at the deep yellow colour of the yolks and the taste of real ham, even the bread and butter was 'home-produced'. If nothing else 'the wife' knew how to cook, assuming she actually did the cooking of course. It all reminded him of home, his real home, the Cliffs.

He finished his meal and took the plate up to the bar where Dai Twice was pulling pints. Kristian was about to order another drink when a tap on the shoulder made him turn around.

"Bugger me! Kris! Kris Treharne! Thought it was you! All the 'air 'ad thrown me, 'ad to come up and take a closer look. Come on, come and sit down with us. It's been a long time. John Eighteen Months is 'ere (the man was called this on account of his only having one and a half 'ears', half of one having been chewed off by an over-playful bull terrier) and the rest of the boys!" Ivor Williams, or 'Ivor Biggun' as he liked to call himself, hauled Kristian over to a table of professional drinkers. "It's 'im. Told you so! Dai Twice wouldn't know 'im, would 'ee? Bloody foreigner from up north, isn't 'ee." All the men stood up, shook hands and slapped backs. Kristian couldn't get a word in. Questions were fired at him from all directions. It was going to be a long night.

The following morning Kristian woke up with a powerful hangover. It was one of the better ones. Roads were being dug up in his head and new pipes laid in his body. He stayed still and tried to come to terms with the drills and sledgehammers. At least his deceased foot hadn't haunted him during the night. Drink was usually the only thing that ever really laid the ghost to rest. The room was warm. A fire still burned but he couldn't remember anyone coming in to refuel it. Whoever it was they must have crept in and crept out. The Welsh were sensitive to a fellow countryman's alcohol abuse, since for them it was an essential part of life that required understanding and respect. Drinking was an art form and to be celebrated at every opportunity. Even its greatest poets were revered for their skills at intemperate alcohol consumption. For a Welshman, getting pissed kept the vocal chords in tune and the lungs free of coal dust. The fact that the mines were on their way out had nothing to do with it.

The curlicued brass bed, starched white sheets and floral piss-pot that he had somehow or another managed to avoid puking into, reminded him of childhood romps and giggles. He moved a hand over his buttocks. They ached. He had a vague memory of falling off the bed. The damn thing was so high it required the skills of a mountaineer and a sober one at that. A half-empty glass of rum sat on the bedside table. Oh well, he hadn't come to bed without a fight, he hadn't surrendered easily. He moved slowly; first division hangovers demanded respect.

Later, when he had dressed and shaved, a burial mound of dismembered pig, gushing rivers of yellow yolk, grease-soaked fried bread and just about everything else that could be fitted onto a dinner plate stared up at him. This should be fun the breakfast thought. Kristian's eyes challenged. His stomach gurgled. His rectum trembled. The food won. With a few sly moves Kristian managed to fill his pockets with tomatoes, mushrooms, sausages, a few slices of bacon and even a couple of eggs. He would dispose of the breakfast later. He was the only guest in the place and he didn't want to offend; after all 'the wife' must have gone to a great deal of trouble to cook all that. At any other time he would have gorged himself silly, God knows, there had been times in the past when he would have given his right leg for such a meal. He drank tea instead, gallons of it.

He needed a walk and to finally address the reason why he had come here. Some fresh country air would hopefully blow away the hangover that tortured and hurt too. The village consisted of one street. Picturesque cottages on one side, purpose-built council houses on the other. The contrast was grotesque. Some council planner had committed an act of revenge on the place. Whatever had the village done? But then, Kristian thought, since when did councils and their employees need an excuse for abject stupidity and frustrated pettiness? There was one Post Office and one shop that sold everything from sheep dip to laxatives. That was it, apart from a small river that had been infested with Coca-Cola cans and worn-out tyres. The once clear and enthusiastic little tributary brought back memories of minnow hunting, leaking Wellingtons, soaking socks and cheap fishing rods. The banks of the river had not altered but its soul had gone on a long holiday.

He walked up a small narrow lane off the main road. Eventually he was met by an old stone farmhouse. He stopped and looked. The walls of the building had changed colour. They were white now instead of pink. The place seemed brighter now, as if someone had tried and succeeded in their attempts at artificial resuscitation. It was not the unwilling and worn-out farmhouse that he remembered. The hedgerows and lane detached it from the ugliness of the main road and the Council's nefarious intent. The farmhouse managed to maintain a unique dignity in spite of its crude and uncouth neighbours. There was no sign to tell the weary traveller that it was a public house as well as a farm, but then there never had been. Everyone who mattered knew that the farmhouse served a good pint – that's if it still did.

Kristian remained where he was. Unsure. Guilty. Did she still live here? A lot could happen in fourteen years. This was worse than any mission he had endured as a soldier. He knew Myfanwy and she didn't take prisoners. Somehow he doubted that fourteen years would have any mellowing effect on the women. He stood still for a few more minutes and then finally mumbled the words of an old Welsh song.

'Why is it anger, O My Myfanwy,
That fills your eyes so dark and clear?
Your gentle cheeks, O sweet Myfanwy,
Why blush they not when I draw near?
Where is the smile that once most tender
Kindled my love so fond, so true?
Where is the sound of your sweet words,
That drew my heart to follow you.'

That was as far as his romantic inclinations went. He finished his romantic soliloquy with "Oh balls to it! It's Monte-Carlo or bust time."

He knew that there had once been a side entrance to the farm so he avoided the main door. He walked through a yard in front of a barn. The place was spotless. Years ago it had been the dumping ground for dung-splattered tractors and worked-out dogs. Everything was quiet apart from the whine of a mangy dog attempting a canine greeting. This wasn't a good start, even the dog couldn't raise an enthusiastic "Hello!" To add further insult, a crow sitting on top of the barn stared at him and squawked "Who the hell are you?" Damn, even the birds were having a go!

His courage stayed with him as he knocked on the door. Nothing. He didn't know whether to be relieved or disappointed. Either way he didn't give up. He decided to walk to the back of the farmhouse, as he did so he noticed a man standing in front of the barn. Where had he come from? The man stood still and watched. He said nothing. He was holding a long-handled axe and moving it from one hand to the other. Kristian put him down as mid 20s and must have been the hired help or something. A farm labourer perhaps. The clothes, the hacked face. The threat. Trouble was the one thing he didn't want but this man looked as if he was about to start some. He walked up to the man and asked, "I am looking for Myfanwy Bowen, I am an old friend of hers, is she in?" There was no response. Not even the curios twitching of a facial muscle. Kristian walked a few more paces toward him. Men never frightened him, women – well that was another matter. As he drew closer he realized how big the man was. He nearly blocked out the barn door. They were about the same height but the other man was broader, there was more raw beef but then size had never bothered Kristian much either.

"Is Myfanwy about anywhere?" Kristian asked again, "and does she still live here?" The man stared, snarled a grunt and walked off. Kristian thought, what is it with this place? I've only dropped in to say "Hello". You'd think I was delivering a bout of foot and mouth or something, even the crows are angry with me!

"Ignorant devil!" Kristian yelled after the scowling hulk. In some ways he wished the man had spoiled for a fight, then remembered his AWOL leg and continued his search. He turned a corner and stopped.

A woman was bending over an outside tap and trying to attach a hose pipe to it, without much success judging by the angry shouts of "*Cachi!*" – Welsh for 'shit'. He stood still. Her small hands struggled. Long black hair fell into her face, seeming to cause her even more annoyance. The vicious red jumper she was wearing failed to thrash the blackness into submission.

She threw down the hosepipe in temper and pushed the hair away. In that single movement Kristian saw again the only face he had ever truly adored. Myfanwy. Feelings and emotions paralyzed him. Fourteen years of the only true and real emotional heartache he had ever known rushed in. Her face was more beautiful now than the young Myfanwy in the tattered photograph that had travelled around the world and gone with him into battle. Her delicate features were untouched by the cynical, ravaged lines of the city dweller. Her beauty was complete, mature. There was none of the unfinished appearance of youth and young womanhood. Strength and spirit shone from her brown, almost black eyes and yet there was a softness in the shine that defied the calculating duplicity of the new 80's women. She had managed to remain apart, alone and unique in her beauty. Her full red lips still begged to be kissed and touched in the surreal moments before daybreak. She was tall for a woman, 5ft 6ins, curved and yet light, there was no hint of largeness or clumsy attribute. Every part of her sang in harmony. She was so utterly beautiful.

She kicked a bucket, swore again and then finally saw Kristian staring at her. Anger, pain and love screamed at him from the blackness of her eyes, "Kristian Treharne . . . the Warrior returns." Neither her voice nor her movements betrayed any surprise: "Are you going to stand there like a fool gawping or are you going to come inside? It's cold out here."

CHAPTER 4

The kitchen was warmer and friendlier than Myfanwy. Antique Welsh pine covered every space.

"What's the matter with your leg? Why are you limping?" she asked as she turned the kettle on. Straight to the point. Fourteen years had not pacified her direct approach to things.

"There is no leg. At least no leg below the left knee. I put my foot somewhere where it shouldn't have been. On it instead of in it for a change. Right now though, I seem to be in it right up to my neck." There was silence for a few moments, then without warning a teacup came spinning through the air and crashed into the wall. It only just missed Kristian's head.

"You bastard, you fucking bastard!" Myfanwy yelled. "Do you know how much you hurt me? One letter! One pathetic letter ending with 'I'll be in touch!' Oh, you've kept in touch all right. Fourteen bloody years too late! Lost a leg have you? Well I lost my heart, you bastard!" By now tears were streaming down her face, the only time Myfanwy used a foul mouth was at times of extreme temper. Kristian knew when to keep his mouth shut where her anger was concerned. He hadn't forgotten much. She was worse than any Argentinian land mine. She seemed to calm down for a few moments but he still remembered enough not to trust her temper yet. "I knew you were back last night. News travels fast around here. I've had all night to think about you, about us. To remember. I knew you would call, no doubt just to say 'Hello', you know, 'I was in the area' etc. etc. Christ, you've got enough nerve! I could kill you right now, I really could!" She collapsed in a chair and sobbed her heart out.

Kristian kept quiet. So much for the sympathy card as far as his leg was concerned. That little ploy had gone right out of the window. He should have known better. Myfanwy was a passionate Celt. All fire and ferocity when required. That had been part of her attraction. She had always fought him, both of them were Aries too which didn't help. A highly combustible combination apparently, not that Kristian believed in such nonsense – until that is, Myfanwy had come along. Fortunately there was also her soft side. The side that would assault and batter any man without the need for brutal force. The side that usually dominated.

They had both been students when they met studying philosophy at Oxford. Kristian was a year older. They had fought, argued and lived for each other for four years; they had loved and neither had ever forgotten. Both were Welsh in different ways and more passionate about things than Heaven and Hell put together or a bunch of manic Pentecostals clapping their brains out.

As Kristian watched her cry he realized for the first time how much he had hurt her. He had been young and like most young people, self centred and self-obsessed. But youth was no excuse. It never could be, not in his world of right and wrong. He remained silent. Words would be a waste of time anyway, he knew Myfanwy. She had to blow herself out.

Eventually the tears stopped. She sniffed a few times and said, "That's better. I needed that." She looked at Kristian, a lost little boy. "Sorry for the outburst. Not much of a welcome I'm afraid but you asked for it Kristian. I meant every word. I loved you. My God, how I loved you! And what did you do? You cast me away without a second thought. That was the thing that hurt most of all Kristian. God it hurt."

She stood up and took another cup from the dresser. "That cup was one of my mother's best. Good job she isn't around, she'd have killed me. Would have killed you too if she could have laid her hands on you." Kristian remembered the mother well. Not a lady to upset. Thank God Myfanwy had some of her father in her. He had been a quiet and calm man. Gentle. Ten Woodbines and a pint of bitter kept him happy for hours.

When his tea arrived and Kristian could see that she had calmed down – best cups but he didn't say anything – he said, "Myfanwy, just sit down for a moment will you? I'm sorry. I'm so sorry. I won't insult you with pathetic excuses. I was wrong. Deeply wrong. The Marines took over. I knew it could be dangerous work. Wives and children just didn't fit. I was too much of a coward to face you. You know what you're like. Those eyes of yours. But know one thing. I loved you too. You don't have a monopoly on the condition. You were always there, at the back of my mind. Always. Especially in times of danger. You see in my own way I never really left you. Try at least to understand that."

He reached across the table and touched her hand. She looked at his fingers for a few moments then stood up quickly and started to clean up the smashed crockery. As she swept the floor she asked, "What exactly happened to your leg? I didn't give you much of a chance to tell me, did I?" Before Kristian could answer she bent down to pick up some broken china. She didn't want him to see the tears that were starting to fall again as she felt the agony of the blast that had maimed him.

"Falklands. It was secret-chaos time. That was my job. Special Boat Service. I hadn't quite counted on putting my foot on a mine though. Invalided out. I am now a man of leisure. You will probably be pleased to know that Queen and Country no longer require my services. It's not too bad really, there were plenty who didn't come back at all and plenty whose injuries were far worse than mine. I've got used to the dummy leg. Bit awkward buying a pair of shoes but that's about it." He grinned but Myfanwy could see the hurt in Kristian's eyes, in spite of his efforts at bravado.

"Marriage? Children? she asked.

"Neither. What about you?"

"There was a husband. It was all very fast and done with little thought. Two years after we were married he ran off with one of the local milkmaids. Don't laugh, I'm serious, buxom wench, like a character out of a Henry Fielding novel. I was too

much for him I suppose. Not really good farmer's wife material."
She looked at Kristian and sighed, "I really pick them don't I?
Here today, gone tomorrow, that's my men."

"There hasn't been much happiness then?"

"Oh, don't worry about Islwyn. That was six or seven years
ago now. The man was a pig and a cow had more brains. He was
one of the farming aristocracy. Kept my parents happy if nothing
else. They both died before we parted company so they were
spared the humiliation. You know what old farming stock are
like."

"Yes. No children then?"

"No. None." There was a finality in her reply that disturbed
Kristian. He knew Myfanwy, something had happened but now
wasn't the time to intrude. "I run this place on my own now. I've
sold most of the farm. The land anyway. I've kept the pub going
though, there would be a riot if I closed it down. Some of the
regulars have been drinking here for more than fifty years."

"So you live alone then?"

"Yes Kristian, and that's just the way I like it."

"Hold on here, don't be so tetchy. I'm not trying to move in
or anything Like you say, you are too much for any man too
handle. I should know." For the first time Myfanwy smiled and
looked directly into his eyes. Kristian's heart nearly broke.

"You didn't do so badly Kristian. Quite masterful if I remember.
Might is Right and all that."

"Still have the philosophy bug I note."

"Haven't you? God you never stopped droning on about
Kant and Bertrand Russell. You used to bore me to death and I
ended up getting a doctorate in philosophy! Fair play though,
I'll give you that, you did get a First. I was only two marks off
though! For all the good it did me. Here I am stuck up in the
mountains, milking cows and beer barrels all day long. Fate
deals out some amusing cards now and again." She smiled for a
second time and Kristian's heart remembered all the reasons
why he had loved so much.

"You should smile more often, Myfanwy. It still charms. It was that smile that bounced me around the Students Union bar when we first met. You're still beautiful you know."

"Oh, shut up Kristian! I know all about your charming, wily ways. You fooled me once. Never again."

"I was only being truthful, you know."

"Well that's fine, just keep it that way. Mind you I'll say that for you, you were never a liar. Which is more than can be said for a lot of men I have known."

"Don't overdo my good points now, will you? My ego might just die of shock."

"I won't, have no fear." Her eyes lied. There was sadness in the dark pupils. The years had not been kind. Kristian knew Myfanwy better than any man on the planet. He may not be able to fool her but the same applied where she was concerned. The veneer of hardness was a sham. A false mechanism to protect against hurt. Myfanwy had been the most sensitive, caring and honest woman he had ever known apart from his mother. There was a depth to her that only he knew how to reach, how to touch. The women would have loved him into battle and back again. She would have stood by him and fought, regardless of the bullets. She knew how to love and she knew how to give.

"So you never married, Kristian?"

"You know, you are still the only person who calls me by my proper name, apart from my mother."

"I never liked 'Kris' and 'Guts' was even worse. 'Kris' sounds so pedestrian. And that is something you have never been nor are ever likely to be . . . more's the pity, perhaps."

"I'll take that as a compliment."

"As you wish."

"Anyway, to come back to your question, I haven't married. As I have said the Forces and marriage do not make happy bed mates. Which is why I . . . Oh, never mind. You aren't in the mood for excuses. Look, why don't you come and have dinner with me tonight. We can go somewhere quiet and talk. No strings, just friends."

"Kristian, you know as well as I do that we can never be friends in the conventional way. Besides that was the one thing we did agree on, if you remember: *amor Socraticus,* sexless homosexual love maybe, but heterosexual sexless love – forget it!"

"I haven't forgotten. *Amor Platonicus* and its corruption by romantic fools."

Myfanwy looked down at her hands and said quietly, "No Kristian. The past is done with. We can't go back. I'm glad to know you are still in one piece . . . well, almost . . . but let's leave it at that." Myfanwy couldn't resist a smile, "And don't get legless tonight either!" This time she laughed out loud at the same time remembering the humour that had always bound them together. That had been a crucial part of their love. The laughter. They had always been able to mock, deride and bite each other and themselves without either taking offence. She still knew that without stomach-stretching laughter there could be no love. No real love anyway. Laughter could hold and imprison two people; it could see them through all the trying and difficult times. It was everything that love should be.

"It's gratifying to know you have at least retained your sense of humour, Myfanwy. Very gratifying indeed." Kristian smiled, he remembered too. Myfanwy became serious again, her humour lost in the sadness around them.

"Try and understand Kristian. Please."

She stood up, the reunion was over. Kristian looked at his cup and saucer for a moment and stood up himself. He went to the door then turned and went back to her. He raised her chin with his hand and kissed her softly on the cheek, "I do understand. I am sorry." He opened the door, before walking out he turned again and asked, "By the way who was that Sumo wrestler I saw lurking around the barn? Had a bloody great axe in his hands. I thought he was going to try and decapitate me! He was like someone out of a Hammer horror film, rude fellow wouldn't tell me anything. Ignored me. Just scowled."

"That's Dewi. Dewi Morgan. Don't judge too harshly Kristian. He's a mute, deaf and dumb. Helps out around here. He's a good man and very protective of me."

"That doesn't surprise me. If looks could kill, that land mine was a waste of time."

"Take no notice, it's just the way he is."

"Fair enough." Before finally walking out he said, "You know, despite what you think, you were the only one Myfanwy. The only one. There hasn't been anyone else before or since. Not like you." He pushed the door open and walked out into a cold that seemed harsher and more violent than before. There was much more of a bite to it now.

Kristian hadn't known what to expect from his reunion with Myfanwy. Certainly not welcoming arms. But there had been a hope. A hope of something more than he had received. As he walked back to the hotel, disappointment walked alongside him. He had never known a woman like her. She had always understood him. Known him. He had given a damn sight more than a leg to the Queen and she was still abusing his generous nature.

As he neared the hotel he determined not to give up. Myfanwy was a tough nut but he had cracked tougher in his time. She had won the first round but the fight was by no means over. Kristian was as stubborn as she was and he was not a man who gave in easily. If ever.

CHAPTER 5

Kristian put the leather gun case on the bed. To anyone else's eyes it could have contained a clarinet or some other musical instrument. For a few moments he wondered if his prosthesis would hinder his dexterity with the shotgun. He had always been a skilled shooter. He put on clothes more suitable for rough shooting – a method of sport that blasted anything that moved, more particularly in Kristian's case, woodpigeons.

Unlike a pheasant or a partridge drive where a visible white forehead was more likely to cause a turn than a furious red hat, camouflage was essential to bringing down 'woodies'. Dressing as near as possible to the soldier in the field came naturally to him. He put on an old, faithful Norfolk jacket. The thick material and heavy lining ensured protection from the wind and cold. The leather gun pad on the right shoulder prevented bruising and rubbing. The jacket also afforded poachers pockets inside the skirt of the coat plus a multitude of other pockets which were a survival from a time when men used to shoot with muzzle loaders and were forced to carry about with them a tool chest of implements and appliances. Later on in the day he knew he would be cursing all the pockets for conspiring to stop him smoking. He put on a brown tweed hat with an all-round brim to prevent water dripping down his back should it start to rain. A yellow scarf and corduroy breeches finished the job.

It had been a long time since he had used a 12 bore shotgun, the Sterling L2A3 sub-machine gun having been more his forte in recent times. He slung a pigskin cartridge bag over his shoulder, picked up his 'bespoke' Holland & Holland and made for the door. As he turned the door knob he paused and grunted. If I must, he said to himself, as he reached for the stick–seat standing in a corner of the room. If I must. He walked out of the room and cursed more loudly than usual.

Kristian left the hotel carrying the gun in the crook of his elbow with the breech open. Comfortable and safe. In this part of the country no one would have felt fear or outrage. His grip on the gun was relaxed. Like having a third arm, a third 'leg would have been preferable though. He was an expert with firearms of any description.

It didn't take him long to find a suitable covert. It lay on the edge of a small wood where 'woodies' would be coming in to roost. He chose this place purely for its tactical value. Aesthetics didn't come into it. For the shooter, landscape became terrain not scenery. Kristian used the clear, pragmatic view of an infantry officer not a poet. He wanted his targets on the wing. Killing pigeons at roost or shooting them off the stooks whilst they fed on corn was no sport. They must be flying and wild. He would be lucky to get a straight advancing bird as nearly all pigeons have a curl on them. They could gain height quicker than any other game birds and on the wing their aerobatics are fast enough to confound even the most determined hawk. For Kristian this was the real beauty and challenge of shooting pigeon, for the slightest mistake in gun mounting and head movement or if his gun alignment was a fraction out of true, then he would miss and the pigeon would be spared.

He sat down on his stick-seat and made himself comfortable. He waited. Most of his time in the Marines had been spent waiting. He was an expert at this too.

It didn't take long for Myfanwy to disturb the peace. She wouldn't leave his mind alone. Her beauty, her wildness. Normally he would be totally absorbed. The target everything. Not today. He remembered her body. The lust. Their craving. Her body had been perfect, rounded in all the right places. Feminine. A baggy red jumper had prevented an accurate view of the past but she had not seemed to have changed in shape or size. She had looked after herself. His memories were not locked up in wool though, and in spite of the pigeons his groin started to twitch. Had she really forgotten so quickly or was it fear of loving him again? That morning he had looked into her eyes – Myfanwy's only betrayers. They couldn't lie. They couldn't deceive. Her eyes told him that there were some things that time could never erase. This certainty made him more unsettled, more frustrated.

His thoughts were interrupted by two wood pigeons coming in low and straight at him, at about 35mph and at a distance of 30 yards. In one movement Kristian and gun became one. He stood up instantly and mounted the gun to his shoulder without any head movement. He placed his left hand well under the stock, thus straightening the trigger finger and clearing the knuckle. The gun was perfectly balanced for recoil. He kept his left hand pointing at one of the nearest moving birds as he swung his body gently into place with the flight of the bird. He made no check for the aiming or trigger pressure, his eyes were focussed entirely on the bird. His muscles tensed in exact timing with the action of the gun's discharge as both barrels erupted, sending the two wood pigeons to the ground in a puff of feathers.

To kill a fast oncoming pigeon required expertise. To kill two was perfection. Kristian sat down pleased with the kill and his ability to use a shotgun. His mastery with the weapon still remained in spite of his absent appendage. He would collect the birds when it was time to leave. The 'Cavalier' or his 'wife' might be able to do something with them. He bagged two more pigeons and an over-curious rabbit during the remainder of the afternoon and then decided to call it a day. Dusk was approaching and with it the damned loneliness. Myfanwy wasn't helping. Bloody women! Crows squawked and chuckled their obscene insults again as he made his way back to the hotel. He stuck two fingers up at them and quickly remembered what had happened the last time he had stuck two fingers up at Nature. He had probably just outraged all the veggies, vegans and animal rights nutcases too. Damn it, he had sacrificed half a leg so that these people had the freedom to eat vegetables, so it was two fingers to them as well!

As he walked back across the tired fields the darkening sky began to grumble with irritation. The heavens were not happy either then. What the hell was happiness anyway, he wondered. Was it simply a momentary frame of mind lifted by some intense euphoria like ejaculation, or was it a lasting experience allowed only to those who had achieved some fantastic perfection in spirit? He had no idea and swore at his idiotic inclination toward existential meanderings. It had never got him anywhere and he had spent years studying the subject. He could only conclude that life was all about love. And laughter. Without both, you were buggered. And right now he was buggered – Myfanwy had given him the two fingers this time. No justice was there. Well he wasn't going to give up yet. The chase was still on.

When he arrived back at the hotel he telephoned Myfanwy in an attempt to change her mind about them seeing each other. After a polite "Get stuffed" he went into the bar to get thoroughly drunk. Even he knew when he was beaten, well on this occasion anyway. Perhaps it really was time to go home. He ordered his first pint and a Woods 100% rum chaser. He walloped back the beer and drank the rum in one gulp. He was on form tonight. Dai Twice had done another of his disappearing acts so he helped himself to another beer and shot of rum. As he was pouring another generous dollop of 100% rocket fuel, Dai Twice appeared from nowhere. He had a habit of doing that.

"Telephone call for you, Kris. A lady if I'm not mistaken. Take the call in my office if you like, more private."

"Nothing is private round here," Kristian muttered and went in search of the telephone. Following the man's pointed finger he found the office which was more like a vet's waiting room. Two cats exchanged pious insults whilst trying to sit on a desk made for a pygmy, a budgie sat in its cage rigid with fear and wondering if he was going to be the cats' next meal, while the frothing St Bernard slouched in a corner looking thoroughly bored and half dead, but nevertheless finding enough energy to raise a respectable fart as a fanfare for Kristian's impolite intrusion. As he picked up the phone a noxious miasma of overwhelming toxicity nearly made him pass out, the stench nearly on a par with one of his own flatulent 'specials'.

"Dirty bastard!" he shouted at the St Bernard.

"I beg your pardon!" Came a shocked reply down the phone.

"What! Oh, I'm sorry. I was talking to a dog."

"Kristian are you drunk? Nothing changes with you does it? Dr. bloody Doolittle now is it?"

"Very funny Myfanwy. I note nothing much changes with you either, you've got to have the last word. You haven't lost your sarcastic edge either I note. So much for fourteen years. This is just like old times."

"Oh, shut up Kristian. Right, I've changed my mind. You can take me out for dinner. The Lake Hotel will do nicely."

"The Lake? It's the most expensive place around here!"

"That's right. You can start paying some compensation."

"Damn it! All right."

"And don't get any wrong ideas. This is just for old time's sake, Kristian, nothing more. I mean it."

"Yes, yes. I'll come round to pick you up at 8."

"Kristian, don't 'yes, yes' me! I mean it!"

"And bugger you, Myfanwy. What do you think I am going to try and do, slip you a length in some passing bush for God's sake? Mind you that wouldn't be the first time now, would it?"

"The last time, I assure you. Like I say, don't get any wrong ideas."

"I won't, so you can stop fretting. Anyway, you should be so lucky!"

"That's a good one. Now shut up. I've booked a table for 9, so be here at 8."

"I've already said that."

"All right Mr Perfect. God, you don't change do you? Always have to be right."

Myfanwy had always been fond of telling him to 'shut up'. He hadn't taken any notice then and he wasn't about to start taking any notice now.

"You seem to have it all planned, Myfanwy? Table booked etc. etc."

"Don't start now, Kristian. I could just use some intelligent conversation for a change. It's in short supply around here."

"Was there another of your esoteric compliments in there again, Myfanwy? Tut, tut, you really are slipping."

"Oh, go to hell Kristian! I'll see you at 8.00 sharp." She disconnected the line. 8 sharp! That was a good one! Myfanwy couldn't be on time if she tried. He remembered the times she used to get on a bus half dressed on her way to lectures. He had tried changing all the clocks in the flat they had shared once and even then she still managed to be late for everything. Her 'punctuality' was notorious; she had even managed to duff a few exams because of her appalling timekeeping. Arriving one and a half hours late for a three-hour exam was not a good idea.

Kristian replaced the receiver. Women. He had come to realize a long time ago that they were all barmy. Every last one of them. Lovely and irresistible with it though, that was the trouble. He looked at the St Bernard and was about to give it a good kick – his nostrils were still smarting – when he realized his bad humour had evaporated. He allowed mercy to prevail.

As he closed the 'office' door the dog let go a mightier and more insubordinate fart than the first, as if to say "And bugger you too!"

CHAPTER 6

As he walked to Myfanwy's he wondered what had brought
about this sudden change of heart. She had always been unpredictable, it was one of the things that had attracted him to her all
those years ago. She had been impulsive too, so it came as no
surprise when she pounced on him as soon as he walked into her
kitchen. It was straight upstairs to the bedroom. Togs off and
down to business. No messing about. No foreplay. No finesse.
She was hungry all right and not in anticipation of dinner at the
Lake Hotel. Their lovemaking had been desperate and crude.
Urgent and unrepentant.

In the early hours of the morning Kristian woke and looked
at the woman who had never left him. A sly moon looked at the
bed and allowed him to see again the whiteness of Myfanwy's
skin and her body. Her thirty-five years had not been unkind.
Her flesh and skin remained firm, there was no stretched fat or
thread-veined thigh. He looked at her face as it shone in the
moonlight and made him love her all the more. Her beauty was
impossible. How could he ever have left her? His fingertip
traced the lines of her face as he absorbed and felt. He ran his
fingers across her belly and to the inside of her thigh, the softest
part of a woman's body. Myfanwy stirred and placed her leg
across Kristian's, opening herself. Gone was the carnality of the
night before. Gone was the urgent depravity. His fingers hardly
seemed to touch as he parted the swollen folds of flesh. His
mind and fingers stroked and held while his lips and tongue
sucked and bit both her nipples in turn. There was a catch of
breath, a moan. His fingers continued to move and explore as his
tongue licked from nipple to navel and beyond. Myfanwy
moved her hips toward his tongue. He knew her. He remembered. He continued to suck and bite. She started to whimper as

her hands gripped his head and pushed his tongue into her. Her juices poured into his mouth. She ground and forced until her hips fell still for a moment. She let out a long sigh and then reached for Kristian. He entered her slowly this time. His strokes were measured. Calculated. He didn't penetrate too deeply. He wanted to tease, to keep her waiting. Myfanwy continued to flow and soak. She gripped his buttocks pulling him into her. This time he would not indulge her impatience. He made her wait. Their tongues kept working together, saliva mixed with the sweet cordials of sex. At last he pushed into her. Up to the hilt. She bit his neck and moaned at the God's. He thrust hard and fast. There was no mercy. Soon they climaxed together, as they had always done. Their bodies had reacted as one, there were no secrets. When Myfanwy's breathing returned to normal she said, "It's been a long time, Kristian."

"For me too," he replied. At least he couldn't remember when sex had been so possessive, so powerful. For once he hadn't wanted to reach for his trousers as soon as ejaculation had reared its impatient head.

"You haven't changed much Myfanwy. You're still as sexy as hell. Still wonderful."

"Are you complaining then, Captain Treharne?"

"No, how could I ever complain Myfanwy? My Myfanwy," he said softly as he looked at the shifting black hair that moved across the pillow.

Moonlight made it shine across his memories as he touched the face that had been with him for fourteen years. He kissed her lips and her cheek as all his phantoms disappeared in her loveliness. He held her body and allowed a gentle sleep to bring them closer. Nothing had changed when they were in each others arms. Nothing at all.

Myfanwy's fingers ignored the white shadows as even in sleep she touched the stump where there had once been strength and agility. Her fingers stroked as she felt again Kristian's pain and his anguish.

The following morning they ate a breakfast of fried eggs and Welsh bacon. There had been a remoteness in Myfanwy ever since they had left the bedroom. A distance. There had been a hint of panic as he had mistaken one of the bedroom doors for the bathroom. Myfanwy had blocked his way far too quickly and her voice had been tight with alarm. "No, not there! Not there!" she had repeated as if he was about to open the door to Dante's *Inferno*.

Kristian met this sudden mood swing head on. "Myfanwy, what made you change your mind about seeing me? Sleeping with me?"

"Oh, lots of things," she said quietly. "Loneliness, the need to be wanted, even loved perhaps . . . if only for a night."

"Just that?"

"Oh Kristian, I don't know. I loved you once – desperately, too desperately. Probably still do. They say the first love is always the deepest. Kristian you are a wanderer, you always have been. You will return to London and find some new adventure no doubt. You would never be happy leading a life of bucolic tranquillity and you know it. You're the proverbial action man. What good is that to me? The last man took off, I'm only just forgetting the bastard. It wouldn't be fair to either of us for me try and hold you. We have both moved on, Kristian. You can't turn back the clock. Last night was lovely but it was a dream. It can't go on, can it? Dreams happen and then you wake up."

Kristian had not expected any of this. It had taken him by surprise. It hurt. "You seem very sure of things, sure of me. For God's sake why don't we just see where things go. Neither one of us is committed in any way. If it helps, Myfanwy, I've done all my 'wandering' as you put it and anyway where the hell do you think I'm going to wander to on one pin! As for the 'action man' bit, well I rather think those days are well and truly over somehow. You know, it's a bit of a struggle playing squash on one pin or embarking upon an idiot adventure through some god-forsaken jungle.

"I still love you Myfanwy . . . even after all these years. I know I can't undo the hurt I caused you but I can at least try and make up for it – if you will let me. Give us a chance woman, we both deserve that! Who knows, we might actually be happy!"

"No, Kristian. My mind is made up. Now leave it at that and let's part as friends." Kristian knew all about Myfanwy's intransigence – it was worse than his own!

"I see, so I'm all right for a quick shag but bugger all else! Damn it women all you have done is use me! What the hell was last night all about then? I thought there was a bit of love here and there. Well, you fooled me good and proper! Ah, to hell with it, I'm off! See you in another life!"

He walked out and slammed the kitchen door as he did so. A few plates nearly fell off the sideboard. Myfanwy sighed. She had seen the tantrums a hundred times before.

Kristian ranted and raved his way back to the Hotel. Women! No wonder he had never married. Probably the only sensible thing he had ever done in his sorry life! They were all bloody mad. Mad! His inherent inclination toward the drama of romance allowed no room for doubt or practicality. For him love would and should always find a way and to hell with everything else. For the first time in his life he felt used. "You're a wanderer," was her accusation and on that outrageous supposition she had decided that only pain would result if they continued to see each other! How the hell did Myfanwy know what his plans were! He didn't even know himself! Women!

The following morning Kristian packed his bags and left the Hotel. He left a letter with Dai Twice to be hand delivered to Myfanwy.

While Kristian sat on the train Dewi Morgan hefted an axe and attacked some logs of wood with a ferocity that only his silent world could understand. He grunted his frustration and anger with each stroke of the axe. He had been up all night. He had seen the light go off in Myfanwy's bedroom and had waited for the stranger to leave. The wait had been endless. His imagination and temper had simmered and then boiled. His precious Myfanwy. She was all he had. The only person he could care for and protect. Dewi had seen the tears in his Myfanwy's eyes. His loyalty and love had cried with her. His eyes compensated for the loss of speech and hearing. He saw everything. He saw the handsome cripple limp. He saw the threat to his secure, loving silence.

He saw hatred in himself.

CHAPTER 7

Gower Peninsula, South Wales. April.

"I'm not sure, Griffith. It's a big step and will cost a great deal of money."

"So what? We can more than afford any losses. And there won't be any anyway. It's time to expand, Lise. We must build on the reputation of the Cliffs. Once people get to know who is running the new hotel, custom certainly won't be a problem, believe me." Griffith Treharne's face moved into an intense frown, the line between his eyes always deepened when annoyance was on the horizon. At least the vivid red thread veins that had been a result of excessive enjoyment were but a distant memory. His drinking days had more or less come to an end sixteen-odd years ago. He still enjoyed a drink, but not the whole bottle. Some fat remained but his Pirelli tyres were an investment as far as he was concerned. Besides, some women liked 'chubby' men and he was after all only chubby, although his stumpy legs didn't help. He had kept all his hair which was something, even though the years had turned it into a silver but distinguished mop. In spite of all these physical impediments and his blossoming age, he was still an attractive man in character if nothing else. His humour and infectious optimism kept him young in spirit and mind even though he was well into his sixties. Right now he was relying on his optimism to convince Lise to expand.

"I'll think about it," Lise Treharne said reluctantly as she straightened the red silk scarf that kept moving across her arms and refused to be kept in place by the beige cashmere jacket that covered her shoulders. "Now we have a new manager to interview, so let's get on with the job in hand, shall we? God knows, this place takes up enough of my time as it is and you want to start expanding into another hotel!"

Griffith tugged at his cavalry twill trousers and noted that his brogues required some immediate attention. The shine wasn't quite right. He often regretted not taking up a commission in the Guards like his late brother Glyn. Mind you, that daft bugger had got himself killed in the war. Fat lot of good a posthumous VC had been to him. Heroism was not for Griffith, he wasn't that much of a fool. Instead he had chosen fast cars, fast women, fast drink and an even faster prosecution for 'living off immoral earnings' by a self-righteous beak in Marylebone Magistrates Court. Thank God his father had handed in his dinner cards by that time. These days he was a highly respected hotelier who was never seen drunk in public or tickling a chambermaid's buttocks in some quiet laundry room.

He shot his starched white cuffs and pulled on the lapels of his Harris Tweed jacket, a sure sign of irritation. "We must build upon our success, Lise, that's all there is to it, so stop being so scared. You know as well as I do that you rather fancy the idea. Since when have you been able to resist a challenge anyway?"

"Oh Griffith, do be quiet will you? As for being 'scared' as you put it, I think not. You know me better than that. Now go and ask Mr Sewell to come in. He comes highly recommended so don't start trying to frighten him off with your hostile and belligerent questioning. Be your normal charming and good-humoured self please, it's far more becoming!"

"If I must, but remember that there's a lot of pressure in the hotel business. Any new manager must be up to it. A little taster of what this place is all about won't do any harm. Don't forget, our standards are extremely high and non-negotiable. I want to find out how he will react to an obnoxious bloody guest for instance. We get enough of the bastards—"

"Griffith! Your language is atrocious. I know your 'tasters' so behave yourself – please." Lise gave Griffith one of her best smiles. Sometimes he was so like his father it made her struggle for breath. The smile had the desired effect, it usually did. Griffith looked at her, his hidden love staying silent and raw.

"Right, well I'll go and get the latest lamb to the slaughter then. Won't be long."

"Griffith, I'm warning you!"

"Yes, yes Lise. See you in a minute. Oh, and one more thing, Lise. Dad would have wanted you to pick up the gauntlet too." Griffith also knew how to achieve the desired effect.

When the door closed Lise sat back in her chair. Her eyes looked around the room that had once been her husband's study. For a few quiet minutes she allowed her mind to wander. William's shadows jumped from antiquarian books and Victorian landscapes while Persian rugs sometimes hopped across a polished oak floor that never stopped groaning each time a human foot was placed on it. There were times when she could still hear the wisdom in her husband's cultured voice and feel the love in a touch that would remain with her until the day she died. He had died in this room, his sovereignty over Destiny maintained to the end. That had been more than twenty years ago.

Lise had changed nothing in the study. It remained exactly as William had left it. She had been neither motivated by any morbid desire to keep death at bay nor indeed to resurrect a memory back into human form. The room was certainly no mausoleum. It was just a place where she could find comfort and sometimes inspiration by feeling close to the man she had loved so deeply.

Shortly after William's death Lise had given birth to Charlotte their only child. She had just graduated in law from University College, London and was trying to become a lawyer. Lise sighed when she thought of Lottie. Her red curls, white skin and incisive mind would have made her father so proud.

He had not seen her born but Lottie was William through and through, so his immortality was quite secure. Lise was not so sure though whether he would have appreciated his daughter's choice of career – he had always hated lawyers! Her only son, Kristian, continued to worry and disturb her. He was so wilful and independent that there were times when she wanted to hit him. For a moment a smile passed across her lips; whilst Lottie may have been all William, Kristian was sure as hell all Lise. Her mind briefly brought back the memory of her rape all those years ago at the end of the Second World War in Denmark, her country of birth and childhood: Kristian being born from such ferocious violence and her brief love affair with Karl.

Lise Treharne had known all the insidious facets of deceit, betrayal and tragedy but William and time had brought balance and Nature had healed. She had forgiven but would never forget. She had learnt.

Her hand moved to a silver letter-opener that lay on William's desk. This small gesture, like everything else about Lise, was elegant and exact. Like the immaculate, tailored suits she always wore, there was a natural bearing of distinction and uniqueness about her. Her finger touched the delicate engraving of her name on its handle. It had been given as a token of love. She picked it up and as she did so she paused to look at the skin on the backs of her hands. Her skin remained slightly tinged by the sun of her ancient Scandinavian ancestors, but it had lost some of the crispness of youth. Sly wrinkles peaked out from a face and dark blue eyes that knew only strength and compassion. Her natural blonde hair, shorter now and less vivid in colour, was still capable of the most outrageous, natural shine when the sun looked favourably upon it. Her body had become a trifle slower and only slightly less vivacious, yet she could still move with a litheness that surprised anyone who was fool enough to believe that Mrs Treharne was getting old. The warrior spirit of her Viking father still clashed with the frantic passion of her Celtic mother on occasions, but at fifty-four Lise was still an extremely beautiful woman to any man whose eyes knew not only how to look, but also to see.

Her hotel, Ragged Cliffs, had become famous. People from all over the globe visited the hotel to experience the wild grip and at other times gentle song of the Gower Peninsula. The house where William had loved and adored her, where he had given her life, was now a renowned establishment where only the finest Welsh food was served and where a new dimension to comfort was experienced. There was no chrome or modern terror in the hotel. Traditional and refined surroundings were the order of the day. It was an environment where people could forget and show who they really were. William's rose gardens had matured and grown into a colourful walk where the guests could look out across the cliffs and see only space and beauty. The stone bench where he and Lise had kissed and laughed still sat amongst the roses, although now other couples enjoyed the fragrances and Nature's blessed touch.

Ragged Cliffs was Lise's creation and far more than a sturdy but refined structure of bricks and mortar. In spite of its past tragedies it still inspired. It still commanded and sometimes conquered the elements that tried to hurt it and Lise's touch still fell upon every nook and cranny as her character spun through every room and closet.

It was Lise Treharne.

CHAPTER 8

"Damn woman!" Griffith cursed as he went to look for Mr Sewell. Too much of my father's influence, he thought, stubborn as hell – and by God the old man could be stubborn!

Griffith was William Treharne's son by a first marriage. There had been a thirty-two year age difference between his father and Lise, thus leading to the unusual situation of his being ten years older than his stepmother. He remembered setting eyes on the shy, magnificent young women for the first time. It had been at his father's dining table. He would never forget how she had totally absorbed him and how he had had to resist any feelings of attraction. Lise was his father's woman after all, and any improper thoughts of his own would have been downright incestuous! At least that's how it had seemed at the time. Over the years this feeling had persisted and continued to trap him.

After his father's death and the calling of time on his own misspent lifestyle Griffith had come to the Cliffs to help Lise with the transformation of his father's house into one of the finest hotels in South Wales. More than twenty years had passed since that chaotic time and he had Lise had come to depend on one another. They had become brother and sister in the most perfect sense. Too perfect for Griffith but these thoughts he kept deep within his own unique private place. Incest again!

His frustration boiled for a few moments longer, then evaporated as he held out his hand in welcome to Mr Sewell who was seated on one of the battered, old leather armchairs in the hotel's reception area. The rich oak panelling was covered with ancient oil paintings of forgotten Welsh legends and surly dignitaries who had died so long ago that no one actually knew who they were. The dead and glorious competed and fought for the light that shone through the French windows facing the reception desk.

"Mr Sewell, I believe. How do you do? Would you like some refreshment before we start? Bit early in the day for booze, but you can have as much tea or coffee as you like" Sewell stood up. The two men shook hands. He was a tall man, early 30s, and tended to look down on Griffith who wasn't sure whether this was intentional or not.

"No thank you to the tea or coffee. I don't need caffeine to keep me alert. Pleased to meet you, and you are . . .?"

"Griffith Treharne, a sleeping partner in the Cliffs, although I rarely sleep. The lazy buggers round here require 24-hour surveillance! Feel like some bloody spymaster out of one of Le Carré's novels sometimes!" Griffith laughed, but his good humour was lost on the man. "Right, well . . . please come with me and we can get all this interviewing nonsense out of the way." Griffith beamed at the man at the same time, hiding his immediate disquiet at the man's handshake. There had been no 'grip', no strength. A sure sign of spineless inclination as far as Griffith was concerned. This, the 'pleased to meet you' bit – in Griffith's preppy and public-school book anyone using this particular verbal response to a first meeting usually confirmed a distinct lack of breeding – and the fact that the man was a long streak of piss did not impress. A bad start.

He led the way to what had once been his old man's study, hiding his annoyance at the requirement for a hotel manager in the first place. Lise had always insisted on a managerial position and he had always been against it. As far as he was concerned it was a family business, so who needed outsiders? Besides they cost too much, and in his view were a waste of money. He and Lise had tooled along well enough since the last bureaucratic incumbent had left, but she wouldn't budge. Kept moaning about the extra workload and their individual ages. God, the woman was a pain in the arse sometimes!

He opened the door to the study and introduced Sewell to Lise. When they were all seated, Griffith sat alongside Lise just to make sure that Sewell was in no doubt as to whom the bosses were in the organization. Lise spoke first, granting the supercilious bugger one of her more devastating smiles. Griffith winced; he hated Lise showing any undue attention to another man apart from himself.

"Mr Sewell – or may I call you Justin?" Justin! What was the woman doing, Griffith fumed and glared. First names already! Bad form. Staff were staff and addressed accordingly. To hell with friendship with the paid help, familiarity and all that. Lise must be letting all this idiotic employment legislation go to her head again!

"Justin will be fine."

"Good. You have already met my partner . . . um, Mr Treharne, so now that the formalities are out of the way, would you like to tell us a little bit about yourself and why you are interested in working for us?"

Justin Sewell coughed into his hand and then began to give a life history that would both impress and secure a job in the prestigious and acclaimed Ragged Cliffs hotel. He wanted this job, London with its monstrous hotels and swarms of vulgar Americans could rot in Hell. This was where he belonged. At the top of the exclusive and rarefied executive market. He kept his almost obsessive ambition under control as he delivered a modest account of his achievements and experience all of which could be backed up by a simple phone call or letter. In the hotel industry he had become a legend and he knew it but now was not the time or place to start lionizing himself. He spoke quietly but with just the right amount of enthusiasm. He would be the quintessential strong and steady pair of hands at the wheel.

Sewell was a handsome man although his chin tended to lack any obvious character. His green eyes were watchful and seemed to quickly note any detail that may be of use to him. His black hair was slightly long but in tune with the fashion of the times. There was charm too in the unassuming demeanour. His smile could be quite dashing and Lise instantly wondered why he had never married. One of her previous managers had been homosexual, it sometimes seemed to go with the job, but being the enlightened woman that she was – she had to be, her children and Griffith made sure of it – the man's sexual proclivities were of no concern to her. If he could do the job and do it according to the exacting standards of the Cliffs then that was fine by her. If he was inclined to prefer men to women on his days off, then so what? She had to admit though there were no obvious signs of the man being other than heterosexual. Time would tell.

When Sewell had finished his verbal job application the three discussed the more detailed terms and conditions of his possible employment. When everything had been agreed in principle they all said their goodbyes. Sewell would hear something within seven days. Lise thanked the man for his time and saw him out through the main entrance. Griffith didn't budge off his seat.

CHAPTER 9

"I didn't like him. Something shifty there – and before you start, you know how you only ever see the best in people."

"Well, Griffith," Lise observed, "at least one of us does. 'Shifty' is a new one. Usually, where any manager is concerned they are either a 'queer' or an 'arrogant bastard', so which category does Justin fall into?"

"Oh God, it's 'Justin' again! That means you want to employ him and no doubt you will get your own way. You always do."

"That's right, Griffith. Will you do the letter offering him the job or will I?"

"You can do it, being as you're so keen, and by the way I do have a say around this place sometimes you know. I have invested a good wad of my old man's hard-earned cash into the Cliffs, after all."

Lise looked at Griffith and smiled with a warmth that could only ever be exclusively for him. "Now don't be childish, Griffith. We need a manager and that's all there is to it. Are you going to do the night duty when one of the porters is off sick? Arrange all the staff rotas? Order all the food? Need I go on? And what happens when you disappear on one of your secret little jaunts and I happen to be away too?"

"All right, all right. You've made your point. You win again." Griffith would never admit it but his resistance to Sewell had been largely based upon the fact that the man was a good-looking sod and charming with it, wet cod handshake or not. Lise may well have been a good bit older than the man, but experience had taught him that one could never predict the wanton ways of human kind. There had been one hell of an age difference between Lise and his father, hadn't there?

Lise stood up from her chair and came around the desk. "Don't start sulking, Griffith. Justin will be fine." With that she gave him a peck on the cheek, sisterly love again. "Now let's go over these accounts one more time shall we? The bar takings seem to be down." Just as they were about to discuss the takings the door burst open and Kristian walked in.

"Well, hard at it again I see. Obsessed workaholics, the pair of you!"

Lise rushed up to her son and hugged him. "Kristian! Why didn't you tell me you were coming home?"

"Didn't want the fuss Mother, you know what you're like!"

Griffith went up to Kristian and shook his hand, wishing as he did so that his own presence could inspire as much enthusiasm from Lise. This time the grip was firm and unforgiving. The two men were extremely fond of each other. They would do the 'men's talk' bit later on in the bar when Lise wasn't around. It would probably be a long night if past form was anything to go by.

"Inconsiderate as ever, Kristian," Lise admonished, "you don't change. How are you anyway? How is the leg?" She was about to ask him if he was doing anything useful in his life but quickly decided against it; he had only just arrived and she was too pleased to see him to start a full-blown row. He would probably tell her in no uncertain terms to mind her own business anyway. God forbid that she should mention anything about marriage or grandchildren as either one really would start another Falklands.

"Fine, Mother, everything is fine. See what I mean? You fuss too much." Lise didn't 'fuss' at all. Her son had nearly been killed in another war. The Treharnes had given enough to warmongering politicians who were never content with just the land they ruled.

"How long are you staying this time, or is this another one of your 'fleeting visits'? You know, say 'Hello', have a few drinks with Griffith, then off again back to some London strumpet, no doubt. And you are still smoking, I can smell it, as bad as your Uncle Griffith. The horrible habit will kill the pair of you one day."

"Oh God, Ma—"

"Don't you call me 'Ma'! You know I hate it. You make me sound like one of those hideous characters in that awful American 'Beverley Hillbillies' programme. God forbid that we should start speaking like those colonial half-wits!"

"Still full of English superiority I note, Mother, and there you are, half Welsh and half Danish. Bit odd that," Kristian laughed. His mother could be so correct and poker-faced sometimes that he enjoyed baiting her. She could also be so wonderfully amusing when it suited her. "A few days, a week even. Oh – and yes, I am still smoking."

Lise gave up. She knew there was absolutely nothing she could do with her son. He would always go his own way regardless of the consequences. All she could ever do was wait for him and love him.

"Where's Lottie then?" Kristian asked. He always missed his little sister. He had changed her nappies many times and by God did she know how to fill them! That had been years ago now, but there was still a highly protective love where his sister was concerned, half-sister or not.

"On the telephone I suspect," Lise replied, "the girl rarely gets off the thing. I dread to think what the telephone bill is going to be like."

"When is she due to be let loose on the general public then? God help them!"

"Don't ask me, Kristian, you know what your sister is like. Everything is left until the last minute. Last I heard she was applying for a pupillage in London – Lincoln's Inn, I think. One thing is for certain, she's not wasting her time around here month after month. Not like me at all. Silly girl will never learn. Try our apartment, she's probably mooning about deciding what dress to wear for one of her latest conquests. God knows how the girl ever finds the time to try and become a barrister."

"You love her really, Mother, so stop complaining. She's just young and full of hell like the rest of her family."

"You maybe, Kristian – oh, and Griffith in his day—"

"Hey, steady on there, Lise, I'm sixty-four for heavens sake! My wild days are but a distant memory and I'm too bloody old to be a playboy now, more's the pity!" Lise gave Griffith a sly smile.

"So you say, Griffith, but given half a chance—" Griffith shut up, he didn't have a leg to stand on. Lise knew all about his blacker days and probably had a good idea where he went on his 'secret trips' too. Nothing ever escaped the damned woman.

"Anyway Mother, before you start casting aspersions on our moral integrity, William was a bit of a lad too I've been told."

"That's none of your business, Kristian, so be quiet!" Her late husband was certainly not short in coming forward she had to admit. He had married a much younger woman and kept her happy in those delicate hours between dusk and dawn, not to mention the occasional and frantic dalliance in the greenhouse when the gardener wasn't watching. Lise started to blush at the memory but quickly composed herself. "Now, go and say 'hello' to your sister, Kristian, and stop annoying me. You know how she misses you. Try and drum some sense into her while you're at it. On second thoughts you two will only conspire to get up to more mischief, so don't bother. Now off you go, Griffith and I have work to do."

"Will do, and what's for supper? I'm starving. Only your cooking will do the trick, Mother, so don't spend too much time ensconced with Griffith, the cooker beckons!"

"Out, Kristian! Out!"

CHAPTER 10

Kristian found his sister in their mother's apartment. She was sitting down reading the law reports in *The Times*. The place hadn't changed. His mother was everywhere as was William. Photographs and piquant pieces of memory charmed the delicate antique furnishings, the evening sun that barged through the air adding a shade of other times amongst the subtle colours of fabric and paint. The balcony doors opened onto the cliffs of the Gower Peninsula, cliffs that had seen and witnessed all the great tempers of the elements and all their benevolence of calm, pride and beauty. The rooms soothed and swooned under his mother's touch. The devoted love of Lise and William moved from space to space and yet there was no bathos, no mourning. Instead there was only celebration, humour, and the moving on into other lives. Lise's memories of these times were happy and alive. Yet like the study, there were no attempts to resurrect the dead, no attempts to achieve impossible immortality.

Kristian stood in the doorway and watched his sister reading. Huge blue eyes that would have offended the seas thrashing the cliffs not far away concentrated and absorbed. Her turret of red curls threatened and challenged as she pushed it out of her eyes. This constant, petty irritation was tolerable as long as her flowing locks attracted the right kind of men. Thank God though she wasn't a carrot head or 'copper crutch'; that really would have been unacceptable and neither did she look like a demented portion of spotted dick. There wasn't a brown or red freckle in sight. Her hair was actually a mixture of gold and red, either colour dominating depending on where the sun blasted it. Her nose and facial lines shouted character not prettiness, which would have been far too superficial and silly for a girl like

Charlotte. There was only sheer, raw beauty and it stood alone, apart.

Her knees were tucked up under her backside as she moved her petite but bountiful body to and fro in an effort to understand esoteric legal bullshit. Her forehead creased as she grunted in frustration: all this just to be a lawyer and to defend all the hopeless misfits who fell foul of the law. She had already decided that criminal defence work would be just the thing. Outwitting all those stuck-up, pompous twits at the Bar would be right up her street. Her right hand scratched the pale skin on one of her legs. As soon as summer arrived the paleness would turn into a lovely natural colour of darkened bronze. Men would die just to stroke, or better still kiss, her irresistible skin. As far as Charlotte was concerned they could all die too – as long as she didn't fancy them, of course. She wasn't that stupid!

"So, Bigjugs, how is my legal genius then? Not Master of the Rolls yet?" her brother said from the doorway.

"Kris! You lovable hound! Where have you been? We haven't spoken for weeks you shit!" Charlotte ran up to him, her plain white dress flowing everywhere, and gave him a kiss and a hug. She didn't let go until she had tousled his hair and pinched his cheek.

"And I do wish you'd stop calling me 'Bigjugs'. I don't call you 'Guts', do I? Mum would do her nut if she heard you, they're not that big anyway!"

"They're big enough to satisfy most men I think, and I've been calling you that since the damn things first exploded, so don't expect me to stop now. At least you don't throw them around everybody's neck I suppose, that really would be tiresome and extremely sluttish."

"No I don't, so think of some other nickname will you, although I suppose that's expecting a bit much . . . Your hair's a bit long for the soldier of fortune, isn't it? What have you been up to then? Tell all! Must be more interesting than my antics. The law is driving me round the bend! Come on, sit!" Charlotte took his hand and led him to a sofa. When they were seated, she said, still holding his hand, "I've missed you big brother, don't leave it so long until you get in touch next time please. How long are you down for?"

"That's the second time I've been asked that today and I haven't been here an hour yet. A few days, a week maybe. Ma will kill me if I don't stay for at least a couple of days and sorry I haven't been in touch. Been a bit busy lately. Now, come on Bigjugs, let's go and take a walk around the gardens. It's a beautiful evening."

As they walked to one of their favourite places they bumped into Will Jenkins, the gardener. The man had skulked, sulked and lurked around the gardens of the Cliffs for as long as Kristian could remember. He had become such a natural companion to Nature that half the time one could hardly distinguish him from the green, browns and vivid colours of the world he cherished and worked in. His flat cap was as old as he was and his wrinkled face so worn by wind, rain and sun that no one yet had been able to determine exactly what age he was. Speculation ranged from seventy to ninety, but no one could be absolutely certain. He had arrived at the gates of the Cliffs some thirty years ago with nothing but a leather bag and a packet of Players. William had taken him on and he had never left. He lived in one of the old outbuildings and never ventured outside the boundaries of his own small world.

"Hello, Will. What are you up to then? Getting ready for Spring, eh? It's already started by the looks of it." Kristian smiled and threw a packet of Old Holborn at the gardener. The old man caught the tobacco with surprising agility.

"Thank you, Master Kristian," he mumbled as he touched his antique flat cap. The old man still lived in a world of fawning deference and doffed caps. The likes of Will Jenkins were rapidly becoming an ancient history lesson.

"How are you then, you miserable old devil? Got a good woman yet?"

"Women! Don't talk to me about women, master Kristian. I was engaged to three of 'em in my time and all the bitches went and died on me before I could get 'em up the altar. Three bloody rings too! Never got one of 'em back! No, bugger women! I have plenty of Nature's love so what more could a man need? Mind you, even she can be a moody cow from time to time, beggin' your pardon Miss Charlotte."

"Oh, don't mind me, Will. You just carry on. I enjoy a bit of misogyny now and again."

"Beggin' your pardon, Miss? *Mis* what?"

"Never mind, Will. Do you think you could find a smile for us on this lovely evening? Go on now, it's a special occasion. The long, lost Prodigal has returned. Go on Will, give us one of your best!"

"Oh bugger off, Miss, 'scuse the language." He couldn't help it but the trace of a smile seemed to remove some of his wrinkles for a brief moment. Miss Charlotte was probably the only person on the planet who could make him smile, or at least try to.

"I'll take that grimace as a smile then, Will, better than nothing I suppose," Charlotte laughed. "Come on then Kris, let's leave the old goat to his earth and manure. See you, Will." She dragged Kristian off by the arm to one of the best places in the grounds of the hotel.

They entered the rose garden and as usual both of them fell silent for a few moments. Sitting down on a stone bench they looked out across the cliffs and sea and allowed the scent of budding roses to infuse and soothe. Forty years ago William Treharne had made this his private place. He had nurtured, coaxed and bullied Nature into creating a haven of peace and colour. His touch and love still remained in all the wonderful shades and riches that would soon blossom into a glorious mixture of the past, the present, the future and the unknown. All the different and cantankerous moods of the weather met up in this one small place. They all fought and struggled, they all tamed and dominated. The sea moaned and sometimes yelled for surrender as the cliffs stood in its way and stopped its imperial conquest. The roses bled and then they healed. Their colours would change with every season, but they always remained. They never stirred from the spot where they had been given life. Their permanence and their endurance inspired those who would sit and listen to their stories, their achievements. For those who could feel and touch, for those who could see, the rose garden was one of the most beautiful places on earth.

Kristian looked out across the grounds and saw so much that had become a part of him. His birth in Denmark, the troubled, pitiful rooms of a tiny terraced house in the more tragic part of Swansea and then the adventure of Ragged Cliffs. William Treharne, his adopted father, showing him the hedges that had been sculpted into Walt Disney characters. Donald Duck and Mickey Mouse still dashed across the lawns to annoy the stubborn and severe bricks of the Victorian mansion that stood behind them. The Cliffs stood still, it never marched into new territory. It was always there when needed.

"Well, Bigjugs, what's happening with you then? Who's the latest?"

"Mind your own business, Kris. You never tell anybody about your women. Not even me. And I bet there are plenty of them too!"

"Come on now, Lottie – there you are, I'm even being polite now – I can see you are dying to tell me. You've got that silly 'in love' look in your eyes and you're smiling far too much. Who is he? Come on?"

"Oh if I must, but you can forget the 'in love' crap. I'm too young for all of that. I don't have the time for any gripping romance. Too much going on. Pleasant diversions are fine, but anything else is off limits. 'He' is a chap I met at one of those post-graduate dos. You know, the things where you meet practising lawyers and they are supposed to tell you what the game is all about sort of thing."

"What's his name then?"

Charlotte paused for a few moments as she fiddled with a gold bracelet their mother had given her on her eighteenth birthday. A sure sign of nerves. "I know you Kris, you will take the mickey and I won't have it. He's great."

"What's his name for heavens sake, girl?"

"Wilberforce."

"What? That's his surname?"

"No, Christian name actually, but everyone calls him Will."

"Wilberforce!" Kristian burst out laughing, "Damn me. Don't tell me his surname is Wooster for God's sake! I couldn't stand it." Charlotte stood up, her hair redder than usual and about to explode.

"You see! I knew you would start! You always go out of your way to find something wrong with my boyfriends." Her pale cheeks were getting redder as she stood in front of her brother hands on hips. Kristian had to admit that she had a point there. He was always being far too protective of his little sister, he just couldn't help it. God help anyone who hurt her or even thought about doing so.

"All right, all right, calm down." Kristian struggled to keep his laughter under control. "'Will' isn't so bad I suppose, doesn't wear a flat cap and smoke roll-ups though, does he? That wouldn't do at all."

"Oh shut up Kris, will you?" He was being told to 'Shut up' a lot lately too. "Actually, he's a barrister. Chambers somewhere in Temple, I think."

"Barrister? I thought you considered them all to be arrogant, snobby devils even though you are hell bent on becoming one yourself. That's a bit of an about-turn, isn't it? Anyway, how old, what's he look like and is there plenty of money in his family? 'Old' money now, Bigjugs, not the fish-and-chip-shop brigade riff-raff. We don't want any fortune hunters now, do we? You are worth a few bob after all. And when Ma dies, look out."

"God, you've got a nerve! Who the hell are you, anyway? You're not my father, William died before I was born! And talk about the pot calling the kettle 'black arse'. What about all the tarts you must have slept with in your time? I bet there's a whole regiment of them and did you ever check up on their financial antecedents? Did you hell! You're just like every other man – your dick rules your head!"

"Now, now, Bigjugs," Kristian replied, trying not to laugh again, "no need to let off steam like a bawdy fishwife is there? Ma paid a great deal of money for your education, Cheltenham Ladies College no less. Anyway all men are 'ruled by their dicks' as you put it, including Wilberforce, so don't knock it. Has he given you a fine old rogering yet then? I am your big brother and entitled to know these things." Charlotte was starting to splutter now.

"Has he what? Dear God, I'm going to hit you in a minute!" He had heard this one again, quite recently." Mind your own damned business, Kris. I may not be Mother Theresa, but I sure as hell don't sleep around either! So sod off and stop calling him 'Wilberforce'!"

"Oh dear. It must be love. Getting in quite a lather aren't we? All right, I promise I won't call your new love Wilberforce" – Kristian started to laugh again – "Oh God, sorry, but that name is a real tongue-stopper you have to admit . . ." At last he managed to compose himself. "Fair enough, it's your life so I won't interfere. I wish you well with Will. Sorted out a pupillage yet? Ma is starting to lose patience. Which is fair enough if you ask me. I mean that Bar Vocational Course was a bit of a joke. All you did was get pissed at all those dinners, learn a bit about drafting legal documents and pick and choose who you dragged in to the nearest bed. And after all that you are 'called to the Bar!' "

"Very funny. I've told you once already I'm not an easy lay. Oddly enough I received confirmation of my pupillage this morning. Chambers in Lincoln's Inn. Haven't seen Mum yet to tell her, at least she can stop nagging now. She won't be too happy when she finds out how much more money I'm going to need though, you know what's she's like. That will teach her to keep going on and on!" Charlotte giggled at the thought of her mother's face when she realized how much it was all going to cost.

"I'm starting in October and, believe it or not, Kris, it's going to be hard work. For the first six months I'll be assisting and observing an experienced barrister and for the next six months, well, who knows, I might even be able to do some court work all on my little own. It's back to London anyway. It's April now, so for the next few months Mum can be my employer. She's already moaning at me to do some work in the hotel so I can't hold out for much longer."

"Well, I'll say that for you, you've always been a grafter in spite of ma's reservations, so do some cleaning or waiting on tables to keep the old girl happy. If I know you, you will probably start getting bored around here soon anyway. You'll be living in the house in London, will you?"

"Yes, I don't have to pay any rent, do I? Mind you, Mum watches the bills like a hawk and I have to pay a contribution out of my allowance. It's no wonder she's such a good business-woman. Anyway enough about me, what's going on with you? You know Mum gets terribly anxious about you. She nearly died when you managed to get your leg blown off. Why don't you come home and help out? Learn something about the business. You're not doing anything else are you, except wasting your time around the pubs in Richmond? You know how Mum would like you to take over the business one day. Getting legless in London all the time won't do you any good either." It was her turn to have a good laugh this time, and all Kristian could do was grunt. When Charlotte had stopped laughing she said, "Sorry, couldn't resist it, no doubt you've heard that one before a hundred times." Hadn't he just, and recently too. "Uncle Griffith hasn't any children," she continued, "at least none that he will admit to, you know how it is, keeping things in the family and all that stuff. Besides – and I don't mean to be brutal – but what can you do with one-and-a-half legs? Your soldiering days are over, so no more 'macho man'. I have to be honest with you though, Kris, none of us have shed any tears over you being invalided out . . . We all love you so much, you know – we really do." The banter had come to a stop as Charlotte hugged her brother. "But we know just how much you hurt, Kris . . . we know," she said quietly.

After a few moments had passed and the two had shared their understanding, Kristian said, "Lottie, that would be my worst nightmare and you know it. For God's sake, I've been a soldier for most of my adult life. I don't know anything else and apart from that, dealing with demanding, chocolate-coated people all day long is not my scene. Forget it. Something will come up, something I really want to do. On second thoughts, I might become an academic – who knows? Anyway, who's to say you won't get fed up with the law and take up the reigns."

"Not likely. We are very much alike in one respect at least. Staying in one place doesn't suit. I have far too much living to do, with the law or without it. I'm too young to settle down, but you're not though, Kris, so think about it. It's time you put down some roots. Had a few children. Find yourself a good woman, someone strong enough to tame you – well, 'taming' is probably being a little too optimistic, but find a woman who can at least cope with you, poor soul. No doubt there's someone out there daft enough to take you on."

"Well, thanks for the vote of confidence."

"My pleasure. Now let's go and see what Mum has made for supper. No doubt it will be something special, it always is when the Golden Boy returns. I expect the chef has already thrown a few tantrums, he hates anyone treading on his territory, employer or not."

"Oh, I expect Ma will hold her own, she usually does."

"And for heaven's sake don't let her hear you calling her 'Ma', otherwise there will be more than idiotic artistic sensitivity, and you know what a temperamental old queen Balzac is!" Honoré de Balzac, as he liked to call himself, had been the chef at the Cliffs for twenty years. His real name was Dafydd Jones and he had been born in the Rhondda Valley. He had never read one word of the master's works, but his food was just as good.

"I know, I know," Kristian grudgingly agreed.

CHAPTER 11

Myfanwy sat in her farmhouse kitchen holding the letter that Kristian had sent to her courtesy of Dai Twice. She had read it a hundred times. Her heart still grieved for Kristian, it had never stopped grieving. He had been the only man strong enough to win her love. She still loved him, wanted him and desired him in a way that no other man had ever even come close to. But she could not go back. She would not go back. How could she place her life, her responsibilities, on a man who lived for action, freedom and excitement? There was her life in the country too. She couldn't move, it was unthinkable, there were too many other people to look after. Country life would kill him sooner or later anyway.

Kristian had always had a way with words; if he was stuck for something to do he should try writing a novel, she thought, it would no doubt be a bestseller. His own life story was enough to keep even the most discerning of readers happy, she concluded. In fact their own sorry relationship would be a good start! She read the letter again; she didn't know why exactly, perhaps it was a way of not totally losing the man she had once loved so much. It read:

My dear Myfanwy,

Firstly, I must apologise for any hurt I caused you by coming to see you. You must believe that I had no intention of upsetting you. Be that as it may, I don't blame you. I know how much I hurt you, I know that more than you can ever realize, but you must understand that at the time I left you there was no other way. Would you have wanted to be a beautiful young widow? A widow without a father for her children?

I know my decision to become a soldier was a selfish one and for this I make no excuse. There are none. I was young and callow but it was something I had to do. I had to, please try to understand.

Myfanwy, I have never, ever stopped loving you. Your photo went with me into many dangerous places. Your lovely face travelled with me all over the world, you never left my selfish heart. Never. There were times when I would look at you and remember so much, the laughter and all your wonderful smiles – and your temper! Although I have missed even that!

Myfanwy I still care, I still love you and I still want you.

Don't throw away the times we have known for the sake of pride and anger. Let these things go, let them die and let us love each other again. Let us love Myfanwy. Let us be again. You and me. We returned to where we had been last night. That place that only you and I know. Such a special place. We can go there again my Myfanwy and keep returning without hindrance.

Allow me to love you as you deserve and I will love you with all that I am, all that I can give and all that I want to be, for you and you alone. When you read this letter think of us and be everything that we have been, everything that we still are and everything that only you and I can ever be.

Forever yours,

Kristian.

PS I am going home for a week or so if you want to reply. I won't ring. If I hear nothing I will try to understand. Whatever your response, you will always be my Myfanwy. Always.

A tear dropped onto the paper. The bastard! As if she hadn't shed enough tears over the man! There had been fourteen years of them on and off! Where had he been when she needed him?

Playing soldier boy! Where had he been during all the times of pain and hurt? Where had he been when . . .?

Eventually she stopped dwelling on the past and stood up. Kristian deserved a reply, that she couldn't deny him. Taking a fountain pen and some writing paper from a drawer she sat back down and started to write.

CHAPTER 12

Kristian was sitting in the hotel bar contemplating nothing but the half-empty pint of beer that sat on the table in front of him. At the moment he didn't want to think too much. His mother had been nagging him about coming in to the business and he still couldn't find a valid excuse for saying no. Myfanwy kept prodding his heart like some squaddie's bayonet on an obliging dummy, and to cap it all the air around his stump was starting to play up. As he finished his pint he looked up to see his mother standing before him.

"A letter for you, Kristian, a woman's hand if I'm not mistaken." As usual his mother didn't miss much.

"Thank you, Mother."

"Well, aren't you going to open it?"

"When I'm ready, Mother."

"Well it might be important, Kristian."

"Well if it is, I will find out soon enough, won't I?" Lise hovered and saw the look of 'what's it got to do with you any-way?' on her son's face.

"Right, well, I'll leave you to it then." Lise knew she wasn't going to get anywhere with maternal curiosity or natural female curiosity for that matter. Still, it was gratifying to know that some woman out there cared enough about her son to write him a letter. Someone needed to look after him even if it couldn't be her. Infuriating boy that he was!

When he had been left alone Kristian opened the letter. The handwriting on the front of the envelope left him in no doubt as to who had written it. He could never forget the firm and yet delicate script. Myfanwy. For a few moments he wondered whether he ought to drink a large Wood's rum before reading it, but decided to go ahead anyway. What the hell, he had known worse dangers in his life. On second thoughts though, perhaps he hadn't. He read the letter. When he had finished he went up to the bar, ordered a large rum, sank it in one gulp, said, "Well, fuck that!" not giving a damn who heard and went off to his room to collect his things. He was off!

CHAPTER 13

When Kristian arrived at the farmhouse, Dewi Morgan was tinkering around in the yard. Kristian raised his hand in greeting but received no response. Well, the man could see, couldn't he? Ignorant bugger. This was turning into another good start. He knocked on Myfanwy's door and waited, hoping that this time his unannounced arrival would not be accompanied by a few china missiles. The door opened.

"Oh, it's you," Myfanwy said with a face as tight as Dewi Morgan's and just as unwelcoming. "Didn't you receive my letter?"

"I did. Can I come in or are you going to keep me standing here like some impatient bailiff about to devour all your worldly possessions?"

"If you must."

"Don't overdo the welcome, will you Myfanwy?"

She turned around and Kristian followed her in to the kitchen.

"Do I get a cup of tea or something, actually a large rum might be more appropriate?"

"A large rum is it? Well, I think I can stretch to that. Wood's only, if I remember correctly?"

"Correct, and try to exercise some 'mine host' geniality as you are serving it please, because at the moment you look as if the skin of your arse has been grafted onto your face. I'm surprised you ever get any customers at all."

"Thank you for that, Kristian. However, I have managed well enough these past fourteen years with or without your caustic wit. I won't be long."

"Oh sit down, Myfanwy, I'll get it myself, I doubt if anything has changed much. In fact I'll pour one for you too while I'm at it. A stiff drink might loosen up that smile of yours which right now is tighter than a duck's arse – and that's saying something."

Kristian was right. The bar hadn't changed. Green walls with a red line pretending to be a dado rail still reminded Kristian of bleach-drenched public urinals. There was no 'bar' as such, it was just a long room with a few trestle tables at the end of it. Behind these tables sat barrels of beer and a few bottles of shorts, nothing fancy, Campari and Pimm's were for teetotallers not drinkers, and this was a drinkers bar. There was no carpet on the floor; tatty, worn-out linoleum seemed to do well enough. The locals would have been most put out if Axminster or Wilton had tried to spy on them, as apart from anything else the floor was a useful ashtray when beer started to make coordination a little hapless. Kristian found a bottle of Wood's and poured a couple of large ones. Two old boys looked up from their dominoes, reddened beer-soaked eyes stared for a few moments then returned to the safety of black and white dots. They had both given up on life years ago, so that whatever time they now had left was just a dismal fugue of hops, yeast and dribbling saliva.

A few minutes later Kristian was back in the kitchen. He sat down opposite Myfanwy. The patched-up antiques in the bar would help themselves as required.

"Thank you for the letter, Myfanwy, it really made my day."

"The army doesn't seem to have taught you any subtlety, Kristian, but then I suppose that really would be expecting too much. You always could switch from intellectual finesse to crude sarcasm in seconds. I thought my letter was perfectly clear so I have no idea why you are here." She drank her rum in one gulp. She knew where all this was heading. Old habits die hard.

Kristian sat opposite her and fumed.

"Why the hell are you being so stubborn, woman? What have you got to lose?"

"Don't call me 'woman'! You chauvinistic bastard! Those days are well and truly over. You bloody men think you control the world – well you don't, and your particular Empire stops at my front door!"

"Oh God, you're not back on that puerile crusade are you? The chains rotted and fell off the railings years ago, and there's me deluding myself yet again that you had grown up, you know, that you had finally left the students' union bar with its sticky, beer-soaked carpet and naïve student fantasy behind. So much for education."

"Grown up! Grown up! How dare you! You're the pathetic little boy who couldn't grow up, had to keep playing soldiers. And where did that get you? No life and no leg, you sad bastard! Now just shut up, Kristian, will you?"

"Never one to pull your punches, were you Myfanwy. Part of my leg did have something to do with you having a right to say what you like, you know." The air around them paused for a few seconds, the anger was wearing it out. Myfanwy stood up and went over to the kettle.

"I'm sorry. That was uncalled for."

"Oh don't mind me. I'm sorry too . . . We aren't handling this very well, are we? Going at each other's throats isn't going to help anything, is it?"

"No, it isn't." Myfanwy sat down and took Kristian's hand. "Look Kristian, it must be this way. I said in my letter that we have no future and I meant it. Can you see yourself being a farmer? Sitting in the pub all night talking about weather, crops and EU subsidies? I don't think so. You would die, Kristian."

"I could try."

"That's nonsense and you know it. You were always inclined to be a bit of a dreamer."

"All right, well, why can't you move? We can find somewhere that we both like and build a life together. I had never actually put you down as a country girl. Too much spirit."

"I know but we change. I can't leave here, Kristian. I can't, and that's all there is to it."

"But why for God's sake? What is holding you here? You have no family here, no children, so what's the problem? We can go wherever you like. Money certainly isn't an issue for either of us and even if you were a bit short I have more than enough for the pair of us."

"I know that. Even so I want to stay here. The life suits me. It's quiet and peaceful. I have only fields and rivers as neighbours. I am even starting to write again, academic papers and so on. I have responsibilities here, commitments, whether you like it or not" There were more moments of silence. Each of them was trying to win their own individual wars.

"You know, Myfanwy, there seems to be one thing we haven't even mentioned here. The most important thing. Love. We did love each other so very deeply once you know. And I believe that we both still do. It might have a different character now but the substance hasn't changed. It's still solid, still touchable. I can see it all there in your eyes no matter how much you try to deny and evade. You can't fool me, Myfanwy, you never could. I may be the hopeless romantic, but we can be together again. Please believe me. How can you ignore the love that is flying around this kitchen? How can you ignore what is so easily within our reach? Don't be a fool, Myfanwy. I know there is something else holding you back. I know. All this tripe about me, the country life, you, the isolated academic, 'responsibilities,' it's all crap Myfanwy and you know it. What is it that you're not telling me, Myfanwy? What is it? None of this is adding up. None of it!"

"Oh God, Kristian, don't you ever give up? Why do you always have to be such a tenacious idiot. For the last time, we have no future! Now go! Please!"

"Myfanwy, I—"

"Go, Kristian! Go! No more!" Myfanwy was shouting now as tears started to stream down her face. Kristian stood where he was. Unsure. Shocked by her outburst. Before he could move the kitchen door flew open and Dewi Morgan charged in. The weight of the man alone nearly knocked Kristian off his feet, false foot notwithstanding. It had been a long time since he had been involved in any close-quarter combat but surprisingly his reactions didn't let him down. As Dewi charged into him he managed to avoid the full force of the man's bulk. He turned sideways with a speed that wrong-footed his assailant whilst at the same time kicking his right foot straight into the man's shin. Dewi howled in agony but remained standing. His clenched fist came straight for Kristian's jaw who managed to duck while at the same time thrusting the side of his right hand into Dewi's throat. The man collapsed onto the kitchen floor gripping his throat and gurgling as he did so. Myfanwy screamed and dashed to the fallen Dewi.

"Right, that's it, Kristian! Get out and make sure I never see you again, Ever!"

"I was only def—"

"Get out, Kristian! For the love of God, get out! And never come back!"

Kristian's response to Dewi's attack had been restrained, the man would have a sore throat for a couple of hours but that was all. He knew that Myfanwy wouldn't see it this way and he also knew that now there really was nowhere to go.

CHAPTER 14

Griffith arrived in Surbiton Station and went straight to a pub just outside the main entrance. He ordered a pint of Guinness, sat down, looked at his pocket watch and decided there was no rush. He hated Surbiton, a place where commuters rested and pretended to live. It was worse than London itself and that was saying something. Vast 1930's semi-detached aloofness sprawled across acres of trite little gardens with their hopeless little gnomes all trying to impress unknown faces and bodies that kept walking nowhere. Comfort and security prevailed in a commuter paradise bereft of sincere love and compassion; it was a safe place to curl up your toes if the boredom didn't get you first.

Griffith was off on one of his 'secret little jaunts'. He wished they enjoyed a tad more humour and enthusiasm, but this was not to be, most of the time anyway. He came to this dull place because he had to. Duty, honour and indeed his own inherent kindness made him knock on a door in one of London's more self-satisfied satellites. His 'secret little jaunts' did have their more satisfying moments though, depending on mood swings, depression, hormones and a menopause just waiting to pounce. He looked at his pocket watch again, finished his drink and made for the door. He was always punctual, booze or no booze.

He walked up a road that was as indistinguishable as all the miserable cars that parked either side waiting for the turn of an indifferent key. Everything about the road was indifferent and everything looked the same, grey, useless and submissive, even the few people who shunted along trying to find somewhere to go. On the other hand, he thought, perhaps their greedy little 'free-market minds' were trying to understand their new status as the 'People's capitalists' as the Chancellor, Nigel Lawson, had christened them in his drive to privatize the nation's assets into oblivion. Thatcher's 'free market' was all very well but Griffith feared the end of his privilege and the comfortable deference he always demanded. Too many shareholders, too many people with money and vested interests meant the end of the proletariat and those who 'did'. Smith, Friedman & Co. were the new government policy-makers: stop the supply of money and inflation would go down and employment up, so that eventually working-class aspiration would prevail and tattoos would be driving Rolls-Royces. As far as he was concerned Lawson and Thatcher were nothing more than closet Commies determined to bring about equality and wealth for all through the back door. Disingenuous bastards!

Eventually he walked up a tidy path with the statutory patch of grass, although thank God there wasn't a red-hatted gnome in sight. He knocked on a door that almost yelled with excite-ment. After a few moments of anticipation the door opened and a woman stood before him. As always memories of more pristine days came back, memories of parties, drink and loose women.

"Hello, Sylvia. How are you?"

"Always punctual Griffith, you don't change do you?" the woman's eyes smiled. So, no hormone imbalance today then. Things were looking up.

"Some things simply aren't worth changing are they? Time does that."

"It can do. Come in then. Paul is out somewhere, I told him to make himself scarce for a bit. Said we had some business to discuss. Do you want to go upstairs or will down here do? You always liked settees." At least she wasn't being too business-like, there had been a smile anyway.

"Upstairs, I think. I'm not so young anymore. Besides I like some comfort, you know how it is. We older boys require more priming." He smiled and for a moment a look of genuine affection passed across the woman's face. The past had been forgiven, sex could be like that, it was better than any Catholic priest or a thousand Hail Mary's put together.

"OK, the bedroom it is. Come on then, Paul will be home soon."

Griffith followed the woman up the stairs. At forty-three, Sylvia Edmunds had not allowed time to get the better of her. He remembered her body, her personality. Twenty years ago she had been the best 'escort' ever to have worked for him. And the most in demand. Arabs used to pay a fortune just for a squeeze of her perfect bosom, let alone anything else. The woman could swing any which way regardless of race, colour, creed, religion or sexuality. He had looked after her then and he looked after her now. Paul, her son, was also looked after, he had to be; Griffith was his father – not that the boy had any knowledge of this. As far as Paul was concerned Griffith was just a distant cousin who called in every couple of months or so when he was in London to say 'Hello' to his mother. They had been close as children apparently. This was the way Sylvia had always wanted it, her past was best left just there, in the past. No other men ever came to the house, so what did the boy care? Griffith was a bit too posh and upper class for his socialist palate though, but he seemed to make his mother smile a lot, which was a damn sight more than he was ever able to do. He wasn't keen on having another man in the house though, cousin or not. His mother was his and no one else's.

Griffith lay on the bed naked and watched Sylvia undress. For him this was always the best part. If a woman knew her business she could turn these moments into an ejaculation all on their own. And Sylvia knew her business. Her tall body was still firm, her breasts didn't fall to the floor with a bang and neither did her buttocks need scaffolding to keep them upright. Short brown hair allowed all her body to be seen and devoured. Nothing was hidden. The black suspenders stretched her white skin and Griffiths eyes at the same time. She stood at the bottom of the bed, legs slightly apart whilst her fingers floated and teased. Griffith watched and absorbed female maturity at its most comfortable and alluring. Her face wore middle age like some triumphant flag after the massacre of youth. Sylvia remained beautiful but in a more certain and understated way. Griffith knew another woman who had managed to achieve this unique status and for a moment hints of guilt coloured his erratic erection. Sylvia came alongside the bed, bent over and kissed Griffith on the lips. Her fingers moved and Griffith allowed time and Lise to stand still.

"Hello, Griffith," four-eyed Paul said in that effeminate, sickly way of his. He sounded like a frustrated transvestite whose stubble was getting out of control. Apart from this, articulate speech was not one of the boy's strong points in spite of all the private schools Griffith had paid for.

"I'm fine thank you, Paul. How is the graphic designing going then? Found a job yet?" Griffith had paid for the boy to go to college to study graphic design. Whatever the hell that was.

The boy fell down on the settee, stuck his Doc Martins up on one of the arms and shouted "Mum, what's for tea?" Sylvia was in the kitchen but she didn't answer.

"A job?" Griffith persisted.

"No. Nothing yet," the boy whined.

Griffith looked at the fruits of his loins and wanted to punch the greasy haired little bastard into next year. Thank God he didn't have to advertise the fact that the objectionable little shit had come from his seed. He couldn't help but remember some words of the old man, how could he ever forget them, he had heard them often enough. "Oh Paul," he said, "I've heard that Woolworths are doing a new line in plastic spines. Quite cheap too. Why don't you go and buy a few, I'll give you the money if you're a bit short."

The boy looked at Griffith for a few moments with a vacancy that would have shamed a normally oversubscribed tart on a quiet Sunday afternoon, then blinked once or twice.

"Plastic spines, eh? Maybe I could make something out of those you know, something artistic." The cretin meant it. Griffith gave up; to add insult to injury the boy would still be scratching his dandruff if you fed him his head. He looked at his lanky offspring. God, what had he produced? Too much female input, that was the problem. Sylvia had always insisted on the secrecy of the boy's paternity and the lack of parental input from Griffith. At first it had hurt him, but being the easygoing sort of fellow that he was he had learned to live with it and not shed too many tears. He had wanted to have the boy properly schooled, public school of course not private day schools, a bit of group buggering might just have made a man out of him. He would have been happy to pay the fees but Sylvia objected, saying "Look how you turned out!" She had a point there he had to admit, although he had never quite gone as far as group buggery. As he looked at Paul he decided that public school hadn't perhaps been such a good idea as the little weed would have enjoyed the buggering far too much.

Later that afternoon he left Sylvia's and returned home. His needs had been seen to by an expert, her finances were fine and so they should be, he was a generous benefactor and his son Paul was happy wasting his money. How he could have produced a son who was too bone idle to wipe his arse and moped around the place all day would always remain an enduring mystery. Thank God he had never become a family man!

CHAPTER 15

"And where have you been then, Griffith? You weren't here last night, I needed to discuss something with you!" Lise was in one of her serious moods.

"London. On some personal business."

"And . . .?"

"And nothing, Lise. That's it, mind your own business." Griffith was enjoying this. Lise always tried to make out that she didn't care where he went or what he did so why should he tell her anything. Not that he would divulge the details of his time spent with his 'family' anyway. No one knew about them and that was just the way he wanted to keep it. "What did you want to discuss with me anyway that was so important?"

"Oh, it wasn't important, I can't even remember now what it was," Lise tutted as she looked down at her desk and started to fiddle with some papers.

"No? Funny that, it seemed a matter of the utmost urgency a few moments ago."

Lise refused to look at him, instead she continued moving papers around. "Well, it wasn't. Now, Justin has started . . . and you weren't here to show him what to do, apart from anything else."

"Oh give me a break, Lise, will you? What the hell do you need me for to do that? You're more than capable, you know the business better than I do. Anyway, I thought he wasn't starting until next week."

"It changed."

"Oh did it, and I'm supposed to have extra sensory bloody perception, am I?"

"Will you stop swearing, Griffith! You know I can't stand bad language – you're worse that your father!"

"Maybe, but at least he was allowed to get away with it! Now stop being so damned contrary, will you?"

Griffith looked at her with one of his most disarming smiles. Very few people could resist them and Lise certainly wasn't one of them. It was William all over again. Damn though, Griffith was so aggravating. She didn't like it when he went away. She liked it even less when he didn't tell her anything. On one of his 'secret little jaunts' again, no doubt. What on earth did he get up to? She didn't want to admit it to herself but it wasn't just curiosity, she was always left feeling quite hurt when he went off somewhere without saying anything. She felt neglected and taken for granted. Was it a woman? Her stomach didn't like this idea at all no matter how hard she tried to rely on feminine curiosity. She and Griffith had developed a deep and affectionate friendship over the years and she had always insisted that it remain this way. She had been married to his father and was his stepmother for heaven's sake! She had known for years that Griffith was in love with her and she had tried desperately hard not to lead him on or give him false hope. She could never be that cruel, but no one could ever replace William in her heart. One man had tried since William's death and she had almost fallen, but it was not to be. Griffith was like a brother and that's the way it had to stay! It had to! Anything else just wouldn't be right, although the thought of being without him wouldn't be right either.

"All right, all right, I'm sorry for being so 'contrary' as you put it. Will you sit down please, Griffith, I've been thinking about your plans for expansion."

"Look out then, it's always dangerous when a woman starts thinking—"

"Oh, sit down Griffith and listen!"

"Very well Lise Treharne, it's about time, so fire away."

"Right, I've jotted down some ideas and some figures. I've worked out how much capital I am able to invest without leaving myself dangerously exposed. I presume you have already done the same."

"I have."

"Good, because I don't want to use any banks."

"Why not Lise, that's what they're for?"

"Maybe Griffith, but I have a bad feeling about the future, the financial future that is. There are too many changes happening too quickly. I don't think the government is being cautious enough. It wouldn't surprise me if we are heading for another Depression."

"What! Good God girl, there has never been so much investment money around since the Tories have been in power. Borrowing is as cheap and getting cheaper as it has ever been and inflation has never been so low."

"I accept all that, Griffith, but my instincts tell me otherwise. How long can the government sustain it? How long will the Stock Market keep going up? I have already moved a lot of capital into safer territory."

"Well, you might as well ask 'how long is a piece of financial string?' and 'who knows?' in answer to both your questions."

"Exactly, that's why I am opting for caution. We use our own money, no interest payments and no nasty shocks if inflation starts getting out of hand. Any bricks and mortar we own will be owned outright as is presently the case, that way we should be able to ride any unpleasant surprises that the economy might throw at us. We don't have to have a 200-room monstrosity with a football pitch as a swimming pool. Besides, the whole ethos of the Cliffs has been about impeccable service, comfort and delicious food. We are more a country house than a hotel, and that's the way we want to stay. At least I do. I assume you are in agreement or do you want us to start competing with Las Vegas vulgarity and ersatz opulence?"

Griffith rested his chin on the palm of his hand for a moment. "Actually, in spite of my economic protestations I am in total agreement with your astute good self, Lise. It seems we both have a great deal to thank the old man for. I am fully aware of the fact that the 'product' we have worked so hard at works and is successful. One would have to be a complete fool to try and change it. So, you have in mind a thirty-five to fifty room establishment in a beautiful setting, and an establishment that will lend itself to exacting refurbishment without having to be virtually rebuilt with all the crippling costs that that would no doubt entail. Correct?"

"Correct."

"I have just the property in mind," Griffith smiled.

"You really do know me, don't you Griffith? How thoroughly irritating." Lise returned his smile, only this time there was just a little bit more than sisterly emotion in it.

It happened from time to time whether she liked it not.

As Lise and Griffith were concluding their discussions on expansion, Charlotte bumped into Justin Sewell. "Hello, you must be the new manager. Justin isn't it?"

"Yes, good morning and you must be Miss Charlotte. It's a pleasure to meet you." The daughter was an unmistakeable presence around the Cliffs, her vivacity and beauty impossible to ignore for long. Sewell held out his hand which Charlotte took, unaware of its limp status. They were standing in the reception area and for a few moments Charlotte felt alone and vulnerable in spite of the fact that there were plenty of people milling around. The feeling was not however an unpleasant one, it was just unusual for any man to make her feel like this.

"How are you settling in then? This old house can be a bit of a handful." Charlotte looked the morning-suited manager up and down, hoping he wouldn't notice her blatant interest.

"Fine thank you, Miss Charlotte. Fine. I have only been here a couple of days so I am just finding my feet as it were."

"My mother looking after you is she? She can be a bit of martinet but take no notice. It's just her way, soft as putty underneath."

"I am sure she is. She and your uncle have been very kind and considerate. Now if you will excuse me I had better get on with managing the Cliffs, otherwise your mother might just decide to ignore the putty that lies under her skin." Sewell smiled and walked off leaving Charlotte decidedly uncomfortable and feeling as if she had just been hit in the face with one of Will Jenkins's shovels. The man was so handsome, so sexy and the charm just poured out of him. No wonder her mother had given him the job. All the female guests would be spitting nails just to get some late-night room service! He was tall too, and she loved tall men.

She walked over to one of the leather armchairs that were dotted about the reception area and sat down. She needed to think. She was on delicate territory here. She had never considered herself a 'brazen hussy' which is no doubt what her mother would have called her if she had been able to read her mind at the moment, but nevertheless Charlotte loved men. She couldn't do without them in fact, not in any nymphomaniac sort of way but she just couldn't resist a good-looking chap in long trousers. In her view she was just plain normal, and at least she didn't go to bed with every male prospect that passed her way, unlike some of her less discerning friends. Apart from anything else she tended to enjoy the company of men far more than women, whom she generally found to be shallow and childish, which was usually the case where her own age group was concerned. Their silliness over men and squeaking immaturity annoyed and frustrated her. This new manager was something else though. Good looking, urbane and great material for a sexual fantasy last thing at night. He certainly wasn't the norm since, apart from the looks, there was something else that she couldn't quite put her finger on. There was a difference about him somehow, a unique quality that she was unable to identify. There was also something fascinating in his green eyes that she simply couldn't resist, something that she had never before encountered. It was all so delightfully unsettling and yet so exciting. There was danger too. Men had always been her weakness. Her nemesis. From her early days of contrived seduction in the stables to the counterfeit impression of drunken ease, Charlotte had always been the one to lead. To conquer at will. Her strength of personality had always controlled, manipulated. She took a deep breath as she recognized that with Justin there was some kind of threat, or that at least she felt threatened. Also she had the intelligence to realize quickly that his strength was something beyond hers, a power that she knew she could never hope to even tamper with. For a moment she shuddered at the recognition of her own weakness. Her weakness for men was being taken into a new and disturbing dimension. The feeling was both delicious and fearful. She also knew that she must go on. Her appetite went beyond instinct as her femininity refused to listen and her youth mocked maturity.

There was just one thing in all this: Justin was an employee of her mother's, delicate territory as she had already surmised. As attractive as the man was, he was basically off limits. Her mother would go berserk if she found out that her only daughter was fraternizing with the staff or, God forbid, that she was having sexual relations with them! It was all right for Uncle Griffith to enjoy the odd tumble in the laundry room, but her own daughter? Her mother would have a heart attack! Still, Charlotte had never been renowned for following the pack or indeed kowtowing to parental authority (or any other authority for that matter) so she allowed her thoughts to run riot whilst she plotted the conquering and seduction of Justin Sewell. She wouldn't say anything if he didn't. In the meantime Wilberforce would have to be put on the back burner. He wouldn't mind, she was sure; he needed some cooling down anyway, at least now he did. His constant phone calls were becoming a nuisance too.

CHAPTER 16

Griffith and Lise stood on the edge of a cliff facing the Bristol Channel. The Gower Peninsula stretched behind them as they cast their eyes downward toward a turreted mansion house that dominated its own private beach. The back of the house was isolated and protected by small clutches of trees, while the front overlooked a senseless grey of rock and pebble. The house and its location were perfect. They had known about this property for years. It had been owned by the government and used as a wartime convalescent home, then as a sanatorium for blackened and clogged up lungs. The government was now selling it off as part of its nationalization of state ownership.

"Why hasn't it been snapped up by property developers, Griffith, it doesn't make sense?" Lise asked.

"Planning permission, apart from that it's a listed building. No property developer can get planning consent to knock it down and split the land into small individual plots for a load of smart new houses or apartments. Some have tried bribing the Council and a few nearly succeeded, they're in clink now by the way, haven't you heard of the Swansea Mafia?"

"No, can't say I have," Lise replied.

"Just as well. Anyway I think the house is just right. Don't you?"

"That depends on all the costs."

"We can do it within our budget. Just. All the specs and surveyors reports are on your desk. I've done my homework, Lise. It won't be cheap but then if I know you, you wouldn't want to cut corners anyway."

"Well, it looks right. In fact I think the house itself is more beautiful than the Cliffs. More character. I'll need a closer look inside of course, but there is definitely potential. When can you arrange a proper inspection?"

"Leave it with me."

"Fine, Griffith. Let's go home now then, the wind is starting to bite. I'll study the paperwork properly over the next few days."

"Ok, but don't take too long about it. No doubt there are other people out there who are having the same thoughts as us."

As they started to make their way down a steep, rocky path, Lise slipped and fell into the arms of Griffith who managed to catch her before she fell and hurt herself. Their faces almost touched and for a few moments the wind stopped ranting, the silence murmured and the cold air seemed to suddenly warm up. They held each other as their eyes reached out and their lips almost met. Neither of them moved. More moments of utter stillness.

"I . . . I . . ." Lise mumbled as she gently pulled away from Griffith's arms.

"Are you all right . . .?" Griffith asked as his arms fell to his sides.

"Yes . . . yes, Griffith . . . I'm fine."

The wind swirled and jostled around them as their eyes met again. They both saw something they had never seen before. Something that was irredeemable, something that could never be recaptured.

They were no longer brother and sister.

Later that day, Griffith stood in a small graveyard attached to an ancient church that continued to fight in the vanguard against national religious torpor and disinterest. The solid stone walls remained straight and true, unlike the religious indifference that constantly spat on them. There wasn't a vicar or verger in sight, they had left the stone with its fantastic delusions to its own devices a long time ago.

His father had bought a large plot years back to accommodate both himself and all the other relatives that would undoubtedly follow him. William Treharne had insisted on a simple steel plaque to celebrate the grand opening of his becoming a fading memory in the cycle of human existence; he had never given a damn about God, Buddha, Allah or any other insecure sop to man's momentous confidence trick. If anyone else chose to continue a morbid journey in fancy marble and delicately inscribed rock that was up to them, what did he care? As far as he was concerned, any so-called God had died along with his own body, so to hell with everyone and let him rot in peace.

Two unobtrusive pieces of rock stood next to William Treharne's steel plaque announcing the end of an era. Glyn Treharne and Megan Treharne. Griffith's brother and sister, lay side by side in their own perfect spaces, perfect in as much as they no longer had to endure the violent upheavals that life had thrown at them. Glyn's body had been riddled with German bullets and Megan's had been overcooked. Neither of his siblings had said a tidy farewell. He knelt down in front of Megan's grave and placed some budding roses into a black pot covered with some wire mesh. In some ways he still missed her bullying antics, her truculence. Her life had been a tragic mess in most respects. Men, money, drink and drugs had all played a part in her ignominious downfall. Her hatred of Lise, her obsessive crusade for revenge and the insanity that had finally finished her off, still lingered in the words chiselled into the rock. If only the woman could have accepted, trusted. But then that wouldn't have been Megan, she had always been such a hateful bitch. Now and again some genuine sisterly kindness would appear for an airing but not often. These were the times that Griffith tried to remember now. The good times when they had all been young and unspoilt by life. He placed some more of his father's precious roses in a similar black pot standing on top of his brother's final resting place. Glyn had been the true innocent out of the three of them. The paragon. Double first at Cambridge, commission in the Welsh Guards, perfect kindness and understanding. Only Death could ever have impeded Glyn's perfection and even then a Victoria Cross had been granted posthumously. Still kneeling in front of his brother and sister Griffith allowed death to bring some balance into his mind for a few minutes longer. Eventually he stood up, lit a cigarette and looked down at his careless handiwork. The flowers flopped about in a rage at having their natural beauty tainted by death, but he could hardly see either his brother or his sister complaining. Megan no doubt would have blasted him with a tirade of angst given half a chance, but not anymore. Her bossy antics were well and truly over. He hoped that all her bitterness and hatred had rotted along with the rest of her body. She deserved some peace. That was the thing about death he thought, sometimes it wasn't quite as permanent as people liked to think. He could still hear Megan's tragedy, her torture, even though she had died nearly twenty years ago.

Griffith was not a man to ponder the great questions of life or death for that matter. He took things as they came, on the chin and without complaint. At least this had been his way for most of his adult life, until that is, Lise Jacobson had confounded him over a leg of lamb. He still remembered that dinner thirty-odd years ago, and her wonderful cooking. The small things about her remained in his mind like limpets sucking the hull of a ship while they waited patiently to explode. Earlier that day he had seen a glimpse of love in her eyes, he was sure of it. There had been real love, love between a man and a woman who were not related in any way. A love that he had wanted and desired for so many years.

Gritfith was an experienced man where women were concerned. He had never married, but by God there had been plenty of women along the way. He knew as much as any man could about the female of the species which, when he actually thought about it, was probably bugger all. Love? Well, that was a different matter. He had always avoided it, until, that is, Lise had come along. What was he to do? How was he to respond to that momentary depth in Lise's eyes. He had no idea. None at all. All his previous romantic endeavours had been uncomplicated and simple. Fine booze, fine food and fine sex, in that order. No dramas and no 'love'. After that look in Lise's captivating blue eyes, he had been left in a state of total flux. What if he was fooling himself? What if he had imagined it all? How was he to react? He couldn't risk losing her friendship, and this is exactly what might happen if he made any unwanted advances. Better to have her friendly affection than no affection at all. God knows he had accepted this state of affairs for years, so why risk losing it? Love, that was why. Love and believing that he might as well be lying alongside his brother and sister without Lise's laughter, her kindness and her sulks. She was all woman too, self-willed, independent, calm where he was all steam and impatience, imperious where he was sometimes diffident, with her anyway. He knew that he could never bear to be without her as a friend, as a lover, it made no difference.

Griffith finished his cigarette, flicked the butt onto someone else's Holy territory and decided to let events take their own course. He would keep true to form and go wherever the Fates decided to lead him. He just hoped that Lise had not forgotten that brief embrace with its moment of truth.

Griffith parked his Jaguar XJ6 at the back of the Cliffs, next to his other Jaguar, an XK 120. At least these two ladies never gave him any trouble. He always knew where he stood with them and they always moaned with satisfaction when he started them up. As he walked to his own apartment he bumped into Gwyn Evans, the maintenance man, another of his father's old retainers. The man's dark and threatening looks had started to fade with age but his humour had remained firm and strong.

"Hello, Gwyn. How are Bronwyn and the children?"

"Still talkin', Griffith. Still talkin'. As for the kids, they're ok apart from Rhys, that boy needs an 'and grenade with the pin pulled out stuck up his arse. Sits in front of the telly all day 'ee does." This sounded familiar.

"Still off the booze, are you?"

"Most of the time, until the missus starts performin'. I just passed your car down by the church as I was coming back from town. There's a temporary vicar shows up now and again. 'Bill the Bible" they call 'im. Got dragged into one of his Sunday sermon's not long ago. I said to the missus as we was walkin' out, an American oilman was once heard to say, 'If you 'aint struck oil in twenty minutes quit boring,' and by Christ did that bugger bore. Turned me to drink it did, got howlin' that night and the missus beat 'ell out o' me in the mornin'. Still givin' me grief. That's the trouble with women, see Griffith. They never forget. Ever. They'll still be remindin' you about the fact that you didn't put the bins out twenty fucking years after the bloody event! Ought to divorce the bitch, that's what. Everyone else is at it these days."

Griffith laughed, "She wouldn't let you, Gwyn, and you know it."

"More's the pity. Less bloody sense than me and that's sayin' somethin'. Moanin' now that I don't give 'er enough of the old nuptials! Reads too many of these bloody womens' magazines. I'm well into my 50s now, what does the dirty cow expect? John bloody Travolta? I tell you, Griffith, she'll be the death o' me. It's 'er age I reckon, forty-plus and look out! Randy as 'ell! She's a dirty cow, into all kinds of different positions now too. Christ sometimes she 'as me stuck up against the wall with both her legs wrapped round my bloody 'ed. Going on manoeuvres she calls it. Manoeuvres, my arse! I'm bloody exhausted I am."

"Well Gwyn, I'm sure you will both work it out. You always do. By the way, was it you I saw the other day doing your flies up as you were coming out of the maintenance shed? One of the older waitresses came out after you, I think."

"What! Me? Perish the thought Griffith. Perish the thought."

"And perish you will, my boy, if Bronwyn ever finds out about your extra-curricular activities."

"Extra what?"

"Never mind, just make sure you don't get caught. You know what a prude Lise can be on these things, not to mention your lady wife."

"Aye, take your point. Well I'm off now things to do. See you again."

"Oh and Gwyn, before you go get a haircut, will you? Might make you look younger, but it's damned scruffy."

"Will do, trouble is 'Deaf and Dumb' 'as been off sick for a while."

" 'Deaf and Dumb'?"

"Aye 'Deaf and Dumb', the barber in Swansea. 'Is missus is deaf and dumb too I'm told, no wonder the butcherin' bastard is always smiling."

"Very funny, Gwyn," Griffith couldn't help laughing.

"It's true I'm tellin' you! 'Ee uses a plank as a chair and a mirror that you can't see bugger all into. Cheap though, and that's what matters even if 'ee does trim your lug 'ole now and again. You ought to try 'im yourself. Very peaceful few minutes too I can tell you. Bron could take a few lessons of 'Deaf and Dumb' that's for sure."

"No thank you Gwyn, looking at your head tells me all I need to know. Now go on, get on with your work otherwise I will set Lise onto you."

"Jesus, not that! I'd rather face Bron in one of 'er extra lively episodes!"

Griffith shook his head in despair as he watched Gwyn marching off cursing and mumbling to himself, a man who had never passed an exam, a buxom pair of buttocks or a pub in his life. And Griffith thought he had been a bit of a boy in his time!

"Enjoying the view?"

Justin Sewell looked up and saw Charlotte Treharne looking down at him. She was a lovely looking girl. The dark blue dress she wore accentuated the clean, pale colour of her skin and the copper redness of her hair. She really was a joy to look at.

"May I join you," she asked, "it's such a beautiful day. Pity to stay indoors even if it is a little on the fresh side. I pinched some chicken and salad from the kitchen so don't tell the chef, you know what he's like."

"I won't." Sewell stood up before Charlotte sat down on one of the stone benches that enjoyed a panoramic view of the sea. On a good day you could see the Devon coast.

"No need to get up, Justin. Very chivalrous and all that but no need for formality. It is your lunch break I assume."

"Yes, but I can't stay long. There's a function tonight. Rotary Club or something. I was just enjoying a bit of peace and quiet."

"Oh sorry! I didn't mean to disturb you."

"No, not at all. Please enjoy your lunch." Sewell gave the impression that he felt awkward being alone with the boss's daughter. His smile was strained, his manner tight. Neither of which went unnoticed by Charlotte.

"Do you want a share?" Charlotte giggled, "Come on, you can be my partner in crime." Sewell nearly found her offer impossible to refuse, nevertheless he declined.

"No. No thank you. I've eaten."

"Not very talkative are you, Justin" This was a statement not a question. Charlotte was not a young woman to hold back. She could see that with this man she would have to take the initiative and yet she felt his reticence was not the result of timidity or shyness. There was strength in his eyes, dominance. He was not a man she could walk over. This made him even more attractive. Most of the men she had known had been young and easy to manipulate. Her looks alone usually beat them into submission, let alone her dominant nature. Justin Sewell on the other hand seemed totally unimpressed with either. His reactions to her advances had been dismissive; if anything he was treating her like some casual nuisance who had to be tolerated. This wouldn't do at all.

"You know, Justin, I may be the boss's daughter but I don't bite and I'm not a sneak. Nothing to be wary of I assure you."

For the first time Sewell smiled, the turning of his lips was genuine.

"Oh, I am not 'wary' of you, Miss Charlotte. I am really quite relaxed. In fact I rarely get worked up about anything. Life is too short as they say."

"And will you cut out this 'Miss Charlotte' nonsense? Lottie will be just fine. That's what my family have called me for years anyway."

"Lottie then if you insist, although your uncle does seem to have reservations about familiarity with the staff etc. I think contempt comes into his thinking somewhere or other."

"Oh, don't take any notice of Uncle Griffith, loveable rogue that he is. He still lives in the age of duels and gallantry. Silly old sod . . . Come on then Justin, tell me a bit about yourself. I'm curious. Reveal all and I promise I won't tell. Girlfriend, family?" In spite of his protestations to the contrary Sewell's body language started to thaw. His movements were more relaxed and his face started to show definite interest. He looked straight into Charlotte's eyes and nearly knocked her off the stone bench. His deep green eyes tore into her and seemed to count how many times her heart was beating. The intensity in his eyes was both intimidating and fascinating. Charlotte felt completely at his mercy. He could have dragged her off there and then to the nearest sand dune and done what he liked to her. Yet again, no man had ever had this effect on her. For a moment she was unable to respond or say anything. Their eyes hung in the air, waiting. Sewell at last drew in his breath and destroyed the moment.

"Family, no. I've always considered such ties to be an irrelevance and unnecessary. Indeed most people I speak with would rarely ask one of their 'family' out for dinner of their own free will, let alone invite friendship."

"God, you are a cynical chap, aren't you."

"Perhaps, although if I am unduly cynical it has served me well during my life."

"So you have no family at all then? Are you an orphan or something?" Charlotte Treharne was not renowned for her tact although Sewell didn't seem to mind the direct approach.

"I never knew who my father was. My mother died when I was quite young, relatives looked after me until I was able to stand on my own two feet. No brothers or sisters."

"Ah, an independent soul like me then. You are well educated. I can tell that by the way you speak, so how did you get into the hotel business? Mum tells me you have quite a reputation, particularly as you are so young. Thirty-odd, isn't it?"

"Thirty-one, and as for the education, grammar school. No university. I wanted to earn a living as quickly as I could, have my independence which is important to me as you have rightly identified. As for the rest . . . well, I would like to think that I am modestly well read."

"Where are you from originally? You don't seem to have any particular accent."

"London. Now have you finished your interrogation, Charlotte – I mean Lottie?"

"Oops! Sorry, I am being a bit rude, aren't I? Can't help it I'm afraid."

"We can all help discourtesy, Lottie, so don't try and excuse yourself with facile excuses."

"Oops again. Not one to pull your punches, are you . . .? Actually I rather like it."

"That's good, we might get on after all then," Sewell smiled and Charlotte made the most of it. They didn't come often. "Now then, I must be off, Lottie. I can't sit here all day telling you my life history."

"You know Justin, not once have you asked anything about me?"

"I don't need to. I know all I need to know. Bye."

"But . . . but, what about a girlfriend?" Charlotte shouted after him. Sewell ignored her question and carried on walking.

"Tight-lipped bastard!" Charlotte said under her breath.

CHAPTER 17

Kristian sat alone returning the stare of a deer who nodded his head with superior wisdom and a hint of contempt. Kristian could almost hear his words, "You stupid, stupid man. Your temper will get the better of you one day!" As far as Kristian was concerned it already had, but what else could he have done? When that big oaf, Dewi Morgan, had come charging at him with murder in his eyes, he had merely defended himself, nothing more, nothing less.

Kristian's eyes moved around the opening blasts of yet another of Nature's coming-of-age parties. Wild flowers, ageing shrubs and spanking new grass sprouted and danced with hope and enthusiasm at the prospect of a sunnier and more benevolent summer than the year before. Richmond Park was the place to be at this time of year. It may not have been the best park in London, but there was something about the clash of Nature with the fumes of car engines that roared through the rural deception that appealed to Kristian's contradictory personality. For some reason he felt at home here and almost enjoyed the intrusive din of ignorant traffic. The place was alive one minute, dead the next. Rather like his own life at the moment.

The park bench, the deer, and Mother Nature forced him to seriously consider what to do next. He had been going nowhere for well over a year now and here he was, no job, no woman and no prospects. At least he wasn't broke though, so he thanked this large mercy. Perhaps he could do some voluntary work to pass the time? Kristian was more a socialist than a Tory. Defending the weak again. Maybe there was something he could do to help the homeless, the hungry, the morally rejected and dejected. He thought about his altruistic tendencies for a few moments, then gave up. He couldn't quite see himself wearing a Sally Army uniform while traipsing around the streets of Soho, dishing out bread and soup to those who were unable to make any grub for themselves. That really would be hypocrisy on a grand scale. No, if anything happened to him, his Will made generous provision for a number of charities. His armchair generosity would no doubt buy him a place at the right hand of God, not that he believed in all that tripe, but at least he was honest with himself which was more than those other unholy bastards in Whitehall could say.

"What to do?" he kept asking himself time and time again, and time and time again no answer was forthcoming. Myfanwy had given him a fine kick up the arse, and as much as it hurt he couldn't blame her. He had asked for it. He wasn't so sure whether he deserved it though, there was a difference after all.

He stood up and continued his aimless trekking around a park that seemed to be the only place where he could find some solace. If he went home, his mother would be at him every five minutes and right now he could do without it. At the moment all he wanted to do was accept rejection by the woman he loved and hang on to his sanity. He knew though that he couldn't take too long about it. Fumbling around in his own darkness was not his way.

While Kristian was trying to bring some sense to his life his mother was rushing past Griffith in reception as she said abruptly, "Griffith, there's a personal message for you. It's on my desk." They hadn't spoken for three days, not since that intimate moment on the cliffs. Griffith was beside himself. Had he offended her? Had he ruined the small hope he possessed? Griffith was not a man who relished confrontation, in fact he hated it. He hated discord of any description and avoided it at all costs. Why hadn't Lise spoken to him, why was she avoiding him? He hadn't really done anything . . . had he? He pushed his confusion aside for a few moments and went to see what this message was all about. He didn't often get 'personal messages', he wasn't that important to anyone.

He picked up the piece of notepaper that had his name scrawled across it. Lise's handwriting. Bloody mess and only just legible. It told him to call back a Mr Paul Edmunds on a personal matter. What could that little shit want, Griffith wondered, and how the hell did he know where I was and get this number? Suddenly Griffith went cold. Jesus Christ, what if anyone finds out about his 'secret family'? The last thing he wanted was Lise knowing about his sexual antics with another woman, and worse still that he had a son by her. She would never forgive him for all the lies and his lack of trust in her. On second thoughts though, what had he lied about? He had never told anybody anything, and more to the point it was no one else's business. After all he and Lise had only ever been close friends. Nothing more. He didn't owe her any fidelity. His real worry though was that any untimely revelations about his 'family' might just jeopardize any chance he may have of winning Lise's heart. He knew what she could be like. Betrayal, in any shape or form was anathema to her. Her life had nearly been destroyed by it a few times. He calmed down for a few moments and decided to ring the boy back when he was in his own apartment. There was no mention of any urgency in the message so his son could wait. 'Son'. Somehow the word didn't seem familiar to Griffith's mind, even though he had always treated Kristian as his son. For the briefest of moments guilt attacked him.

Later that afternoon Griffith called his 'son'.

"What?" Griffith could hardly believe what he was hearing.

"Well, Griffith, Mum reckoned it would give me a chance to find out about the hotel business. I can't seem to get any work with the designing bit so she thought I might just try and do something 'constructive'. To be honest she's pissed off with me dossing about the house all day, and I'm pissed off with her nagging me all the time. Thought a little coastal air would do me good whilst at the same time doing a bit of work for you. Everybody's happy, if you see what I mean." By this point Griffith had nearly dropped the phone in shock. Sylvia had broken all her own rules. The boy knew what Griffith did and where he lived. The woman must have been desperate!

"Well, to begin with you can start talking about your mother in a more respectful manner and cut out the bad language (Griffith was the consummate hypocrite when it suited him). You are talking to me now, not one of your mates down the local boozer. You speak with your elders and betters with respect, boy, and don't you damn well forget it! You also know that I object to you addressing me by my Christian name. You haven't earned that privilege yet. So it's 'Uncle Griffith' if you don't mind. As for having a paid holiday while you breathe in the coastal air, you can forget that one too! If I have you here, and it's a bloody great 'if,' you will be here to work not to enjoy yourself!

"I need time to think about all this, Paul. To date your track record has hardly been impressive. At twenty-two, you have some poncey degree in 'graphic design' which appears to be no good to man or beast, you certainly have no training that I can use, navvies are two a penny and you wouldn't be much good with a pick and shovel anyway as you'd probably be running off to the nearest wash hand basin every five minutes to wash your little pinkies!" As Griffith banged away with the insults, he thought if this didn't put the boy off such a harebrained idea then nothing would. Surprisingly the line wasn't disconnected and the boy stood his ground. Maybe there was some of the Treharne in him after all. "Are you still there, Paul?"

"Yes I am. No need for all that though, Uncle Griffith, I was only asking for a job after all." The timid response surprised Griffith and made him feel a right shit, the boy's speech had been clear and really quite articulate too for a change. It had even lost that effeminate twang that had always made Griffith despair. He was obviously trying. Maybe he had seen some sense at long last. Perhaps he had been too hard on the boy, everyone deserved a chance after all and the useless bugger was his own flesh and blood, like it or not. Not that the boy was aware of it. Another problem to worry over.

"Look, all right I'm sorry. You've caught me at a bad time. I'll think about it, all right? No promises. I mean it."

"That's ok, but thank you for taking the time to talk to me anyway." Oh God, Griffith began to feel even more of a shit.

"Good. I'll get back to you in a few days. I promise."

"Fair enough. Thank you for listening and I apologize for disturbing you at a busy time." What! The boy was actually being humble now! This really was too much. He must be trying out a new line in dope or something. Before ending the call, Griffith's dominant soft side appeared again.

"In a funny kind of way, Paul," he said more gently," I'm quite impressed that you are finally trying to do something with your life. I'll see what I can do. By the way, tidy yourself up and wash that oil slick you call hair. Goodbye."

Griffith put the phone down and wondered what the hell to do next. He was in a right pickle. Paul Edmunds was his son, his only child. So far he had been a lousy father although that hadn't really been his fault. Sylvia had squeezed him out from the beginning. How was he going to explain all this if the boy came to the Cliffs to work? How? He poured himself an Irish whiskey, large and overflowing, sat down and tried to decide on the best course of action. His son had to be given a chance. Griffith himself had been a highly successful waster for a large part of his adult life, so who was he to start lobbing self-righteous and hypocritical bricks about the place? How could he close a door? He might even enjoy getting to know the boy properly. The trouble with all this of course was the fact that Paul didn't know that Griffith was his father, so how the hell was he going to deal with this minor little detail? Lise couldn't be unkind if she tried, but how much should he tell her?

A bottle of whiskey and an ashtray full of cigarette butts later Griffith was still in a mess. Old times had returned with a vengeance.

CHAPTER 18

While Griffith was depending on a bottle of Irish whiskey and a packet of cigarettes to sort out his fate, Lise lay in bed and tried to resolve her own troubled mind. That moment on the cliffs had stayed with her for the past few days. The sudden desire to kiss Griffith, to touch him, had been overwhelming. She had never felt this exposed with him before. Over the past few days she had avoided talking to Griffith too which hadn't helped, and this in itself annoyed her. She was not a woman to avoid an issue, to prevaricate or to turn away from sensitive difficulties. She had come this far in her life by being bold and strong. Always strong.

Lise sent her mind back to all the tragic attacks and assaults that life had inflicted upon her. She had been a victim of the most violent and appalling facets of the human condition. She had experienced betrayal and death in all their most heinous forms. She had survived and lived. She had known the most intense and wonderful happiness only to have it stolen from her, again in the most brutal way.

Griffith had been with her throughout all the years of healing and recovery. He had always been behind and in front of her. Her success had been his too, her peace had also been his. She had known of his love right from the beginning, she had seen it every day for the past twenty years, every morning, every night, without fail. Her husband had been his father, she, his step-mother. Anything beyond friendship would have been a betrayal of William's love, it would also have been improper. How could she make love to both father and son? The conundrum disturbed and absorbed her. And yet it had been so long since she had enjoyed the touch of a masculine fingertip. Lise had been taught to celebrate sex by her late husband. He had taught her how to enjoy both her body and a man's. She missed the physical joy of a man's body. She missed it so much but more than anything else she missed the love of a man's eyes and a love that she could return without condition and without guilt.

Lise looked at the ceiling of her bedroom and said out loud, "Griffith, dear loyal Griffith, what am I to do? How am I to treat your love? Can I love again in the only way I know how to, with all and everything that I am. Can I love you in this way. You, my husband's son?"

As sleep began to calm her mind and bring some balance to her emotional secrets her fingers moved to the inside of her thighs. It really had been such a long time.

The following morning Griffith and Lise were finally left alone in the study, and this time neither one of them did a bolt for the door. The atmosphere in the air around them seemed awkward and cumbersome, it had an idea of what was about to come.

"You don't look well, Griffith," Lise looked concerned, "what's the matter? Do you need a doctor, you really do look awful?"

"I'm fine, don't fuss."

"Your father always used to say that."

"Oh to hell with my father, Lise! Do you always have to keep comparing me with him for God's sake? That's all I ever hear about, my bloody father! He's been dead for years, woman, so stop resurrecting his ghost. For Christ's sake move on, will you? There are other men out there you know, they might not all be paragons of virtue or up to the old man's standards but do they have to be?" Lise sat back in her chair in a state of shock. She had heard Griffith shout and yell many times but never at her. Never. Years of pent-up frustration and unrequited love were finally starting to come to the surface. Griffith's heart and his mind had finally snapped. Now was the time to lash out, to hurt. The whiskey had done a good job.

"I was only—"

"Well don't, Lise! I'm just not in the mood!"

"Griffith, have you been at the bottle?" Lise said quietly with no hint of accusation in her voice. She cared, that was all.

"Actually, yes I have and damned enjoyable it was too. Smoked forty fags while I was at it! What the hell has it got to do with you anyway? You're not my wife!"

"Griffith, what on earth is the matter with you? Why are you shouting at me like this. There's no need. Please stop it."

"Oh there is a need. For twenty bloody years I have loved you. Twenty bloody years, and all you have done is wallow in the perfect safety of your 'friendly' little world. Good old reliable Griffith, good old loyal Griffith. Have you ever wondered what it's been like for me? Have you? Like hell you have. You're too damned selfish and self-centred to ever consider my feelings and the best bit is you have known all along! Christ, how the hell have you managed it? The cold Scandinavian blood I suppose. There Lise, I have finally brought this sickening charade to an end. It's out in the open. I love you, woman, and have done so since the first time I met you. You have known it all along, so stop looking so stupefied will you, it doesn't suit you. For once I've taken control of things, now what are you going to do about it? And let's have a straight answer, shall we?" Lise looked at Griffith, her eyes gripped his, this time there was nowhere to hide.

"Well, Griffith, I must say you have a way with approaching these things!" Lise was returning fire now. "Of course I have known about your feelings, what do you think I am? And do you honestly believe that I have ever wanted to hurt you? Don't be the usual idiot that you tend to be most of the time! You must give me time to think about all this, Griffith. You must!"

"Think! Think! Jesus, you've have had a lifetime to think! You're fifty-four and I'm ten years ahead of you. How much time do you think we've got for Christ's sake?"

"Right then, well you can go to hell right now Griffith! You don't swear at me like this, you ignorant bastard!"

"Swear! Swear! Jesus I haven't even got out of first gear yet! And look whose bloody talking! 'Bastard' am I? Now who's the worn-out old tart from Townhill?"

"How dare you! Get out, Griffith, will you? Get out of my study!"

" 'My' study! Since when? 'Our' study, or more accurately 'my father's' study!"

"You're still drunk, Griffith, now for the last time get out!"

"When I'm bloody well ready, now—" Suddenly Griffith's hands clawed at his chest, "Oh Jesus . . ." he managed to moan, "oh Jesus." His face had gone white and he was struggling for breath, agony contorted his facial muscles as his hands clawed and gripped his chest. He collapsed on the floor as Lise ran to him. She took one look, dashed to the telephone on her desk and dialled 999. Next, she ran into reception.

"Bethan, find Dr Rees! It's an emergency! Quickly now! It's life or death. Bring him to my study. I saw him in the restaurant half an hour ago!" The look on Lise's face was enough to make the girl run. Lise ran back to Griffith who was writhing on the floor. She knelt down beside him and grasped his hand as he spat through clenched teeth, "Lise, Lise . . . I'm sorry . . . I'm so sorry." Dr Rees dashed into the study as Griffith fell unconscious and his lips started to turn blue.

"Have you phoned for an ambulance, Mrs Treharne?"

"Yes."

"Good." The doctor felt for a pulse. There was none. "Quick, Mrs Treharne. You know how to give mouth to mouth?"

"Yes."

"Then start. Now!"

As Lise put her mouth to Griffiths in order to push oxygen around his blood supply the doctor thumped Griffith's chest and tried to massage his heart.

"Oh God, Griffith! Don't die, you mustn't die! You mustn't!" Lise pleaded as a past already tight with tragedy and death battered her heart into more grief and hopelessness.

CHAPTER 19

Lise looked out of a window from a sterile room that overlooked Swansea Bay. Tankers, Irish ferries and gruesome maritime dredging machines criss-crossed the Bay and competed with the industrial might of British Steel that looked on through a haze of poisonous smoke and the sweat of worked-out bodies. Her eyes moved to the other side of the Bay and saw the jutting rocks and sturdy lighthouse that had haunted and confounded truck loads of paint brushes, water colours and reams of canvass. The holiday giggles of Mumbles sat and mocked its neighbours on the opposite shore, who could only steam and groan at their own complete ugliness. The Bay was a sea of amusing contradictions and sat in its own memories of anti-aircraft batteries, bright yellow sewage slop and delicate trains that had once simpered around the Bay in their attempts to accommodate the adventure and mystery of childish minds, parental cynicism and a half-decent memory of at least one happy 'stop fortnight' holiday.

Lise had taken her own children on the Mumbles Train. She remembered Griffith carrying Kristian on his broad shoulders, the two of them grinning and self-conscious as she and Griffith had tried to take some family photos for a past that could never be forgotten.

She thought of all the years Griffith had been by her side. She thought of all the devoted love that he had given to both herself and her children. She thought of his sacrifice. Tears rushed down her face and fell upon a floor that was used to flooding by human guilt and remorse. How could she have taken Griffith's love for granted for so long? How could she have been so cruel? Her eyes cried and cried as she was unable to excuse her selfishness. Griffith had been right.

Lise stood alone in Singleton Hospital and wondered why she had been so fearful of allowing what had been so deep within her to surface. Over the years she had come to love Griffith but her sense of duty, her sense of loyalty had always overwhelmed and subdued the natural inclinations of her heart. She had kept Griffith at arm's length, away from her heart and away from the betrayal of a profound love that had been snatched so mercilessly away from her. And yet hadn't William himself told her not to grieve, hadn't he demanded that she find happiness after his death? Would he have been outraged if Lise decided to love his son too?

All these thoughts rushed through Lise's mind and forced her to finally address the suppressed love that she had fought against for so long. Her mirror was forcing her to confront, to obey. To seek who she really was and who she had become. There could be no escape this time.

The door behind her opened and a doctor walked up to her. His face gave nothing away. A stethoscope hung round his neck and seemed to glare at Lise. The device threatened and warned. Lise looked at the man's face and despaired. There seemed to be an air of finality in the man's eyes. She had lost Griffith. Her body shook as the depth of her love for the man strangled her vocal chords and almost made her feint. Now that he was gone, dead, she knew how much she had truly loved him.

"Mrs Treharne?"

"Yes."

"It was touch and go in there but he's a tough devil. He's lucky you and a doctor were on hand. We thought we'd lost him a couple of times. He's not out of danger yet but he's through the worse. I'm sorry but that's all I can tell you for now."

Lise nearly collapsed with relief, instead she sat down in a chair and said, "Thank you, Doctor. Thank you." When the shock of near sudden death at last started to wear off and Lise's mind began to clear, she collected her thoughts.

"Can I see him, Doctor? I must see him."

"Yes. Yes of course. I believe you are his next of kin. He is conscious but you mustn't be too long. Five minutes. We don't want him talking too much, as I say his condition is still critical. Now, I must be off, we will speak again later on when he has stabilised."

Lise walked into the private room where Griffith lay like a man set upon by some science fiction fanatic. Tubes, plastic bags, saline drips, bleeping monitors and electronic wizardry played evanescent tunes while green and red dots winked their confidence that all was well. At least they hoped all was well. She sat down on a chair next to his bed and took his hand.

She put her other hand over his and looked at the silver strands of hair that fell in ungainly steps across his forehead. His face looked calm, the narrow wrinkles unleashed from pain and imminent death. Her deep blue eyes ravished his breath and renounced a past replete with her own doubts and delusions. She loved Griffith and knew that a life without him would be no life at all. A morning without his tweeds and cavalry twills would be no morning at all. A day without his bad language would be no day at all and a night without his laughter and smiles would be a night where darkness would never end. Her finger touched his cheek as she whispered, "Oh God, Griffith, I love you so much. So much. I'm so sorry, so very sorry. Please forgive me. All these years that I have let pass us by. How can I ever make them up?" Griffiths eyes opened for a moment and he looked at the woman he adored and cherished.

"By being you, my beautiful Lise, just by being you." His eyes closed as his hand gripped Lise's and he fell back into a deep sleep. A contented sleep.

Lise stayed for a few more minutes and reached her decision. She was a determined woman and when her mind was made up there could never be any turning back. She and William had caused plenty of tongues to waggle and spit, and no doubt sharing her bed with his son would produce more smoke and fire than British Steel on a particularly productive day. Well, it had been to hell with them then and it was to hell with them now. Ever the pragmatist Lise also considered the fact that her wanton notoriety might even be good for business. She was sure that no doubt Griffith would fully approve too!

CHAPTER 20

It was the beginning of July and an unruly rogue day had decided to slap itself down on the Gower. The heat and sun threatened anything that moved too quickly or ventured out of the shade. It was early evening and Charlotte had finished her work for the day. The starched whites and jet blacks of servitude had been thrown into the nearest laundry basket along with her mother's constant nagging. She sat on one of the hotel's verandas, sipped a Campari and soda and settled down to unwind. It had been a swine of a day. Guests perspired ill humour by the bucket full, staff complained and jostled for the cool air of the air conditioning and Justin Sewell was still determined to ignore her subtle and sometimes not so subtle advances. What was wrong with the man, for heaven's sake? Was he playing hard to get or what?

Charlotte wasn't used to rejection. It hurt. Normally she could pick and choose, but not this time. The man was infuriating her because she knew damn well that he fancied her. The look of desire in his eyes every time she purposefully bumped into him was unmistakeable. The only thing that could be holding him back was the fact that she was the boss's daughter. What else could there be? She knew that just about every man she ever encountered would give his eye teeth to get her knickers off, so why was Justin being so un-cooperative? For a moment the ice in her Campari turned colder at the prospect that the man might bat for the other side. No, that couldn't be. She had known plenty of homos and Justin just didn't fit the bill. She knew that overt masculinity meant nothing in deciding whether a man was the other way inclined or not, but she also knew that the lips, voice and general demeanour could say it all. No, Justin was straight she was sure, in which case she had to continue with her assault until his defences were finally breached. She was irresistible after all! She was also one of the new breed of 80's women. Liberated, emancipated and entitled to love and screw whom she liked.

As she allowed a cool evening breeze to massage her face an opportunity she couldn't resist presented itself. Serendipity arrived in a blaze of fortuitous coincidence. She had decided earlier on to go for a swim when the heat had calmed down. Her bathing costume and towel were sitting along side her. Just as she was about to finish her drink and make her way down to the beach who should she see but Justin Sewell. He was making his way down the steep path toward the sea. He was wearing bright red shorts and carrying a towel. He too had decided to take a swim but had no idea that a pair of predatory eyes were follow-ing him on his journey.

"My God!" Charlotte almost gasped, the body on the man was exquisite. She had wondered often enough what his flesh looked like underneath the black jacket and grey pinstripe trousers, and now she had seen it with her own eyes she was even more determined to catch her man.

Charlotte allowed twenty-odd minutes to tick by – she didn't want to seem too obvious about things, 80's woman or not – and then followed Sewell down to the beach.

The place she was heading for was more a cove than a beach, one of those tiny inlets that dotted along the peninsula every now and again. It belonged to the Cliffs so was spared the seasonal onslaughts of livid varicose veins waiting to burst, wasp-infested ice creams clinging on for dear life to worn-out soggy cones and over-boiled reddened faces with heads covered by all kinds of knotted handkerchiefs and silly hats. Not to mention, of course, bleached white hairy legs – this included the women – huge flip-flopped big toes, tits that abused Newton's theory on gravity and the pulsating mounds of insulting pale flesh that stretched and outraged tiny pieces of brashly coloured lycra that yelled and shrieked for mercy. The cove was normally deserted at this time of the day, most of the guests would be getting dressed for dinner and the evening staff would be too busy preparing food, cutlery and drinks. It was an ideal time for Charlotte to make her last throw of the dice.

She arrived at a small area of sand that stood in between some defiant rock and a few belated puddles of sea water. She laid out her towel on a lump of sand that was as hot and as dry as a sunburnt cork, took off her baggy smock and lay down, at the same time glancing with nonchalant interest at the irritable waves that titillated the shore line. For a moment she smiled to herself, titillation was the name of the game all right. She and the sea had a lot in common it seemed. Her eyes quickly scanned the surface of white crests and falling waves. Where the hell was he? For a few moments disappointment trimmed her ardour, then she spotted a towel sitting in front of a rock to her right-hand side. Justin was around here somewhere, but where? Her eyes went back to the sea, and at last she spotted a mop of black hair bouncing around with the waves.

Now that the prey was in her sights she relaxed and allowed her body to do the rest. He couldn't stay in the water for ever and he couldn't miss her when he stopped swimming and returned to terra firma.

With one eye closed and the other ever so slightly open Charlotte saw her man coming out of the water at long last. She lifted a knee, breathed in for maximum breast effect and waited.

"Hello, Lottie. I didn't see you there, I nearly stepped on you!"

Charlotte opened her eyes. Sewell was looking down at her. His body was a masterpiece and parts of her tingled at the immediate impact. "Oh hello, Justin. Been having a swim, have you? I was just about to have one myself but I dropped off. The heat has been a bit much today."

"Hasn't it just." Justin's eyes did an unobtrusive examination of the body lying down in front of him. He didn't need to exercise much imagination. Charlotte's blue bikini would have shamed a mint condition Penny Black. Her 'bikini line' must have been executed by a demented Lady Shaver on full throttle too and the nipples on top of her straining breasts stood up like Baptist chapel hat pegs. She was a sight all right and even his hitherto indifference took a belting.

"Come on, come and sit down Justin. You're no where near the Cliffs now so relax." Sewell sat down next to her, this time unable to resist a smile accompanying the body that would have destroyed any man's gentlemanly intent.

"Near enough. Your mother has eyes everywhere. Keeps me on my toes I can tell you."

"And the rest of us too I assure you. Actually she speaks very highly of you, and to impress my mother takes a bit of doing. Have you settled in ok now? How long has it been, three to four months?"

"About that."

"Is your flat comfortable? Mum has always had a thing about looking after people she works with, says that this is a sure way of maintaining loyalty. Pays over the odds too."

"Yes she does, but she has the right idea. If there were more employers like her in the hotel business there wouldn't be so much of the constant staffing problems. People move on too quickly. They are never given enough incentive to stay on. Long hours, low pay and no thanks. Your mother has recognized these things and remedied them, thus the fact that we have staff who have been here for years."

"Like Mr Jenkins, Gwyn and his wife Bronwyn," Charlotte replied. Justin beamed for the first time, up until this point his smiles having been their usual awkward affairs.

"Ah, Gwyn and Bronwyn. Now there's a pair. Have you heard them? God she gives the man hell. And talk? By God the woman could talk a donkey's glass eye to sleep and that's a fact. No wonder the poor blighter hit's the booze now and again. The woman is always on transmit!" Charlotte was laughing with Justin now. There was a change in his attitude toward her. Something had happened, she could see it in the way he looked at her. There was a difference in him, he was warmer and more responsive than he had ever been. She didn't believe it was just her body either. His fingers had actually touched her arm! He was becoming more tactile, intimate.

"You are happy then, at the Cliffs? I know Mum would hate to lose you."

"Yes, yes I am. It certainly beats London."

"Ah, London. I have to go back there myself in October. Starting my pupillage." Charlotte was sitting up and as she spoke her fingers played with her toes. She looked distracted for a few moments.

"You don't seem terribly enthusiastic about it."

"Oh it's ok, it's just that I get used to the slower way of life back home. I've already done a few years up there so there are no illusions. Having said that it can be fun. Plenty of life."

"Providing you have money."

"Well . . . that's not really a problem and I have Mum's house to stay in, so I don't have to pay any extortionate rents."

"You're lucky then."

"Yes, I suppose I am but don't think my mother is an easy touch. Believe me, she gets her pound of flesh. I had to pay for my old banger, she made me work for the money. No loans. And as for lazing around watching the television all day and going out enjoying myself, forget it. She pay's for my education but damn all else. Any luxuries I have to pay for out of my modest Trust allowance or at least work for, she even charges me for using the telephone. Her motto is and always has been 'if you can't afford it go without!' And by God does she mean it! No loans, no handouts, no sod all, that's my mum! She doesn't even part with any money out of my Trust fund without wanting to know the ins and outs of a donkey's backside. And it's my money! Have to prove myself first apparently."

"Quite right too, if I may say so, because at least you haven't turned into a spoilt brat who thinks the world owes you a living and is too high and mighty to even catch a bus. Good for your mother I say, at least you have learnt to value things and are no doubt a better person for it. Anyway, I have every confidence that you'll be ok up there in the Big City. Plenty of boyfriends to keep you occupied too, I expect."

"I won't have time for boyfriends! A pupillage is no picnic I can tell you. And I want a junior tenancy after it. So I have to impress. Anyway, what about you? You never did answer my question . . . Is there anyone in your life . . . anyone important?"

It was time to stop messing about. The question and Charlotte's demeanour could leave no doubt as to her intentions. She put her hand on Sewell's arm. His forearm was strong, the muscles taught and in peak condition, like the rest of his body. There wasn't an ounce of fat anywhere to be seen, all his limbs and torso fitted together like port and stilton. He wasn't muscular in the obscene, weightlifting sense. He was slim and firm, his muscles agile and trim. Charlotte didn't dare look at the red bathing costume, she had already made a furtive appraisal and had an idea that it wouldn't disappoint, like her own bikini it didn't leave much to the imagination. Sewell spent some time thinking about his answer. Oh God, Charlotte thought, don't tell me you really do prefer men . . .

"Actually, at the present time the answer must be 'no'. There was someone up in London but she didn't want to move so that was the end of that. Things had started to go wrong before this job came up so neither of us shed many tears."

"No heartbreak then?"

"No. None."

"Glad to hear it. I can't abide these people who work so hard to obtain a first-class honours degree in self pity. Although I must admit to date I have managed to escape such emotional tribulations, so perhaps I am not best placed to comment. My God, that's a bit humble, not like me at all. Now, fancy another swim?" Before Sewell could reply Charlotte stood up, removed her bikini and started running toward the sea, yelling as she did so, "Come on! Take your trunks off! It's much more fun and healthier!"

Sewell stayed where he was for a few moments, thought 'to hell with it', removed his trunks as ordered and ran after the nymph who had appeared from nowhere.

Charlotte was the first to arrive back on land. They had cavorted and flirted without any intimate touching. Only their hands and an occasional leg had made contact. She was drying herself when Sewell turned up. He took her towel without asking and started to dry her back, her buttocks and legs. Still his hands didn't touch. Neither of them said a word when he turned her around and kissed her cheek.

"You are beautiful, Lottie. Quite beautiful." He kissed her on the lips then gently played with her tongue, as he did so he pushed her back onto the sand, knelt alongside her and started to lick and kiss her breasts. Charlotte moaned and placed her hand on his hardness, she fondled and stroked as she took his hand and placed it between her legs. They stayed liked this for some time, kissing, licking and absorbing until Charlotte couldn't stand it any longer. "Now," she pleaded, "Now, for God's sake. I want all of you!" Sewell teased her for a while before entering her. Charlotte gasped, he was big. His thrusts became faster as he too started to lose control.

"Oh God Lottie! Oh God! I have wanted this for so long!" he moaned.

"Me too, darling Justin, me too. Don't stop, please don't stop!" Sewell pushed and pushed, withdrew and withdrew until he felt like exploding. At last he let go. He had to.

"Oh God Lottie. Oh God!"

"Yes, yes Justin! Now my darling. Now!"

"Griffith what are you doing?" Lise scolded, "you mustn't overdo it, you stubborn man!" Griffith was sitting down at her desk pawing over some paperwork and trying not too perspire too much. Irish linen jackets creased up enough all on their own without his sweaty skin adding to their unkempt intent.

"What's it look like? Some work. I'll start going mad soon if I don't start doing something. I'm just checking what the builders are up to. They cost enough. What's for supper?"

"King prawns and salad."

"What? Rabbit food again!"

"Doctors orders, Griffith. No cigarettes, no alcohol and no piles of treacle pudding drowned in custard."

"You know, sometimes Lise I wish I'd pegged it. Life is so damned miserable and thoroughly tedious without any kind of vice in it."

"Don't be silly Griffith, besides you really would be bored if you didn't have anything to moan about, now stop being your usual cantankerous self and put those papers down, there is something we need to talk about. The new hotel will be completed in the New Year and we haven't decided what to call it. Any ideas?"

"Now you're asking a fine one, Lise, you know I'm not the most original or, come to that, imaginative of thinkers. How about Ragged Cliffs II?"

"Very funny."

"Well, you asked."

"Ok. How does . . . 'The Gower Rose Country House' sound? The Cliffs is renowned for its rose gardens, and I'm sure William would have liked it. He created them after all, you know how obsessive he was over pruning and cross pollination. The gardens were his 'pride and joy' as he never stopped telling us all." For once Griffith didn't sulk at the reference to his father's memory, instead he came over to Lise and kissed the back of her hand. This small, unobtrusive gesture, declared everything in its gentle simplicity.

"The Gower Rose is a charming name, Lise, and the Gower Rose it will be."

"Good. That's settled then. There is something else we need to discuss, Griffith."

"Oh, and what might that be?" Lise had on one of her serious faces.

"You and me."

"What about you and me, you're happy aren't you?" There was a tinge of fear in Griffith's voice. It was still early days after all.

"Yes. Yes of course I am, but . . . well . . . sooner or later we are going to have to tell people that we are . . . well . . . together as it were. It's been fine so far, you have been ill and need the peace and quiet of your own apartment, but this can't go on forever, can it?" Griffith sighed inwardly with relief, he had been waiting for this, in fact he had wanted to broach the subject for some time but had felt it better for Lise to make her own choices and in her own way. The secret nightly journeys between each other's apartments were becoming tiresome as was their initial desire to keep things from people until he felt better. Soon after his massive coronary Lise had finally accepted that they both loved each other, that they should be together and on a more 'biblical' basis at that. Powerful thing, death, Griffith had thought at the time, who the hell needed a God and prayers?

Griffith looked at the woman he had loved for so long. Lying in bed with her had been everything he could have imagined. Touching her skin, feeling her body, waking up to her morning smiles had made all the years worthwhile.

"I have left these delicate matters to you, but of course you are quite right," Griffith said. "Somehow though, I suspect people will not be as surprised as you think. We have been exceptionally close for many years, Lise, albeit like brother and sister. I would hope that anyone who matters will simply wish us well and probably say 'about time too'! Don't worry, Lise, everything will be fine."

"As may be, Griffith, but you know I'm not terribly comfortable about this 'living in sin' bit. It may be permissible for our 80's children, but not for me."

"Good God, Lise! Was there a proposal in there somewhere? Perhaps you are more a child of the 80's than you think!"

"Don't tease now, Griffith, you know exactly what I mean!"

"Maybe – but let's not rush things. I know you, Lise, you like to think about things long and hard. Sometimes too long I grant you, nevertheless I'm not having you turn round on me in a couple of years time and accusing me of coercion and force. No, tell everyone we are 'together' as you so delicately put it but leave it at that. We will just have to continue with the creaking floorboards and furtive giggles of the staff for a while longer, that's all. It's not really much of a sacrifice, Lise, is it? I've waited this long so what the hell difference will another year or so make ay?"

"What about Lottie and Kristian?"

"Oh God, Lise, what about them?"

"Well, they might not like it. You know what children are like . . ."

"Not really, never had any of my . . . at least I don't know much about fatherhood, do I?"

"Oh don't talk nonsense, Griffith, for a start you're the only 'father' Lottie has ever known, and as for Kristian you treat him like a son and always have done."

"So what the hell are you worrying about woman? Dear God, you're infuriating! Look Lise, both your children are adults, Kristian has led his own life for years, Lottie is about to begin hers. They have left the nest. They have good and decent hearts, there isn't one drop of overindulged selfishness in either of them, both of us have seen to that. But Lise, most importantly of all they both love you and they both care about you. All they will want is your happiness, nothing more, nothing less. Trust me, I know the pair of them, like you say I have been a father to them for many years. I have every confidence in them and I have every confidence that they will be quite delighted to know that we are at last 'together' properly. This is the way it should be and I have no reason to think that either of them will behave otherwise. If they do, then we have made some awful mistakes somewhere along the way and I have to say that I would be deeply, deeply ashamed of what we have created."

"That won't happen, Griffith, and you know it."

"Exactly, so stop fretting old girl."

"I wish you wouldn't call me that, 'old girl' makes me sound as if I have just joined the Womens Institute."

"Now that, Lise Treharne is extremely unlikely. You are far too young in spirit for that . . . and sexy!" With that, Griffith made a lunge for her breasts.

"For God sake's, Griffith, not here! Behave yourself!" Lise scolded as she pushed his hands away . . . mind you she could lock the door for a short while, it was the quiet time of the day after all. "No, get thee behind me Satan," she whispered to herself. "Besides you're not supposed to overdo things!"

"You didn't say that last night, did you!"

"Oh be quiet! Now sit back down will you, before you have another heart attack. Right, it's decided then, we will tell the children when I think the time is right."

"Fine by me. Now that we have sorted out your paranoid anxieties, how is young Paul Edmunds doing? I haven't seen anything of him lately." This wasn't strictly true. Griffith had been keeping a watchful eye on the boy and had been surprised at the way he was shaping up. They had spoken on many occasions and Griffith was actually starting to like the lad. They had even gone out for a drink together on a couple of occasions, and as they had gradually become more familiar with one another Griffith had come to realize how much his son was like him. What the boy lacked in looks he made up for in humour and natural charm, and there was also a subdued kindness in the way he talked about people and the way he treated them. There had been many occasions when Griffith had felt an overwhelming sense of pride and fatherly love for the boy. One day soon he knew that he would have to tell Paul the truth, it would be an appalling betrayal to do anything else, regardless of what Sylvia thought.

So far Griffith had kept his son's antecedents a secret from Lise too, but the pressure was building up on both counts. If he didn't say something soon, any marriage to Lise would be blasted out of the water. His lack of honesty would appal her and he knew it. The whole business was giving him sleepless nights.

"Very well, Griffith," Lise answered his question, "very well indeed. I have had nothing but good reports. Hard worker, the staff like him. He's been with Gwyn the past couple of months learning new skills, although if I know Gwyn all the boy will end up knowing is how to be an expert drinker, smoker and womanizer. And before you say anything, Griffith, I know all about Gwyn's antic's when Bronwyn's eyes are somewhere else. Actually the boy is doing rather well, he's bright too. I have plans for him. What did you say your relationship was to him, Griffith?"

"Er . . . oh, one of my second cousin's sons. All a bit complicated really, you know what extended families are like."

"I never heard your father speaking about relatives by the name of Edwards." Lise looked at Griffith for a few moments and allowed silence to push him further back in his chair.

"Well . . . er . . . no, you probably wouldn't have. On my mother's side and my father hated anything to do with that lot. They were all scoundrels and villains as far as Dad was concerned."

"Oh, all right then . . . Anyway, so far I'm quite impressed with the lad. We'll give him a year and see what we can do with him after that. Might be an idea to train him up for management. We can think about it then."

"Yes, good idea. Well I'm off for my afternoon nap now so I'll see you later Lise."

"You do that. Enjoy your nap."

Griffith closed the study door and felt again the death throes of a defunct heart. His pulse was racing faster than his ardour to get Lise into bed! The damned woman could spot a rumpled skirt at 300 paces and a whiff of fag at 600! Bloody Lise! She knew something was up he was sure. It was in her lovely blue eyes. He had seen that all-knowing look more times that he could remember. She had known about Gwyn and his randy antics in the out buildings so why not his lusty adventures in the laundry rooms? Oh God, this notion didn't bear thinking about! She had slipped that question in about Paul like a real pro too. All innocence and light. My arse! He knew Lise. The crafty bugger knew more than she was letting on but how, for crying out loud? How? She was making him suffer, that was a certainty, dangling him on one of her sadistic strings. God, she could be a vicious bitch when she wanted to be. He collected his thoughts over a disgusting orange juice and finally decided that perhaps things weren't as bad as he thought. If Lise smelt a paternal rat then his eventual exposure and admission may not be so bad after all, as for his adventures with bed linen and black skirts, well, Lise knew all about his weaknesses where women were concerned, at least when he had been young anyway. Hell, there had only been one or two romps in the laundry cupboard after all . . . well, maybe more than one or two over the years and then there had been . . . Whatever she knew she had obviously decided not to get in a lather about it, so that was in his favour. One thing he did know, he had better come clean and fast. He wasn't so sure about Paul though. Would it do more harm than good? What about his mother, she had insisted on secrecy from day one and even now Griffith wasn't entirely sure why. The blood tests at the time had been unequivocal.

He left the hotel bar and went up to his apartment. As he poured himself a small whiskey he looked over his shoulder, Jesus he wouldn't have been surprised if Lise had discovered one of the few bastion's of vice he had left, a hidden bottle of Irish whiskey. Damned woman probably knew about the sly fags that Gwyn smuggled into his desperate hands every now and again too! And God knows what she would do if she found out about the little arrangement he had with the chef!

CHAPTER 21

Kristian's head hurt. This one was a real beauty. The Wood's was getting out of hand and he knew it. His chest heaved for breath as his lungs started to inhale the only few minutes of carbon monoxide-free air they were likely to get for that day. He moved his stump in a westerly direction and felt it struggle with some hot flesh, or was it fooling him again, he could never be too sure. One eyelid popped open, two at the same time may well have caused serious damage. The ceiling was still in one piece so that was something. He moved his eye sideways and saw a mound of long brunette hair attached to one of the pillows. Where had she come from he wondered? At least he hoped it was a 'she'. The state he had been in last night it could well have been a 'he' and he probably wouldn't have known the difference!

Kristian tried to recall the events of last night. They were so vague that he began to wonder why he was bothering at all. Spiv passed briefly in and out of his dubious recollection, words about some unhealthy African independence, money, an international corporation requiring his expertise . . . For a moment his stomach lurched as drunken memory returned with a clarity that made him wish for an early grave. Oh God, his anxiety moaned, he hadn't signed up for some stupid war had he? That's all he needed!

He sat up slowly and moved his one and a half legs to the edge of the bed. His head required a great deal of respect at the moment so quick, agile movement was out of the question. As he bent over to strap on his peg leg a vicious expulsion of wind nearly blew his poor unsuspecting bed-mate out through the window and onto the pavement one storey below. There was a mumbled, "Did you say something?" from the river of brunette hair. Kristian replied, "No, just 'Good morning'," and carried on strapping himself up. Just as he was about to negotiate a standing position, his balance was all to hell, there was another mumble from the hairy pillow.

"I wouldn't do that too often if I was you, that arsehole of yours will crack the fucking mirror! For one moment there I thought I'd been shot!"

"Wait until the stench hits you, my girl, my farts are for the benefit of the deaf too! My god, this one has started to curl my moustache!" He heard a giggle crumple the bed sheets. Oh well, Kristian thought, whoever the woman was she had a sense of humour, she spoke well too. Traces of public school had meandered through the 'fucking'. "Er . . . do forgive me, but I've forgotten your name. Have we been formally introduced?" Kristian asked.

The woman's head refused to move so he had no idea what she looked like. It may be best if it stayed that way, he thought, God knows he had woken up to a few frightening 'night before' surprises in his time. False teeth, hair lips and rear ends that needed a crow bar to get them out of the door to name but a few. Some of them had even looked as if they had overdosed on steroids, and he wasn't thinking about their bodies either!

"No, we haven't been formally introduced as you put it, unless you call that flatulent bowel motion an introduction," the woman finally replied, "or for that matter a first meeting between my aching right hand and your useless boozed-up winky."

"Oh, like that was it?"

"It was."

"My apologies. Nothing personal you understand. Too much drink."

"That's all right, you're forgiven. You made me laugh which is something I suppose. My name is Zoe by the way." The face underneath the brunette hair finally made an appearance. It didn't disappoint.

"Ah, 'Zoe'. Greek for 'life' if I remember correctly."

"You remember correctly . . . ugh! Dear God, you were right about the stench! I should have stayed beneath the quilt. I deserve the Victoria Cross for enduring this . . ." Zoe jumped out of the bed and opened all the bedroom windows. When her nasal passages had finally calmed down and the air around them refreshed itself she said, "Now where do you think you are going, Kristian, stink notwithstanding you filthy bastard, note that I do at least show you the courtesy of remembering your name? I think some compensation is in order here what with one thing and another and I'm feeling as horny as hell!"

Kristian looked at the dark eyelashes, the pretty face and the naked bosom that had jumped over the quilt. Her body would ruin any man whether he loved or not. Mindless dicks again. He sighed with resignation, undid his peg leg and hopped back into bed. A few moments later Zoe murmured, "You know, darling, that half leg of yours allows for some cracking fucking positions!"

Later that morning Kristian sat alone in his sitting room drinking strong coffee and swearing at the tremors that raced through his fingertips. The 'shakes'. He had never experienced such an outrage being inflicted on his body before. His nervous system felt as if it had been riddled with armour-piercing bullets and his stomach insisted on retching every ten minutes or so. He was a wreck. Over the last few months all he had done was drink, smoke, feel insanely sorry for himself and curse Myfanwy. He would be running off for some counselling next, or worse still a dose of pathetic, self-inflicted bleating at one of these new fangled 'support group' things. The world, his world, was going mad, no wonder Thatcher was banging on about personal responsibility. The Brits were becoming a nation of lily-livered, gutless wimps, intent on their own destruction. 'Syndromes', 'support groups', 'self-esteem', it was all bollocks.

He thought about the young woman who hadn't long left his bed. She had been a diversion, a mere receptacle for the necessary offloading of natural male testosterone. They had both known the rules, there had been no declarations of intent, no sweet kisses of undying love and certainly no future. They had both been quite content with the mutual use and abuse of each other's bodies.

Zoe was not Myfanwy nor could she ever hope to be.

Kristian had telephoned Spiv earlier that morning and confirmed that their merrymaking had not resulted in Kristian pledging his services to some mineral-grabbing corporation intent on stirring up rebellion in some remote African fiefdom. So, what next? He looked at a half-empty bottle of rum sitting on the coffee table and for a few moments was tempted to immerse himself back into the gory and emasculating war zone of alcoholic delusion. No, he decided, this was not the way. He needed a clear mind, clarity. Enough was enough. The only option he had left was to return home, for a while anyway. Perhaps there was something he could do there, even if it was only some building work. At least this would help to get his body back into shape. It would be something physical and something that would avoid having to sit behind a desk, which is exactly what his mother would have him do.

It really was time to get his act together, his body into some semblance of offensive good health and his mind away from Myfanwy . . . well, maybe that was pushing it a little.

CHAPTER 22

"We really must stop meeting like this you know, people will start to talk." Charlotte laughed at her own clichéd remark, she couldn't care less whether 'people' talked or not. Justin looked at her and once again found it impossible not to grin and kiss her on the lips. He was about to pull his mouth away when Charlotte pulled his head back and said, "Not so fast!" before exploring his mouth with her tongue. They kissed for a long time, and as usual their mutual lust reduced them to a pair of rampant stoats about to be placed on a farmer's execution list.

An hour later when each of them was finally satisfied, 'quickies' had yet to appear on their performance programme, Charlotte remained half dressed and Justin looked ridiculous. His shirt was tied around his neck, his trousers and pants were strapped to the car pedals and his socks were gradually reaching the ends of his toes. Although they had been enjoying sexual discovery for a month or so, their enthusiasm had yet to refine their lovemaking or enjoy the comfort of a proper bed. They both lived at the Cliffs, so urgent copulation had to be carried out where and when they could manage it. On this occasion the car was parked right at the back of a car park abutting Caswell Bay. All this of course annoyed Charlotte and frustrated Justin.

"You know I'm getting thoroughly fed up with all this, Justin. What the hell are we hiding for?"

"I agree but the point is, Lotte, how will your mother react if she finds out. I could lose my job you know, and I really don't want that to happen."

"I understand that, Justin, but I'm not so sure my mother would react in that way. I know she can be a prude sometimes but she's really not that bad. I'll say that for her she has never interfered in my private life, so perhaps we are exaggerating things. I say, let's have it out in the open once and for all because all this back-door, MI5 stuff is seriously pissing me off. What the hell are we hiding like a couple of criminals for any way? We are both adults for heaven's sake!"

"That's as may be. But like it or not I am 'staff'. Your mother and Griffith are my employer's and they're both old school, say what you like. They just might not take too kindly to my being intimate with you. Let's face it, I'm only a grammar school boy with no rich family behind me and certainly no money in my bank account, at least not the sort of money that you are used to."

"Look Justin, I think I need to say something here." For once Charlotte seemed to be struggling for the right words. There was a calmness to her face matched only by the intensity of her blue eyes.

"You know Justin, all we have done so far is meet up and screw. Well, at least that's what it feels like. I know we talk for hours on end but our time together always seems to be limited. We are both constantly looking over our shoulders and this can't be right. You see Justin . . ." Charlotte started to play with her bracelet again, "I don't want all this . . . because . . . well . . . I have fallen deeply in love with you . . . and sod your modest bank balances." She moved her eyes away from the bracelet and looked directly into Justin's eyes. He said nothing. He took her hand and kissed the back of it.

"Well then, we had better be a bit more open about things then hadn't we because . . . I love you too, Lottie. More than you can ever know, believe me." There was that moment of complete silence that only two people deeply in love can understand. The mutual knowledge was total and special. It was secretive and unique. They held hands and tried to come to terms with the emotion that tumbled between them. Charlotte would be going away in a couple of months and Justin being the older of the two knew only too well how fickle and transient young love could be. He had been hurt in the past and knew the dangers. Charlotte so far had always been in control of her loving inclinations. She had led, she had taken and she had decided. Justin didn't doubt her feelings for him now, but would they be strong enough to withstand the attacks of distance and absence? He wasn't so sure. London could taint a genuine love, it could also obliterate it. His eyes looked out of the car window at cliffs and waves that offered no answers.

"What's the matter, Justin? You have gone all quiet."

"Oh, nothing much. Just wondering about you going away."

"Oh, don't worry about that. It's only for a year or so and I'll be back at weekends."

"Will you?"

"Yes, of course I will. We'll be fine."

"Yes, but what about afterwards? Your tenancy and so on, where are you going to do that? I know you want to do well."

"Oh God, Justin, don't worry. If push comes to shove there are a couple of chambers in Swansea and Mum has all the right connections." This was not a particularly attractive idea but for now it would have to do. Charlotte didn't want to upset her loving apple-cart and besides, a lot could happen in a year.

"Swansea is hardly the hub of legal glamour is it?"

"Maybe not, but the Welsh are just as villainous as everybody else so it doesn't really matter where I am. Besides I will only be happy if I am with you, so like I say, don't worry about it."

"Are you sure, Lottie? Because I don't want to stand in the way of your career. You're a bright young woman with the world at your feet. Our love may hold you back."

"I'm sure, Justin, a career isn't everything you know. There are . . . well . . . children, family. Now let's leave it at that." She kissed him while her hand checked for more enthusiastic life in another part of his body.

"Oh God, Charlotte, you are such a slut!"

"I know, but don't you just love it?"

"Oh, I see."

"Is that all you have to say, Mum?"

"Well what else can I say? You are a big girl now, far be it from me to influence your romantic endeavours."

"Romantic endeavours? God Mum, don't overdo the good wishes, will you!" Lise sat opposite her daughter and remembered for a few moments. Charlotte may well have been the physical reincarnation of William and very much like him in more ways than one, but there was the odd gene in her that belonged to her mother. All her life Lise had followed her heart, could she now blame her daughter for following hers?

"I'm sorry Lottie, but this has come as a bit of a shock. Justin after all is our manager and an extremely able one. How will all this effect his position here?"

"I don't see how 'his position here' has anything to do with it. We're not about to enter a business relationship, are we? God Mum, is that all you can think about? We love each other and that's all there is to it! Now, you could at least try and be happy for us instead of worrying about your bloody profit margins!"

"That's enough, Charlotte! Watch your tone of voice when you're speaking with me!" In times of anger 'Lottie' always became 'Charlotte'.

"Tone of voice! Who are you to judge anyway? You married a man years older that yourself and in those days housekeepers and their employers usually stuck to quick 'getting to know your betters' in the stables! You married the boss, didn't you?" Lise stood up from her chair, anger warned her daughter.

"That's enough Charlotte! I'm not telling you again!"

"Well it's true and you know it, so don't start pontificating with me or lecturing. I'm a 'big girl' now as you put it and I will make my own decisions. If you don't like it, then hard luck. I love Justin and want to spend the rest of my life with him and that's all there is to it!" Charlotte stood up now, this was a battle to the death. Mother and daughter confronted each other, both strong women, both self-willed and both capable of the most loyal and profound love. They stared at each other for a few moments, fists almost clenched – not that either of them had ever hit anyone in their lives. Nevertheless, like most people, the capability was there.

"Don't you ever speak to me like that again, Charlotte! Ever! Do I make myself clear?" Charlotte wasn't going to give way, she was far too much like her mother.

"I'll say what I feel whether you like it or not, Mum. We love each other and to hell with everyone and everything else!" There was a hiatus of silence for a few moments as the air gripped the pair of them and threw their tempers around the room. Neither of them said a word. They just stared at each other and waited. At last age with its hopeful wisdom prevailed. Lise spoke quietly.

"Lottie my girl, your impertinent and objectionable nature drove me to distraction even when you were a child, adulthood and a modicum of maturity seem to have had little if any effect on these less endearing qualities of yours. You are certainly your father's daughter, I'll say that for you," a smile touched Lise's lips, "yes, you are most certainly his daughter. Now come here and let's give each other a hug. I hate quarrelling as you know."

It was Charlotte's turn to be humble now, and as usual her mother made her feel like a right bitch. Lise always won in the end, her mother was one person she would never beat. The same applied to Justin she suspected.

"I'm sorry for being so horrible, Mum, I really am." They hugged each other as Lise said, "You are also too much like me in some ways my girl – at least where matters of the heart are concerned. Far too much like me. You and Justin love each other and be happy. All I ever want for you is happiness, and don't you ever forget it. He seems a good man so don't play him up too much, although I suspect he is strong enough to handle you . . . he will need to be!"

"Oh, he's strong enough all right, I wouldn't love him if he was anything else."

"No, I don't suppose you would. One other thing, what about your career?"

"Nothing changes."

"I see . . . simple as that is it?"

"Look Mum, I have my pupillage to finish first and I'm not going to let anything stand in the way of that. I've spent years studying and I'm not about to throw it all away for a man, as much as I love Justin. These days it is possible to have a career and a family you know. I want to be a criminal advocate who's hotter than Coleman's mustard, Mum, that's what all these years have been about. And believe me that's exactly what I will be one day."

"Good, I'm glad to hear it." The determination in her daughter's words came as a relief. "Now go on, I have work to do. This new hotel is taking up a great deal of my time. It's meant to be opening in the New Year and the work isn't half finished. No doubt you and Justin will give the staff plenty to talk about for a while so enjoy the attention, oh and don't allow your relationship to interfere with Justin's work – or yours. Believe me, I will be keeping a careful eye on you both."

"Oh, we are not the only ones they talk about, Mum," Charlotte said with an inscrutability that would have embarrassed a Chinese brothel-keeper. "I don't think we will steal the limelight from you and Uncle Griffith anyway. Both of you are far more important than Justin and I. Oh, and Justin's work won't suffer I promise you." With that Charlotte left the study, along with a slightly bemused Lise.

There were few secrets at the Cliffs and Lise had not really been surprised by her daughter's comments. Well, if Lottie already had some idea that things other that friendship were going on between she and Griffith, then the truth would come as no surprise. As for Kristian, she doubted if he would even raise an eyebrow, she knew her son was an utter rascal – albeit a loveable one – and that like her daughter he would probably be glad that the farce of she and Griffith was over once and for all. He was due home at the weekend. She remembered his phone call. The boy was troubled, his voice had lost some of its usual levity and humour. Something was wrong but her son had never been too quick at revealing whatever it was that was bothering him, in this respect he had always been so independent, so self-contained. It may have served him well in the military, but now he had to live in the real, civilian world. The normal world.

Lise had been worrying about Kristian for a while. He was obviously drinking too much, his voice had slurred once or twice on the telephone and this was a bad sign. He had always managed to hold his drink well and as far as she knew rarely over-indulged, but she had noticed that on the last few occasions he had been home there had been a greater intensity to his alcohol consumption. It had been more desperate, more isolated. Bottles of rum had been taken up to his room by the staff too, and this had never happened before. What was wrong with the boy? It couldn't be the amputation, he seemed to have adjusted well enough to that. Was it the boredom, the feeling of being unable to do anything constructive or at least anything he would be happy doing? She didn't like it, but deep down Lise knew full well that her son could never sit behind a desk all day, such a prospect really would kill him off. Even so, he was capable of doing almost anything if he put his mind to it, so why wasn't he even trying? That left one thing. The only thing. A woman.

Lise sat at her desk and worried. Lottie was jumping into love head first, and her son, she was convinced, was suffering from a broken heart, not that he would ever admit it, but she knew her son in a way that only a mother can. Both her offspring were making her anxious, and to top it all Griffith could die from a heart attack at any moment but still insisted on his contraband cigarettes and Irish whiskey! And he thought she didn't know!

Lise sighed and picked up her faithful, silver letter-opener. She looked at her name that had been engraved on its handle and allowed her mind to reflect. There was the playground love of unknown implications, both pretty and innocent, there was young love that was thoughtless, destructive and less innocent and then there was the love of middle and latter years. This love was perhaps the best, especially if it was new and without the coercion of children, relatives and financial commitment to things that neither party would ever really choose if they were given the chance. This older love lacked the rapid deluge of passion and suspect emotion but it knew its place. It knew what to do and how to behave. It rarely tore apart with treasonous vows and impossible promises. It could survive in spite of doubt and ridiculous aspiration, in spite of cynical winks and thread-bare delusions. Lise knew and had learnt that love in her prime could only ever be a grand finale, a finishing touch to all the love she had ever known. The childish, the young and the middle aged all came together to construct a holistic bond of finality and pristine hope. Her heart still begged, still yearned but it was quieter now and more complete. She knew the touch of Griffith's skin was all she would ever need to be who she was and who she had ever wanted to be. This was enough and she was grateful.

CHAPTER 23

August was drawing to a close as Griffith nearly puked when he saw the green salad and boiled haddock staring at him. To make matters worse, Balzac, their prancing chef had been got at. Griffith's supplies of sweet, lard-coated treats had been mercilessly cut off. Lise had exercised her brutal prerogative yet again. Even Gwyn and the nearest off-licence had been warned off!

He looked around the dining table. All the surviving Treharnes were present and correct apart from one. There was Lottie, presently being serviced by the paid help, not that he could say anything about that; Kristian, drying out after a broken-hearted bender; and he and Lise, about to declare that they too had joined the sexual revolution in their bloody dotage – not to mention of course the fact that the missing Treharne was his bastard son who lurked about the place with covert pretensions of becoming the best hotel manager this side of the United Kingdom. Oh well, he thought, nothing changes where the Treharnes were concerned. All in all, apart from the money, they were just like any other normal, average family.

Grithith seethed while everyone enjoyed a leg of lamb roasted in herbs and apple crumble and custard to finish. When they had all stopped gorging themselves Kristian, looking a lot fitter since he had started directing the building work on The Gower Rose and pitching in himself when required and sometimes when not, lit up a cigar and poured his sister and Lise a brandy, five star just to annoy and torture Griffith even more. Kristian was sticking to iced water; going without the booze didn't seem to bother him Griffith had to grudgingly admit, the smug sod. His own tongue was almost falling out just looking at the bottle. The smell of sweet, perfect cigar smoke didn't help either.

"Now then, both of you, your Uncle Griffith has something to tell you . . ." Lise paused, giving Griffith time to counter-attack her ambush. Nothing happened. "Griffith . . . you do have something to tell Kristian and Lottie, don't you?" Griffith's shin received a painful kick.

"What? Yes . . . oh yes, sorry, er . . . damn it, this teetotal and tobacco-free regime is killing me! You're running a bloody police state here, my girl. You'll be inviting Oswald Mosley for tea next, God help us!" Lise looked at Griffith and said indulgently.

"Now that would be a trifle difficult, Griffith, being as the man died back in 1980."

"Did he? Bugger me. Well his Brown Shirts still live on and that's a fact!"

"Griffith, stop blustering and tell them what's going on, will you? Dear me you are the most irritating man I have ever known! You're worse than Kristian! Now get on with it!"

"Very well."

Both Kristian and Charlotte were quite used to their mother and Griffith arguing so they took no notice. They just sat and waited patiently. Griffith leaned in a little closer to Kristian in an attempt to secure at least a few surrogate puffs of cigar smoke.

"Right . . . well . . . er . . . it's like this. Your mother and I are getting married." Straight and to the point, Griffith was on form.

Silence.

More silence.

"Did you both just hear what Griffith said?" Lise asked.

"We did." Kristian and Charlotte replied in unison.

"Well!" Lise was getting exasperated now. "Is that all you have to say?"

At last Kristian beamed and Charlotte got up and gave them both a kiss. As she hugged Griffith she said, "About time too, if I may say so. My God, Uncle Griffith, you do take your time about things, don't you? That's a point, what on earth do I call you now?"

"Well, I suppose you're old enough now to be granted the privilege so 'Griffith' will be just fine, thank you Lottie."

Kristian pulled out a bottle of the best champagne from under his seat.

"Come on Griffith, you've suffered enough for one night. Let's finish this off and you can have one of my cigars too, and Mother, you just keep quiet please."

For once Lise gave in to the occasion. As the cork erupted Lise remarked, "The pair of you knew all along, didn't you?"

"We did indeed, Mother," Kristian replied as he gave his mother a kiss, "you're not the only one with X-ray vision as it were. Now here's to a wonderful future for you both and look, even I am jumping off the wagon for this one night!" He shook Griffith's hand and said, "Rather you than me Griffith, so good luck, you're going to need it!"

Later that night when all the grandfather clocks could be heard ticking the guests to sleep Griffith put his arms around the woman he loved. They were lying in bed enjoying those delicate moments when breathing calmed and love could be touched and held.

"Lise," Griffith murmured, "there is something I have to tell you . . . Paul is my son." Once again that night Griffith threw subtlety to the winds as he hung on to his pyjama trousers and hoped that his parachute would open. He held her more tightly, hoping to pre-empt any anger that may be waiting to attack him.

"I know."

"What?"

"I've known for quite a while. Woman's intuition, Griffith. You're in the boy's eyes, his expressions, his mannerisms. Your father is there too."

"But . . . but . . ."

"All those secret little jaunts to London, Griffith? And wasn't there a vengeful woman at the back of all those horrible court proceedings you were involved in all those years ago?"

"Yes but . . . you remembered all that?"

"I forget very little Griffith, you should know that. Thank you for finally telling me though, I was wondering how long it would take. As Lottie commented earlier on, you do tend to take your time about things but you get there in the end, I suppose."

"You're not angry?"

"Why should I be?"

"Well, you know what you're like about honesty in all things and so on."

"Griffith, all that business was a long time ago. You didn't really do anything wrong, and I know what a decent man you are. And an extremely loveable man at that. Paul doesn't know, does he?"

"No."

"Well that can't go on forever. It's not right so you had better start thinking about it. Now give me a kiss goodnight and go to sleep. We're both tired."

Griffith kissed Lise and was yet again surprised by her tolerance and understanding, no wonder he loved her so much. The woman was unique.

PART II

June 1984

CHAPTER 24

Southwark Magistrates Court, London

The two male magistrates stared down at an unusual sight. Both had bid farewell to the last vestiges of middle-aged virility, but even so they could still allow their minds to imagine all the tremendously perverted things they could once have done to the disgracefully sexy young barrister that stood before them. Advocates like Charlotte Treharne didn't come before them too often, most of the female lawyers who bristled before them were an unwholesome lot to put it mildly, and if they were caught on a day when their hormones were jumping about in a frenzy, then look out. This Miss Treharne was an absolute tonic though, even if she did remind them of younger days and make them despair at the prospect of returning home later that evening to the gritty tongues and sour faces of the old boilers who would dump their supper in front of them.

Charlotte looked up at the bench and tried to remember all the things she had learnt. This was her first case, her first modest chance to start building up her reputation, a crucial step for the future. The case had been thrown at her the day before with the words, "Don't try and be Edward Carson or Lawrence Olivier, Charlotte. The beaks have heard it all before and seen it all before a thousand times, so don't piss them off by trying to be a tedious smart arse. They aren't a jury, so make damned certain that you don't try and pull the wool over their eyes."

She had read the brief and hadn't known whether to laugh or cry. The client, whom she was defending, had been charged with causing a breach of the peace. A minor tickle where the criminal law was concerned but a start for her, if nothing else. She was still, after all, a mere 'pupil'. The lowest of the low.

Her client, a Mr Hoult, had apparently called the police following the removal of his car from outside his front door by persons unknown. These 'persons' were still 'unknown' as far as Charlotte was aware. Two policemen had duly arrived to take down a statement and pretend that they would be able to do something. Mr Hoult lived in one of the less salubrious areas of London so as far as they were concerned the vehicle would no doubt be discovered soon enough as a burnt-out wreck on some local piece of wasteland. They would go through the motions of filing a report, Mr Hoult would go through the motions of claiming the insurance money and everyone would be happy. Nothing unusual.

The two policeman had turned up at Mr Hoult's house and been cordially invited in. An Alsatian dog had followed the two officers through the door.

Good manners and polite conversation had prevailed while one of the officer's had proceeded to take a statement from the outraged Mr Hoult who was beside himself with anxiety at the loss of his only means of transport. How was he going to get the missus to the hospital now? he had moaned Of course everyone in the room, including Mr Hoult's arthritic, Disability Living Allowance wife, knew damn well that the whole 'crime' was a total fiction. Mr Hoult had paid someone a few quid to torch the car in order to make a fraudulent claim on the insurance company and allow him to buy a newer model. This was the way things were done around here after all. To put it in legal terms, it was common 'Custom and Practice', as it were. Anyway, while everyone played a well-known game, the Alsatian had by this time parked itself down on the Chinese rug in front of the fire. He was more than happy to allow the 'crime' to take its natural course.

When at last all the paperwork had been completed and Mr Hoult had expressed his desire to have the perpetrators of this heinous crime caught and 'strung up by their balls' the two officers stood up, said their goodbyes and made their way to the front door. The Alsatian, on cue, obediently left his place of comfort and started to follow the officers out – not before leaving a huge, warlike turd on the Chinese rug in front of the fire. No one said a word. Everything had been so polite and civil so far so why spoil things. The dog got as far as the doorway, decided that it was too cold outdoors after all and returned to the sitting room with its Chinese rug.

The officers were about to jump into their squad car when Mr Hoult shouted after them, "Hey, aren't you going to take that dirty fucker of a dog of yours with you? The bastard's left a bloody great steaming turd on my brand new Chinese rug! It cost a bloody fortune!"

"What do you mean?" one of the officers shouted back. "It's not our dog! It's yours!"

"What? What do you mean, 'mine'?" Mr Hoult shouted back angrily, "The dirty bastard is yours, he came in with you, didn't he!"

"But we thought . . . the dog was yours!" the same officer yelled back. "He seemed quite at home, after all."

Next minute Mr Hoult blew a gasket and started throwing flowerpots around his garden while he cursed and defamed anyone who came near, including the two officers of the law. He was duly arrested, taken to the local nick and charged with a breach of the peace. While all the shouting and swearing had been going on, the Alsatian, proud of his handiwork and unrepentant, had sneaked away from the debacle never to be seen again.

Charlotte had advised her client to plead guilty. It was the only sensible course. Needless to say he wasn't having any of it. As far as he was concerned the police had mislead him and in the process had desecrated his property. No way was he going to plead guilty to a justifiable reaction to police intimidation and brutality!

Charlotte stared at her blue legal pad and pleaded for inspiration. The prosecution had laid out the facts of the case, it was now down to her to get her client off. Fat chance! And how the hell was she supposed to litigate the 'the case of the bloody great steaming turd' as it had been referred to in the police statements. She had tried to convince her client to go quietly, hands up to the court, look all humble and diminished, apologize as if your life is in peril, pay the fine and go home. This was the way to deal with the bench, on this particular matter anyway. The magistrates would give credit for the contrition and humility and no doubt order a small fine with a binding over for a year or so. Not likely, Mr Hoult was determined to have his day in court and that was that.

Charlotte coughed delicately into her hand. "Your Worships, we seem to have here a case of mistaken identity."

"Really, Miss Treharne?" the Chairman of the bench enquired as he looked over his half-moon spectacles. "Would that be of the defendant or the objectionable calling-card left on his Chinese rug?" The magistrate could never resist making these new bright sparks earn their fees, but apart from this it was plain heaven just watching the young woman's chest heave and strain against her white blouse. What he wouldn't do to get his hands on that glorious pair of Bristols!

"Neither, your worship. Mistaken identity where the dog was concerned."

Charlotte knew that she mustn't be intimidated even if the beak was trying to unsettle her, while at the same time keeping his eyes glued to her tits. Well, two can play at this she thought. She pushed her bosom out a little further. Take that you perverted old bastard!

"So, there you have it your Worships," Charlotte concluded after she had outlined her client's defence of provocation, self-defence and anything else her imagination could conjure up, "a perfectly understandable case of mistaken identity. The police officers thought the dog belonged to my client – the animal seemed to know the house and to be at ease in front of the fire – and my client thought the dog belonged to the officers. Again a perfectly reasonable assumption bearing in mind the dog's pedigree and the fact that he came in with the officers. Police dogs are a familiar sight on the estate where my client lives due to the general lawlessness that sadly seems to prevail in what can only be described as an underprivileged area of London.

"All I can finally say in my client's defence is how, your Worships, would you feel if a strange dog walked into your sitting room and left, I quote, 'a bloody great steaming turd' on one of your rugs?"

Charlotte lost the case but started to gain a reputation.

Later that day Charlotte and Justin were sitting down in the Hard Rock Café, Piccadilly. Thumping great bottles of tomato ketchup rocked to the drums of raucous shrieks and the wails of people trying to make themselves heard. American-style burgers raced around the place searching for early heart attacks whilst drinks bubbled and squeaked in mounds of rock-hard ice that fizzed and popped to the trendy music that refused to go away. And this was supposed to be a place to relax and enjoy intelligent discourse with one's girlfriend on a Friday night out, Justin thought as he looked around the walls that were covered from head to noisy toe with pop paraphernalia. Being hip and groovy was not quite his style, neither were the incessant vibrations that travelled along the floor and ended up trying to bash his brains out.

"Aren't you enjoying yourself Justin? Come on loosen up, you old curmudgeon!" Charlotte loved it when Justin went into one of his sneering moods. She had to admit though that mischief had prevailed when she had suggested coming here. Justin hated London but now and again he would give her a break by coming up to see her. He appreciated that travelling back and forth to Wales on the weekends could be tiresome for her.

"Loosen up? What the hell does that mean? I'm not a leather belt!" he shouted back at her. Before he was able to shout anymore a plate of so-called 'American buffalo' trapped between a hefty bread bun and thin, fat-saturated 'French fries' nearly landed in his lap. The odd slice of tomato and recalcitrant string of lettuce added to the outrage that he was supposed to eat and enjoy. A monolithic glass containing reservoirs of caffeine-overdosed Coca Cola arrived alongside the food. Charlotte really was enjoying herself. She had ordered.

"Am I supposed to eat this Yankee rubbish then? Am I?" Justin moaned. He had always been proud of the fact that he was a fully trained cordon bleu cook and an Epicurean of the first degree. He knew about good food, he also knew about pigswill. Charlotte giggled above the din.

"Oh stop moaning, Justin. Eat and be quiet, you might just enjoy it."

Justin picked up his knife and fork and stared at the new food. He was damned if he was going to pick up the beefy brute with his fingers; apart from anything else he doubted whether he would be able to get the thing anywhere near his mouth anyway. This was going to take some negotiating if his table manners were to maintain their dignity. Eventually he managed to place some beef and chips in his mouth. He chewed for a few moments and surprisingly didn't need to rush off to the nearest toilet. Twenty minutes later his plate was clean.

"See now, that didn't hurt, did it?" Charlotte remarked, "you pompous old fart!"

"I had to eat something I was hungry."

"Nonsense! You enjoyed it so don't lie."

"Well . . . I . . ."

"'Well I' nothing. Right, how about some flapjacks with lashings of maple syrup to finish off?"

"Oh God, if you must—"

"I must. Two helpings then and I'll eat yours if your ever-so discerning palate is unable to cope."

Later that evening they arrived back at the house just off Kings Road in Chelsea. It was one of those typical Georgian affairs that seem to go on forever. There were loads of upstairs, downstairs, back rooms, front rooms, basements that disappeared into nowhere and attics that were always having a good laugh at history.

The drawing room was typically Lise. All elegance and refinement, with no room for flippant remark or crass comment except of course when Charlotte was around. An elderly couple who were permanent fixtures looked after the place when it wasn't being used by one of the family. Charlotte was certain that they ran their own 'hotel' when no one was around, pre-packed shampoos, soaps and a plethora of fluffy towels tended to leave little to the imagination, but Charlotte being Charlotte had decided to give the old sods the benefit of the doubt and keep her mouth shut. Her mother rarely if ever used the house and so as far as she was concerned good luck to the pair of aged entrepreneurs – Thatcher would have been proud of them after all, so who was she to give their game away?

When the two of them were seated and enjoying Lise's champagne Charlotte asked, "Well Justin, how is the Gower Rose Country House doing? Is my mother allowing you to have a life?"

"So far very successfully. Your mother and Griffith know what they are doing. No expense was spared on any of the reno-vations and refurbishment. I have to say that the house is an absolute joy. Like the Cliffs but better – if that's at all possible. It's bigger, more rooms and so on but somehow it just seems to have the edge. For me, anyway. Maybe it's the overall style of the building, slightly Gothic and yet not forbidding. The turrets with their green copper roofs make it special, unusual. Guests can be taken back in time whether they like it or not. As with the Cliffs, each and every room has its own character, its own unique perception. Some are modern but most are four-postered and delicate. You know what your mother is like, vulgarity and brashness are strictly no-go areas."

"That's my mother for you, she's never been renowned for going off at things half cock. All or nothing, that's Mum. I haven't had a proper look around the place myself yet. Next time I'm down we can test the four-posters out . . . talking of which it has been nearly two weeks now, Justin, so if you don't mind this lady is in dire need of some rather filthy servicing . . ." With that Charlotte started to undo Justin's flies and like the attic, the rest as they say is history.

The following morning they were sitting up in bed having finally finished the marathon romp they had started the night before. They were eating some toast and Fortnum and Masons thick-cut orange marmalade along with a jug full of fresh orange juice, provided courtesy of the 'Entrepreneurs'. Charlotte had a feeling that they suspected she knew about their profitable sideline so keeping her happy was in their interest, while the thought had occurred to her that maybe she should demand a cut, God knows her mother kept her short enough, the parsimonious old devil. On second thoughts though, such a demand would be tantamount to extortion or worse still, black-mail. She was trying to become a barrister after all, so such criminal endeavour wouldn't do at all. Still it was tempting for all that.

"You haven't told me yet, Justin, if my mother is putting on you," Charlotte said with that post-coitus reddish veneer of satisfaction still glowing from her face. "I know she's a real gem underneath the hard-nosed exterior, but even so I know she can be unreasonably demanding when she wants to be. What's she got you doing, she hasn't lumped the everyday management of the Cliffs on top of the Rose on you, has she?"

"No, not at all," Justin replied. Unlike Charlotte he was not one to glow, sexual gratification or not. "To be honest with you I see very little of her at the Rose. The same goes for your brother, since all the building work finished. Griffith noses around from time to time but to be fair short of our monthly meetings they leave me to it. I think your mother has a soft spot for the Cliffs. She is certainly very attached to it."

"Yes she is. My father, William Treharne, and she were married there."

"Ah, that explains it. I thought there was some strong sentimental attachment there." Justin paused for a moment. "You don't say much about your father, Lottie."

"No, well there's not much to tell. Only what Mum has told me. He died before I was born. Quite a man apparently, mind you it wasn't all roses at the Cliffs believe me, but that's another story. It's had its share of tragedy. My father. His only daughter from a previous marriage. Megan. She was a right nutcase apparently and a violent one. Drink, drugs, men, you name it. One day I will tell you all about it, you will just have to be patient. Griffith is the one who has really been my father, he's always been there and he's such a softie, not like my mother at all. I could always get around him. I love him desperately, old rogue that he is."

"Fair enough, Lottie." Justin didn't push. He was coming to know every twitch of facial muscle, every expression and every movement that passed across Charlotte's face. Her look had told him that the history of the Cliffs needed understanding and compassion and that right now she wasn't prepared to revisit that history. She changed the subject.

"How is the new lad Paul . . . what's his name . . .?"

"Edwards."

"Yes, Paul Edwards. My mother and Griffith seem to have high hopes for him."

"Yes they do, but I'm not so sure."

"What do you mean?"

"They've kept him at the Cliffs. He is learning a lot, but I'm not so sure whether he is strong management material. He seems too relaxed about things, too easygoing."

"What makes you think that? Mum and Griffith seem to think he has loads of potential."

"Yes I know but they aren't always right about these things. Don't forget their experience is limited to a small corner of

159

Wales. Granted they are experts in their particular area but nevertheless their opinions are limited."

"Limited? I don't see how you can say that. Their hotels or country houses if you prefer are renowned throughout the country. They also have age and experience on their side and one thing I have learnt from studying law is that there is no better or complete knowledge than experience, so whether you like it or not I would rather put my money on their judgement than yours."

"How very loyal of you." The sarcasm in Justin's voice hit more than a raw nerve.

"Oh for God's sake Justin, stop being so bloody arrogant and such a damned know all. Dear God they were running hotels before you had jumped out of your pram." Charlotte was loyal to her family and didn't like what she was hearing. It was fine for her to call them everything, but not anybody else and that included the man she loved so deeply.

"Lottie, just because they have run a couple of small hotels in the middle of sheep-shagging land doesn't mean to say they know it all." This time Charlotte didn't rise to the bait, she was far too clever for that.

"Small hotels? You seem to have changed your tune. Not so long ago they were the best hotels in the land for you to further your career. Do I detect a hint of jealousy here, Mr Forte?"

"What . . . what do you mean?"

"Could it be that Paul Edwards is a threat to your empire building?" It was Charlotte's turn to strike where it hurt, perfectly aware that Justin had designs on things other than her love. Even so she believed in the sincerity of his feelings for her. If it brought some perks, then so what? Who was going to take over the Cliffs when her mother and Griffith were too old or too infirm to carry on anyway? She and Kris didn't want to know. There were a few moments of silence as Justin looked at Charlotte in a way that she had never seen before. There was utter contempt, even loathing, and a ruthlessness in his eyes that she had never before encountered in her young life, there was something else too that she just simply couldn't fathom. It was there but she didn't know what is was. Remoteness perhaps, cruel detachment? She just didn't know. For a few seconds his whole mind seemed to lose control. His mental resources had gone haywire. His look stopped her in her tracks. She had gone too far but wasn't entirely sure why. She had only made a facetious remark, she didn't even really mean it. An inexplicable fear pounced on her and for a few moments she felt like running away. Then as quickly as his look had warned her it disappeared.

"I'm sorry Lottie . . . I am overreacting. You are probably quite right. I suppose I do feel a little threatened by Paul. God knows why . . . It's just that I have worked so hard for your mother and Griffith, and yes . . . one day I would like to have more control over the hotels. There is enormous potential just waiting to be exploited, though sometimes I get this feeling that Paul is being overindulged. Don't ask me why, it's just a feeling. Your mother and Griffith seem too keen to push him upwards and yet he has little if any experience. I have earned my position, he hasn't and that galls me."

Love can be full to its nonsensical brim with fraud, denial and irrational delusion. Charlotte looked into her man's eyes again and this time saw only love and utter devotion. She quickly convinced herself that her momentary fear had been a figment of female exaggeration, an aberration. This is exactly what she wanted to believe and her love allowed this to happen without complaint. Why should it do otherwise?

"Now come on, Lottie, enough of my stupidity, what are we going to do today? How about a trip around an art gallery or two? I feel like some culture and beauty. You can't always provide it all, you know!" Justin looked at Charlotte and smiled. As usual his lips destroyed her.

The two of them held hands as they walked alongside mankind's greatest efforts to define a reality that could only ever confound and a beauty that could only ever be felt. Rubens watched and felt sympathy while Turner could only bluster and moan. Constable felt nothing at all except superior security in his rural utopia of yellow hay and holy spires that reached up to a heaven that only he knew about. People whispered and gaped, some pretended, this was the place to be after all, and some were fool enough to even try to understand. Justin watched the pretentious wine tasters with their exclusive golf clubs and portraits of Margaret Thatcher hanging from their estate agent's walls mill around and stare at their own self importance and their victory over fraudulent education with its odd page of Conrad. They had all come out of the darkness and wanted the whole world to celebrate with them.

Justin and Charlotte sat down on a bench and held each other. Frightened footsteps walked around them, voices sometimes passed through them, paintings continued to observe and swipe away their initiative. Neither of them really cared, they had each other, so sod the Great Masters. Charlotte briefly thought about forensic evidence and hearsay testimony, both of which had been driving her around the bend lately. The late-night briefs faxed over to her the night before the hearing, all the travelling and hours spent waiting dragged her mind from the magnificent to the mundane, maybe it had something to do with the artistic atmosphere which could both uplift and ruin. She was still trying to make up her mind when Justin said, "Right, I think that's enough culture for one day, let's go back to the house, freshen up and go somewhere decent for dinner, my treat. How about it?"

"Fine by me," Charlotte replied unconditionally.

As long as Justin was by her side she didn't really care where she was, although she couldn't quite bring herself to tell him that. Somehow she felt that an over-effusive love would turn him away. He was so serious about many things and seemed to find it difficult to laugh at life. His humour and sense of fun were never given unconditionally, but when he did smile or laugh then Charlotte immediately understood why she loved him so much. She recognized that she was a handful for any man and in some respects she secretly preferred playing a more subservient role. She knew that her strength of personality could overwhelm if not intimidate and this was one thing that she didn't want inflicted upon her relationship with Justin. Even so she was brave enough to appreciate that she probably loved him more than he did her. This imbalance hurt her and left her slightly unfulfilled, but there was nothing she could do about it. Most of him was better than anything that was left. As much as her personality rebelled, deep down she recognized that Justin's strength sapped her own and left her feeling weak and vulnerable.

The following morning Charlotte's hand reached out for Justin. It touched only crisp white sheets and the smell of their own bodies. Her head ached and her stomach rolled back and fore with nausea. She vaguely remembered bottles of her mother's champagne and for a brief moment her mind determined to replace whatever she and Justin had drunk. Charlotte wasn't a big drinker, in fact the occasional glass of wine was all she ever indulged in. She was suffering now though and required some immediate pain-killing medication.

She swung her long legs over the side of the bed and made her way to the bathroom. Dizziness and hangover made the trip an exercise in endurance but she managed to reach a bathroom cabinet and hunt around for some aspirin. As her left hand picked up a bottle of aspirin it stopped in mid air. "What . . . what on earth . . .?" she managed to whisper to herself. She dropped the bottle of aspirin in the sink and rushed up to the bedroom window. Sunlight was shining through the window as she lifted her left hand up to the light just to make sure she wasn't sleepwalking or something. The solitaire diamond beamed back at her and almost sent a wave of excruciating pain through her fragile head. The size of the diamond was impressive, but how on earth had Justin afforded it? He must be mad, she thought! Mad maybe, but she couldn't help but sit down on the bed and try to recover. And to think she had doubted his love. God, what a bitch! For a few moments her heart dived from chronic guilt to ecstatic euphoria. She looked at the ring again, she couldn't take her eyes off it, it was so beautiful. There was a dullness about the gold band for which only time could have been responsible. She remembered telling Justin once how much she hated the glittering arrogance of spanking new jewellery with its lack of history and elegant proportion. The antique ring that fitted perfectly and now sparkled along with the sun could tell so many stories, so many tales of happiness and heartbreak, this was part of its allure, its fascination.

"Does it suit then?" Charlotte heard Justin's voice come from the doorway. She immediately jumped up from the bed and ran into his arms.

"Does it suit? God, it must have cost you a fortune! That was sly of you, taking advantage of a drunken young woman, you should be ashamed of yourself and how did you manage to get the right fit?" She kissed him as hard as she could.

"I'm a resourceful fellow, that's all you need to know." He returned Charlotte's kiss and said, "I take it that's a 'yes' then?"

"Oh yes! Most definitely . . . but not until I am fully established and have my own tenancy in chambers. Agreed?"

"Agreed." Justin held her in his arms and kissed her again just to make sure.

"What a wonderful, wonderful man you are! I love you so much Justin, God I love you!"

"I love you too Lottie, I really do." As Justin rested his chin on Charlotte's shoulder his eyes looked across the bedroom and observed other things.

CHAPTER 25

"Right, Paul my boy, you can down tools and come with me."

"Well actually, Uncle Griffith, I am quite busy at the moment, can it wait for half an hour or so?"

"No it can't young man. The stocktaking can wait. Come on now, I'm the boss so don't damn well argue." Paul Edwards stuck his pencil behind his ear and did as he was told but not without a grunt of protest. He had been sorting out the bar stock all morning and didn't appreciate being disturbed. He took his duties seriously and had come to love hotel life. He wanted to move higher up the ladder but his ambition was restrained and slightly on the plodding side. He enjoyed working with different people, the girls were lovely too and seemed to think a lot of him. He never quite understood why, but then this was his inherent nature. He rarely held himself up in high esteem being a rather artistic and sensitive soul. He still loved to sketch and draw during his time off, particularly if Bethan could sit alongside him on one of the cliffs. Bethan Jones, one of the receptionists, had caught his eye when he had first arrived. The young woman had the most honest smile he had ever seen and her laughing face often sent him off to sleep. Small and chubby was Bethan. No one would have said that her looks were inspired but nevertheless her simple, plain features were irresistible, to Paul anyway. He often imagined cuddling up to her warm, rounded buttocks and letting her long strands of mousy hair tickle his nose as he fell asleep. He had wanted to reach out for her hand on a number of occasions but his shyness had stepped in between them. He was twenty-three now but still a bit useless when it came to the opposite sex. His virginity haunted him and his gentle manner sometimes frustrated him. There were many times when he wished he could be a bit more like his Uncle Griffith.

Griffith's bright red Jaguar tore around the narrow, bending roads of the Gower oblivious to any oncoming traffic. And he was supposed to avoid stress Paul thought, but kept quiet. He had grown fond of his uncle and would have hated to see anything happen to him, but he also knew him well enough to know when to keep quiet.

"Where are we going then, Uncle Griffith?"

"You'll find out soon enough. How is your mother by the way, I haven't spoken to her for quite a while?"

"Oh she's fine. Nags me to go home more often but apart from that she's ok. Has a boyfriend now apparently." Sylvia hadn't been in touch for some time so the new boyfriend must be preoccupying her. Good for her, Griffith thought.

"Does she now, are you ok with that?"

"Yes, as long as she's happy and the man is kind to her, then good luck to her." Griffith marvelled once again at how much the boy had grown up in such a short space of time.

When they arrived in Swansea, Griffith parked his car on a couple of yellow lines and made his way to Wind Street.

"You'll get a ticket for parking on double yellow lines, Uncle Griffith."

"Balls to 'em. The Chief Constable rings me up now and again to remind me that there's an Arrest Warrant out for me so he gives me a bit of grace. I only fork up when there's an imminent risk of being locked up for a few hours. The grub is appalling in those places, you know. Now come on, Lise's eyeballs are off the ball for a while so I think a gentle livener is in order."

"Uncle Griffith, you're not supposed to drink."

"I'm not 'supposed' to do a lot of things, young Paul, now stop talking like that nagging bloody woman of mine and keep your mouth shut. First stop the tobacconist's."

Griffith marched off with Paul trailing behind. It was pointless trying to dissuade his uncle, and he knew full well who would be driving them home too. They called into the No Sign Bar, a scruffy watering hole halfway down Wind Street, a place where banks competed with one another and where a Post Office annoyed the hell out of everyone who had just enjoyed the healthy ambiance of a stroll through Salubrious Passage. As soon as Griffith walked into the bar he was greeted by lawyers, accountants, architects and anyone else who felt like being crammed into a tiny space to enjoy the antiquated bottles of dusty wine, the bare floorboards of a drinkers' paradise and the renowned toleration by the Welsh for anyone sensible enough to be pissed before the sun got anywhere near the yardarm. Courts, plans and balance sheets all disappeared into empty wine bottles that would eventually be slung back on the shelves. The greens and browns provided the only decoration available, but at least the place had character and a smoky deference toward the good, honest boozer.

Three hours and twenty Benson & Hedges later, Griffith and Paul walked up the Kingsway to the only decent off-the-peg men's outfitters in Swansea.

"Right my boy. We have finally arrived at our destination. Time to have you properly togged out. Would have let my own tailor get at you, but no doubt his particular cut with a piece of cloth would have been too old fashioned for you younger coves." Griffith let loose an award-winning belch before lighting up another cigarette and pushing Paul through the doors of Calders.

A tall, bald-headed gentleman stood behind some glass showcases displaying leather gloves and self-tie bow ties. None of the clip-on or elasticated monstrosities were allowed in this hallowed place of gentlemanly distinction. The man looked up and over his bifocal spectacles.

"Ah Mr Treharne, what a pleasure to see you again." Griffith marched up to the counter.

"You too, now sort this young fellow out will you? Formal wear, casual stuff, the works. I'm off to the Hanbury (another boozer) for an hour or so and will expect young Paul here to have at least some idea of sartorial propriety by the time I get back. Is that all right with you?"

"Leave it to me, sir." The man looked Paul up and down and quickly decided that he was going to have his work cut out. "Perhaps a little longer than an hour Mr Treharne, young men these days are a little more demanding than we . . . er . . . more mature gentlemen. We have started to stock some more fashionable menswear so I'll see what I can do."

"Very well. I'll leave it to you. See you in an hour or so, Paul."

"Oh, before you go sir, all items to be charged to your account?"

"Of course." With that Griffith walked out leaving Paul to the tender mercies of a genuine gentleman's outfitter. The young man was also mystified as to what was going on.

As expected, Paul had to drive home. Griffith still hadn't told him what all this new wardrobe stuff was all about and the car was packed with dinner suits, formal suits, casual wear, shirts, ties, overcoats, scarves, gloves, you name it. The whole lot must have cost a fortune. What was going on? Griffith hadn't been plastered when he had taken him into the shop and he didn't seem to be plastered now – mind you, Griffith's capacity to hold alcohol was legendary, or so he had been told by the staff anyway. Apparently he could put away a shed load and no one would be any the wiser.

Paul loved driving the Jaguar and even dreamed of having one himself one day. He wouldn't be able to pay for one pulling pints and mixing up cocktails all day long though, that was for certain. His daydreams of Jaguars with Bethan sitting alongside him were interrupted by Griffith.

"Now then Paul, Lise and I have decided to let you manage the two bars and the restaurant at the Cliffs, that's what all the clobber in the car is about, what do you say?"

"What . . .! But I've only—"

"No 'buts', my boy. You just get on with it. Plenty of people around to give you a helping hand. That prancing prat Balzac is being shifted over to the Rose. He can exercise his puerile spleen over there, by the way any idea whose bowels he's bashing these days?"

"Pardon?"

"Oh God, Paul! Wake up boy, won't you? Our chef prefers tender male rumps, haven't you spotted that yet?"

"Well, it had crossed my mind."

"Crossed your mind! Christ, you didn't let Balzac cross your arse, did you?"

"No, Uncle Griffith . . ." Paul sighed, his uncle was beyond sometimes.

"Anyway we're appointing a new prima donna, Lise will be showing him the way we do things, if the self-important bugger thinks he can go berserk with a load of Froggy crap he can think again. Good honest Welsh grub, that's what we've prided ourselves on all these years and that's the way it's going to stay. By the way have you got used to laverbread and cockles yet?"

"Sorry, no. Can't stand the stuff. Laverbread looks like a recently delivered simmering cow pat and cockles remind me of something removed from someone's stomach. No thanks."

"Philistine!" Griffith moaned. "So what d'you say about your new promotion?"

"Well, I . . . I'm very pleased. A little shocked if you must know, I'm not even certain if I can handle it. I mean, there's ordering the staff around, making certain that we are properly stocked with everything, the wine cellar, all the stuff needed to run a good restaurant, the list is endless . . ."

"I know, and you are just the young fellow to do it. You're a hard worker, Paul, and we've already seen how quickly you pick things up. You'll be fine. Lise will be backing you all the way, so don't worry. Once she is satisfied that you know what you are doing then you'll be left to your own devices. The responsibility will do you good. Now stop worrying and just get on with it . . . Oh, and don't forget there's always me. I still know how to run a good show. I know what people want and how to deliver it."

"The two bars and the restaurant . . .? Thank you, Uncle Griffith. I will try to do my best."

"You won't 'try' to do your best my boy, you will, it's as simple as that and by the way you're on a salary now, pension, the whole lot.'"

Paul continued to drive and come to terms with this new change in his life. It was so unexpected. He didn't feel the least bit flattered, if anything he was scared to death. There was Bethan too, he was now one of the bosses, how was this going to effect their sketching sessions out on the cliffs?

CHAPTER 26

"Now look Lise, I may have been a *bon vivant*, a thorough and drunken bounder, a pimp extraordinaire – of the up-market variety I stress – but I have always been a man of my word. Always! I promised Paul's mother that I would never let on and that's all there is to it."

"Did you actually 'promise', Griffith. I doubt that, I know you too well. In fact I don't think I have ever heard you 'promise' anything in all the twenty-odd years that I have known you – for the very reason that, as you say, you don't break your word. Now, admirable as all this is, Griffith, sometimes life makes certain . . . er . . . how shall I put it? . . . moral commitments . . . a little difficult to keep. Let's face it, you hadn't planned on Paul coming here and the only reason you allowed it was because of a 'moral commitment'. You are the boy's father after all whether his mother likes it or not, and from what I can gather you have looked after the pair of them for years. The mother has never even had to work and you gave Paul a good education. Private schools and all the rest of it, why do you think he speaks so well and is so good with the guests?"

"Damn it woman, I've made you a promise haven't I? And I sure as hell don't intend breaking that! We are supposed to be getting married in a few weeks time!"

"That's as may be, Griffith. Now enough of your procrastination. You tell him or I do. Tonight."

"Tonight!"

"Yes Griffith, tonight." They looked at each other for a few moments then Griffith grunted.

"Tonight it is then."

"Good. Anyway have you considered what is going to happen when you and I are no longer able to run things or God forbid that one of us should die. It will happen you know, Griffith."

"Christ, first of all you're making me break my word now you're bumping me off! I know I've got a tricky ticker but steady on girl, I'm not dead yet!"

"Will you do something about your language Griffith! You're incorrigible!"

"I know but you love me."

". . . Sometimes, only sometimes . . . It doesn't alter the fact that we need to think about what will happen after our days. Apart from this, I think we should be starting to take less responsibility for things."

"What! Did I hear you correctly? You're not actually thinking about retirement, are you?"

"Well, semi-retirement maybe. I thought you and I might start to do some travelling. A couple of world cruises would be nice. They would do your health good as well. You don't get enough sun."

"Fine by me."

"Paul is part of the family and I believe he will do well. He's taken to his new duties like a duck to water. Another reason for you being honest. Kristian has settled down a little but I don't put much faith in that, no doubt he will be taking off again somewhere or other soon. As for Lottie . . . Well, she does seem determined to become a Queen's Counsel at the very least. She's in love with Justin too and he seems to be in love with her. So who knows?"

"That's still going strong then?"

"As far as I know. They don't say much the pair of them. I know one thing though, her pupillage is coming to an end October–November time. What's going to happen about a tenancy I just don't know. I know that she is committed to carry on with her career, whether she will stay in London or come back to some chambers here remains to be seen."

"Well, Justin's got the right idea if he marries the boss's daughter, hasn't he?"

"Oh Griffith, stop being so cynical. He's a disgustingly good-looking chap and seems to treat Lottie well. They both seem very happy. What with Paul and Justin we might just keep the Cliffs and the Rose in the family yet."

"Dear God Lise, you're building up a bloody dynasty here! I'm still not so sure about Justin though."

"What do you mean?"

"Sorry, but I've never liked him. Not from day one and you know that. There's something there. Something shifty, as I said at the time. I'm still not convinced."

"Oh, you're being paranoid now, Griffith. The man has worked wonders at the Rose, he makes Lottie happy and at the end of the day that's all I really care about. Her happiness."

"You're entitled to your opinion, Lise, of course you are, but my radar's up and it's never let me down. The man needs a close eye."

"Oh stop your nonsense . . ."

They talked about business for another hour or so when their conversation was interrupted by the telephone. Lise picked up the handset.

"Lottie! About time too . . . Take your time, girl . . . What . . .? When . . .? Well I . . . congratulations!" The conversation went on for a few more minutes then Lise replaced the handset.

"Well Griffith, it looks as if we have another wedding to arrange, and if I know Lottie it will be a big one."

"Oh God!" Griffith moaned. "The bugger moves fast, I'll give him that, they haven't known each other that long."

"Griffith! That's an awful thing to say! They have been together a year or so."

"A year! It took me twenty years to get your knickers off!"

"Griffith! Be quiet, the staff might hear you . . .! Now then, you might not like him but you keep that blunt tongue of yours quiet, do you hear me?"

173

"If I must."

"And try and smile, will you?"

"If I must."

"Oh dear God, Griffith, there are times when you drive me to distraction!"

"When is all this going to take place then?"

"Not for a while. Lottie has to establish herself first, so you'll have plenty of time to get used to Justin being part of the family."

"And the business."

"Oh do be quiet. Nothing is certain, Griffith. They both might well decide to live in London, it's hardly unfamiliar territory for either of them, is it?"

"That's as may be but Lottie is far too young to be thinking about marriage for heavens sake. Far too young. What is she? Twenty-three, twenty-four? And being a successful barrister can take years."

"Twenty-four next month, September 10th. And she's not too young either. The girl is a mature young woman now and certainly knows her own mind."

"You can say that again, she's just like her mother . . . and her father, come to think of it."

"Well, I think it's wonderful news, the girl needs a strong hand now and again and I believe Justin is just the man to do it. Anyway they're not rushing in to anything. She mentioned something about a year to eighteen months, so presumably during that time they will make up their minds where they want to be."

"That's something then. Plenty of time for her to see some sense."

"Griffith, I'm warning you! Now stop it! You should be delighted for the girl."

"Oh I'm sorry, but I just have a bad feeling about the man. Can't get rid of it. Come here and give me a kiss."

"You don't deserve one."

"Right then, I'll come to you." With that he chased Lise around the room until he finally got his way.

"Oh Griffith . . ." Lise moaned when he finally got to grips with her. "You really are a naughty man . . ."

Later that evening and after swallowing a sly, large whiskey Griffith found Paul washing some glasses behind the bar. At least the boy hadn't let his new position go to his head, he thought as he walked up to him. You reap what you sow, Griffith my lad, he also thought as he girded his already tightened testicles.

"Paul my boy, pour yourself a drink and come and sit down. I want a word." Griffith went off to a quiet corner of the bar that overlooked the rose gardens. Memories of other 'Confessions' came back to him when his father had been the priest. This time, he hoped, there would be a little more sympathy. Eventually Paul came to sit down next to him, tomato juice in hand. As the boy walked across the bar Griffith noted how smart he looked. Professional. The dark mohair suit played in tune with the rest of his body which wasn't as lanky or as thin as Griffith remembered. His face had filled out into a healthy glow too and there was an aura of maturity about the boy. His skin didn't look like one of those disgraceful pizza outrages that were inundating the town either. There wasn't a yellow-topped spot in sight. The sea air and good wholesome grub had obviously done the boy good. 'Boy', Griffith thought for a moment as he looked at Paul, although he wasn't really a boy at all now, he was a man in his own right.

"How is Bethan then?"

"Pardon?"

"How is Bethan? I saw the pair of you out on the cliffs the other day. Buxom wench. You have taste, my boy."

"Well I . . . there's nothing like that, we're just friends."

" 'Just friends'. No such thing my boy, not between man and woman anyway. Do you like her?"

"Well . . . I . . ." Griffith was trying to relax the boy with some man talk. He wasn't having much success. Paul wasn't like Griffith at all where woman were concerned. When Griffith had been in his early 20s, no woman under forty was safe. Sketching on the cliffs be damned! Griffith would have been doing a damn sight more than sketching! Paul was obviously the shy type so he gave up on that line of enquiry. He took a gulp of orange juice, winced, and decided to come straight to the point. Tactfulness had never been one of his strong points besides he just couldn't be bothered with polite platitudes and chasing elusive bushes. "I've got something rather important to tell you, Paul." This was not going to be easy. The boy looked uncomfortable.

"My work is ok, isn't it?"

"Yes, yes. Your work is fine. Look Paul . . . oh, to hell with it. . .! I'm your father. Your real father. Your mother and I were good friends many years ago and well . . . these sort of things sometimes happen. We decided to go our separate ways for one reason or another, but I still always looked after you both. Financially anyway." Paul took a sip of his tomato juice and said nothing. He looked at Griffith. Looked at his tomato juice. Looked around the room then took a deep breath.

"Excuse me, for a moment," he said as he stood up. He then ran behind the bar and poured himself a large whisky which he downed in one gulp. Like father, like son. He came back and sat down opposite Griffith, another large whisky in his hand.

"Well this is a bit of shock, Uncle . . . er . . . what on earth do I call you now . . . I . . .?"

"Griffith will do, I think 'Dad' is probably pushing it a bit." Griffith tried a half-hearted smile, God this was hard. He felt for the boy, understood his confusion. Griffith wasn't all shallowness and 'Hail fellow, well met'. Guilt and regret tore at his weakness, the ease with which he had let Sylvia have her own way. He could have fought harder and he knew it. He should have fought harder. Now as he looked at his son's face, his eyes, he realized how much damage he had left in his irresponsible wake. He wanted to reach out to the boy, to hold him, to say, 'I am your father and I am so very sorry'."

"Why didn't Mum ever tell me?" Paul asked. The boy was remarkably calm. "I was always led to believe that my father just deserted us, never to be seen again."

"Not quite," Griffith replied quietly. "I had wanted to play a more active part in your life but the brutal truth is your mother wouldn't let me. That's not to say that she has ever been a bad mother, it was just the way she wanted to do things and I respected her wishes."

"So it was you who was paying all the bills? Mum just said that she had inherited some money and as long as we were careful everything would be fine. Actually I always thought that was why you came to the house every now and again, to discuss her investments." Not quite again, Griffith thought, but kept his mouth shut, there was no need to add insult to injury. Paul was obviously in a state of shock, the truth was taking time to penetrate. Griffith remained silent to allow the boy time to absorb.

"Is this why you and Lise have been so good to me?"

"What do you mean?"

"Well, you have promoted me rather quickly and I've never been too sure whether my abilities were truly up to the task." There was no recrimination in Paul's voice, no accusation.

"Now let me put you straight on this, Paul, once and for all." Griffith's voice hardened, it had to. "You have been given extra responsibility for one reason and one reason only. Your competence to do the job, full stop. And I assure you that neither Lise nor I have been disappointed. You are a manager because you are extremely good at it, not because I am your father. You have worked hard and hard work usually pays off, at the Cliffs anyway. So you can forget any stupid notions of nepotism or favouritism. You will do well, young Paul, and your achievements will have absolutely nothing to do with the fact that I am your father."

"That's something then. Look . . . er . . ." – he had no idea what to call his uncle, now father – "do you mind if I take the evening off to think about all this. It's a bit of a shock."

"Of course. If you need to talk you know where to find me. And don't blame your mother. I suppose she just didn't want an absent father. Think about it before you start bashing away with recriminations. She did what she thought was best for you. At the time you were born I would have been a pretty useless father. Women, drink. You name it. She's a good woman your mum and don't you forget it." Paul stood up and left the bar, leaving Griffith feeling like the biggest shit on the planet. Worse still, he deserved it.

"Well?" Lise was waiting for him in the study.

"Well what?"

"I presume by your surly face that you have told Paul. I told you it wouldn't be easy, nevertheless it had to be done. You couldn't possibly have carried on this charade for an indefinite period." Griffith sat down and sighed.

"I know, but that doesn't make me feel any better. Poor bugger has just had a bomb dropped on him and there's nothing I can do to ameliorate the damage. Nothing at all. If you must know I feel a right royal shit and yet you know, Lise, I never wanted to keep his paternity a secret. Spineless waster that I was at the time That was all Sylvia's doing, believe me. Even so I still blame myself, I mean I could have been a bit tougher about it all." Lise went over to Griffith and knelt down on the rug in front of him. She took his hand.

"Griffith, you know we can all look back and regret. We can all look back and despair at our mistakes. Regrets and despair, they both make us what we are, what we become. God willing, we learn or at least try to and even then sometimes we go back to where we were and often start all over again. It's what makes us so ridiculously human. You did your best by Paul, he never went without, you didn't desert him. Now Griffith Treharne, you stop looking back. You make up for lost time. Paul is your son, you love him and care fore him. That's all you can do. He's a decent boy, I don't think he's the sort to be bitter about anything. He's like his father there . . ." Lise smiled. "Give him time and he will come round, just let him get over the shock and a shock it must be to suddenly discover that your long-lost father is the reprobate Mr Griffith Treharne!" She kissed Griffith on the cheek. "Now come on, let's go out for a walk. Get some air. It's a beautiful evening. We also need to discuss the arrangements."

Griffith stood up. "Where would I be without you, Lise? Where would I be? The thought terrifies me."

"No it doesn't. You would probably enjoy the peace and quiet, not to mention your surreptitious cigarettes and Irish whiskey."

CHAPTER 27

A month later, in the middle of July, top hats, tails and a nonsensical barrage of female colour and tears rampaged around the tiny church in an attempt to convey eternal happiness and congratulations for the newly-weds and their future. The vicar dropped words of perpetual harmony on the replies of 'I do' and kept his fingers crossed. Griffith stood before him and damned all papists, bible thumpers and Church of England catechisms to hell and back. He smiled all the same and still felt a tear or two well up in his eyes as he looked at the woman who was now his wife. Lise stood next to him and looked into his eyes with a serenity and love that only he could truly know.

"I now pronounce you man and wife," the vicar concluded. Lacy handkerchiefs mopped away tears of female regret and delusion while men sat back and remembered. Some turned their heads slightly to remind them of their foolishness, some looked straight ahead not wishing to be reminded at all. Days of fun and laughter sought out bitter memory while love endured or at least tried to hang on. They had all been here once before, and for most once was certainly enough. Matrimonial harmony survived for the day of union, then it was all downhill at least for most of the morning suits and most of the frilly hats. Masculine torpor clashed with silly romance and wondered what it was all about. Wedded veterans lifted eyes up to the heavens and whispered abuse while at the same time wondering how Griffith could be such an idiot at his age. Younger men looked on and waited for their day. Would their brides be as beautiful as Lise? they pondered. Old enough to be their mother she may have been but by Jesus, given half a chance . . .

As Lise and Griffith walked up the aisle as man and wife everyone felt, everyone believed and everyone wished they could start all over again. That was marriage for you. Insane, deliberate but profoundly necessary.

Paul drove the new Mr and Mrs Griffith Treharne to Heathrow Airport where they were to catch a plane to Miami. The boy had accepted Griffith as his father and his mother's mysterious love without anger and jolts of self-pity. Either would have been fundamentally against his nature. From Miami the newly-weds were to join a cruise ship that would sail them around the world for three months. At the terminal Paul hugged his father and stepmother and told them not to worry about a thing. He, Kris and Justin had everything under control even if Kris was an unwilling participant.

They said their goodbyes and Lise and Griffith began a journey that needed to make up for twenty years of lost love.

CHAPTER 28

Summer was dying away at the Cliffs as October started to curtail and ration sunlight and winter coldness began to breathe on the sea and cliffs. For some this was the best time of year. The brashness and frivolity of summer had to give way to the more serious shedding of autumn waste and surplus. The gardens of the Cliffs closed their eyes and waited for sleep while Will Jenkins collected their clothes by the barrow load. He adored their red and brown goodbyes and always treated their interring with respect. He wandered around the gardens, roll-up stuck to his lower lip, and waited for another year of life, another rebirth.

Kristian watched Will scraping up the leaves and decided that the old boy had got it right after all. Simplicity was pure joy and that's all one needed to know. Will always knew where his lover was, he always knew what mood she would be in and he always knew when she was about to be peevish and awkward. Sensible man.

He stepped back from the French windows and sat behind his mother's desk. She had managed it after all, manipulative woman. Here he was, holding her fort while she and Griffith travelled the Seven Seas. Justin and Paul (his new step-cousin and Lottie's nephew, although he still wasn't entirely sure how the hell they were all related, William Treharne had a lot to answer for), saw to the everyday running of things, but the last word remained with Kristian. Ultimate responsibility was all his. He didn't like it and intended to jump ship as soon as he was able to, but at the time how could he have refused his mother and Griffith? They deserved time together on their own, the pair of them, God knows they had waited long enough, he just hoped that his mother wasn't beginning to think that he would keep his hands on the wheel until he died. If she did, she was in for a shock. He still had no idea where his life was going to take him but it sure as hell wasn't taking him down the road of respectable hotelier.

Kristian was thirty-eight now, tinges of grey were beginning to appear at the side of his head, distinguished looking it might well be but he could do without it. He remained unloved and unfulfilled, but who was he to complain? As he started to fight the soldiers of self-pity there was a knock on the study door.

"Come in."

"Ah Kris, I thought I might find you in here," Paul said with his usual good-humoured smile, "there's a lady in reception asking to see you. She didn't give her name."

Oh God, Kristian thought, it wasn't that woman he had entertained the other evening when he had been in Swansea, was it? That's all he needed. These days his philandering never went further than 'love 'em and leave 'em'.

"OK Paul, tell her to take a seat. I'll be out in a minute." He needed a few minutes to collect his thoughts, this could be delicate. He remembered the woman. Good looking, good sense of humour. But not for him. He hated rejection. Whether it was he who was being rejected or the other party it made no difference. As far as possible he tried to avoid hurting people, he certainly didn't enjoy telling a woman he wasn't interested, more so if he had slept with her, which he had done with the woman waiting to see him. He had made it clear at the time that there was no commitment, no future but she obviously hadn't listened. The women in his life rarely did. Oh well, he thought, better go out there and do the dirty deed, he really did hate doing these things but it served him right for having a wandering dick in the first place. All women loved a bastard, at least the ones that mattered, the trouble was he wasn't really a bastard. Quite the opposite. He sighed with resignation, stood up and walked out of the study.

There was no one in reception apart from Bethan. Kristian was about to ask where his visitor had gone when he saw a woman standing over by the French windows. For a moment his heart leapt across the huge hallway as disbelief stopped him taking another step. It couldn't be. The woman's back faced him but the raven coloured hair and straight posture were unmistakeable. He walked up to her and dared to say "Myfanwy?"

Myfanwy turned around and faced him. There was sorrow and a terrible apology in her dark eyes as she put her hands on his arms and said. "Kristian, there is someone I want you to meet." Kristian followed her eyes and saw Dewi Morgan standing behind a wheelchair on one of the verandas facing the sea. A mountain of wool hid the body beneath. "I'm so sorry, Kristian. I should have told you before. You have a right but . . . forgive me. Please forgive me. I couldn't stand not telling you any longer . . . Come and meet your daughter." She took his hand and led him outside. Kristian was unable to say a word.

Dewi moved alongside the wheelchair, his eyes watchful and wary, but this time there didn't seem to be any threat or hostility. A few feet away from the wheelchair Myfanwy let go of Kristian's hand and said, "Go on, say hello, her name is Angharad. She doesn't bite." She stood back. Kristian didn't know what to do, he was in a state of utter shock. He looked into Myfanwy's eyes, her love and beauty pushed him forward. For a moment he paused. Uncertainty, panic and a frightening unknown gripped his footsteps. He had no idea how to be a father. What was he supposed to say? What was he supposed to do? Why was his daughter in a wheelchair?

He walked to the front of the wheelchair and saw a young girl with blue eyes and long blond hair. Her hair was covered by a bright red bobble-hat and the rest of her body by a thick, Welsh-wool blanket. There was a seriousness about her expression which at first intimidated Kristian and almost made him turn and run. But before he could say anything she said, "Hello, you must be my father, Kristian Treharne?" Her eyes nearly blew him off his feet as did her confident manner. One look left him in no doubt as to whom the father was. He stood before her like some tongue-tied teenager on a first date.

"Er . . . yes. And you must be Angharad."

"I hope so," she smiled. Kristian knelt down in front of her and rested his hands on the arms of the wheelchair. At last confusion and panic gave way to his inherent instinct for leadership. The hardened war veteran and father became one as control, calm and overwhelming love prevailed. He touched her hand and said, "That pretty little nose of yours is going to be frozen off soon if you stay out here for much longer. Come on, I think we'd better get you inside." With that he stood up, leaned forward and held out his arms slightly, as he did so he looked at Myfanwy who smiled carefully as she nodded her head, she had had no idea how Kristian was going to react to her sudden revelation. She had struggled for weeks to discover the best way to tell him. A letter? A telephone call? They had all seemed so dishonest. So wrong. There were times when she damned him to Hell for turning up at the farm in the first place. It had taken years for her to get over him or at least for the pain to subside. There had been Angharad. Life had been simple. Lonely but simple. Then they had slept with each other. His touch, his love had demolished all her resolve. She had tried to resist, dear God she had tried. But he had a right, a right to know. She couldn't deprive him of his fatherhood. She just couldn't. She couldn't deprive her daughter either. She couldn't lie any longer. She couldn't deceive. Myfanwy watched Kristian take his daughter in his arms. He picked her up in one strong movement. Angharad went to her father without any objection, for her it was the most natural thing in the world.

As Kristian carried his daughter back into the warmth of the hotel a love that he had never thought possible drew some tears from his eyes. The purpose in his life that he had been so desperately searching for was now being held in his arms. As long as he lived he would never let this lovely treasure fall from his grasp.

He now had his reason to be.

CHAPTER 29

"How old is Angharad?" Kristian asked when he and Myfanwy were finally alone. They hadn't seen each other for eighteen months, there was an awkwardness between them, a brittle truce.

"Fifteen soon," Myfanwy replied. They were sitting on the settee in Lise's study drinking coffee. Angharad was fast asleep in one of the hotel rooms. The four-poster bed had eventually managed to send her excited eyes to sleep. Dewi Morgan was content to sit in one of the bars drinking beer and enjoying his own special silence.

"I noticed how light she was when I carried her. Her legs were thin, from the waist down there's something wrong." Myfanwy looked at the man she had never stopped loving. His eyes were pleading, almost begging.

"About four years ago I took Angharad on holiday to India. A treat, you know somewhere unusual. She contracted tuberculosis which needed frequent lumbar punctures to diagnose and treat it. Unfortunately an intraspinal dermoid tumour has developed on her spine. The doctors tell me that this can sometimes develop from implanted skin fragments attached to the needles that are used for the lumber punctures. Of course this can be avoided if only needles with well-fitting stilettes are used. This obviously wasn't the case with Angharad, no one is to blame apparently. It's just one of those things. Anyway I noticed something was wrong when her thigh muscles started to develop an awful weakness, they seemed to be just wasting away. She also started to complain about having a stiff back. It wasn't long before she was unable to walk. That's the bad news, Kristian. The good news is that surgery can sort it out. The tumour can be removed and the success rate is extremely good. Hopefully as we've caught the tumour at a relatively early stage there shouldn't be any permanent damage. Angharad should make a full recovery and lead a perfectly normal life. It is major surgery though, and there are always risks."

"When is this operation taking place then?"

"In a month's time. Great Ormond Street, London."

"She's getting the best then?"

"Oh yes."

"Good . . . Myfanwy, I have to ask. Why now? Why didn't you tell me that we had a daughter? Why didn't you tell me you were pregnant?" Myfanwy stared down at her hands, unable to look Kristian in the eyes. She knew how much her actions had hurt him. His face, his eyes, the way he had looked at Anghared, told her all she needed to know. Her guilt tore at her while her love tried to explain.

"Kristian, you had left me. Not for another woman in the physical way perhaps, but for me it felt like another woman. The marines took you away and they weren't prepared to give you back to me. Ever. I was bitter. Angry. So angry. I wanted to lash out, to hurt you. I had never experienced such terrible betrayal. For a while all I wanted to do was to tear you apart. Then I found out I was pregnant. I even began to take out my anger on the baby growing inside me. I wanted to terminate the pregnancy, kill the product of your betrayal. Why should you be a father, why should you receive the loveliest and most powerful gift that any woman can give to a man? You did not deserve it. You had cheated me in the most appalling way, you had already abused and thrown away the most valuable thing I had to give. My love. Why should I give you my child too?

Then you came back. Oh God, did you come back. That afternoon in the back yard. You were standing there, the man I would have given my life for, the man I would have protected to the end. All the years of bringing up Angharad, seeing you in her every expression, her every smile. Day in, day out. I couldn't even have a child that looked like me. She's you through and through. There has never been a day in the past fifteen years when I haven't been reminded of you. When I haven't been reminded of what we once had. Can you imagine the torture, the agony? Then after all the years you decide that you want to love me again. Well, this time I wasn't going to give in without a fight. I still wanted you to suffer. My revenge wasn't quite complete. The months have gone by, and try as hard as I have I am simply unable to punish you any more because you see, Kristian Treharne . . . I still love you. I love your child with all that I am. I want us to be together again. The three of us. There has never been a man in my life who can compare with you, there has never been a man in my life whom I can love so much. Only you, Kristian, only ever you." Tears started to fall down Myfanwy's cheeks as she put her arms around Kristian, kissed him on the lips and said, "I have been so wrong and I am so desperately sorry. Forgive me and let me love you again in the only way I know how to."

Kristian returned her kiss, touched her cheek and said, "I will never leave you or Angharad again. I promise you."

Later that night Kristian and Myfanwy went to find Dewi. He was still sitting in the bar drinking. He looked up when he saw them coming. Kristian couldn't help but tense his muscles; the last time he had met Dewi Morgan the man had wanted to kill him. Myfanwy sat down next to Dewi and started waving her hands around like some demented ruffian at a football match.

"I didn't know you could do sign language, Myfanwy" Kristian said with a look of amazement on his face.

"Oh, there's lots of things you don't know. I haven't just been driving tractors and drinking Wood's rum for the past fifteen years you know." She continued to talk to Dewi. When she had finished she said, "Right, shake Dewi's hand Kristian and don't damn well argue!"

"Didn't take you long to get back on form did it, Myfanwy? Still a bossy cow."

"Excuse me but I need to be, with you. Now go on, shake his hand."

In spite of the fact that Dewi was unable to speak any words, his face and eyes were able to signal a certain respect for his erstwhile adversary. Their eyes met and in that moment a truce was called. It wasn't over yet, as Kristian had the distinct feeling that he was still on trial, though oddly this didn't make him angry, in fact he rather admired the man. Dewi cared, loved even. Why should Kristian condemn the man for that? He did as ordered and shook Dewi's hand. Where Myfanwy was concerned he usually did, at least some of the time, and on things that he felt weren't worth fighting about, which, when he came to think about it, weren't many. She knew however that she could never 'boss' his will or determination; if Kristian didn't want to do something then hell on earth wouldn't make him. Although he and Myfanwy were two strong characters, Kristian was the strongest. He had to be. Myfanwy wouldn't have loved him as much as she did if she was able to dominate him. She would never admit it but she knew who was really the boss and in her own way was quite comfortable with the arrangement. It didn't mean to say that he could do what he liked though. She would always fight him tooth and nail where necessary. In the past their relationship had blossomed and thrived on contention. They had done nothing but argue and failed to agree on just about everything. Even two flies buzzing their way up a window pane was enough to start a war. Despite this, they both knew that any other type of relationship would bore the pair of them to death and they also knew that it wouldn't take long for them both to settle back into their usual easy habits of mutual insult and general contrariness.

They said their goodnights to Dewi and went up to Kristian's rooms. As they were walking up the stairs of the hotel Kristian asked, "Does anyone else, apart from Dewi, know about Angharad being my daughter?"

"The locals at home have always known that there was a soldier in my life years ago, but that's about it. Why?"

"Well, let's keep it quiet for now, shall we? My mother and Griffith are back soon and I'd rather they hear the news from me instead of anybody else. I don't think Ma will be too impressed to discover second hand that she is at last a grandmother."

"I understand. Still the matriarch then, is she?"

"In some ways."

"Actually, I rather liked her on the few occasions that I met her. She's a bit of a sweetie underneath the hard businesswoman exterior. Beautiful too if I remember."

"She still manages to keep her looks I think, but then she's my mother so what would I know? There have always been beautiful women in my life you see." With that he stopped Myfanwy in her tracks and gave her a long kiss on the lips. As usual he didn't give a damn if anyone was looking.

The sex between them that night took them back to their younger days. Laughter kept throwing romance out of the window and stopping the urgency of carnal lust. Neither wanted these precious moments to end. In spite of the now-fifteen year gap, they both knew and they both enjoyed. They also knew with a certainty that usually plays havoc with love that they would never be parted again.

Early the following morning Kristian went into his bathroom to relieve himself. As he hopped through the bathroom door he let rip a fine expulsion of flatulent outrage.

"Dear God, Kristian! I wanted an early morning call not an ear drum shattering fart! And knowing you, it probably stinks too! You're such a filthy bugger, do you know that? It always was all right for me to put up with your farts, your sweaty balls and hitting me around the face with your winky first thing in the morning but God forbid if I should ever be anything but the perfect lady. You're a pig!"

Kristian looked back at the bed. "It's my chauvinistic prerogative to fart at will, Myfanwy, and don't you forget it."

"Oh shut up, Kristian, now hurry up, I want to use the toilet. We might just have time for a quickie before I go to our daughter and make sure she's all right."

"Still as randy as ever, Myfanwy, still a dirty harlot and you have the nerve to talk about my foul habits!"

"Oh shut up!"

This time he did but not before hitting her with another barrage from his anal howitzer and this time Myfanwy couldn't help but laugh, even she would have been proud of that one!

CHAPTER 30

Kristian struggled with the wheelchair. The sand was making any kind of progress almost impossible. He had brought Angharad to one of his favourite places, a remote and unspoilt beach that very few people knew about. Local knowledge was jealous of this place and allowed few visitors. Eventually he stopped pushing the wheelchair and allowed it to settle on top of a moss-covered sand dune. The ground underfoot was firm so the wheelchair and more importantly his daughter were not at any risk. He sat down on the spindly grass next to the wheelchair and looked out across the sea. It was late afternoon, a time when the beach reflected and thought about other things.

During the past week Myfanwy had left Kristian and Angharad alone. They were both on a journey of discovery, both finding out about being a father and daughter. With each minute that they spent together a greater warmth and ease developed between them. Sometimes it seemed as if Kristian had never really been away.

"Are you warm enough, Angharad?"

"Yes, thank you Kristian . . . er, Dad." She giggled as she called him 'dad'.

"What's so funny? I am your father you know."

"I know, I know . . . Dad, I'm sorry I just can't help it. Mum never allowed me to call Islwyn 'dad', that's all. It just seems a bit funny using the word. Odd I suppose. I'm very mature you know. Can't I call you 'Kristian'."

"You certainly cannot."

"Oh all right then, I suppose I'll get used to it after a while. I know lots about you, you know Dad." It was interrogation time. Kristian had wondered how long it was going to take. His daughter was a bright little thing.

"Do you now."

"Oh yes. Mum often spoke about you." Kristian's nerves were starting to jump. How much had Myfanwy told the child? "I knew from the beginning that Islwyn wasn't my father. Mum just told me that you had to go away and that one day you would come back. You were a soldier and couldn't help being away from us. She was always certain that you would come back you know. And here you are. It is lovely to know that I have a proper father now. Mum . . ." – Angharad paused for a moment as she struggled to find the right words – "also told me that you didn't know about me. She felt it was best, that's all she would say. I'm not so sure though whether that was the right thing. I didn't know whether to believe her or not. I used to think that she was just protecting my feelings and that you had just left us. It hurt."

Kristian didn't know what to say. Part of him understood Myfanwy, part of him didn't. Whether he liked it or not Myfanwy had deprived her daughter of a father, and there would be consequences. Even he couldn't miss the resentment in his daughter's eyes. No poison had been placed in the child's mind though, which must have been hard for Myfanwy. Although he didn't agree with the way Myfanwy had handled things, at the same time he couldn't blame her. How could he?

"Yes, Angharad, the military can be a selfish master. I am sorry for being away from you all these years. You mustn't blame your mother though, she did what she thought was best for you. You see my work was sometimes extremely dangerous. I could have been killed at the drop of a hat. Try to understand. I didn't desert you, Angharad, that I could never have done, believe me, I just didn't know. It's hard to understand I know, but don't be too harsh on your mum . . . or me. We adults usually make far more mistakes than callow youth. It's the nature of idiot maturity, though the trouble is maturity has no excuse. I'm sorry, Angharad, I really am."

"Oh I know, so don't worry. I'm just glad that you have finally come back to us. Mum seems so much happier now.

These past few days all I have seen her do is smile. She's not even shouting at me!"

"Well, that's something I suppose." His daughter was a forgiving child, although he had a feeling that her forgiveness would come in fits and starts. She was a young woman, an adolescent. Trouble. They stopped talking for a few moments. A light breeze washed the long, almost yellow strands of hair that fell across Angharad's face. Cold sunlight shone upon her delicate features and highlighted her Nordic blood. Her blue eyes stared out across the sea and seemed to see far more than they were letting on. Kristian absorbed the perfection in his daughter's face and felt an untouchable pride.

"Did you do Latin at school, Dad?"

"Yes I did. Know your Latin and you will know your English."

"I love it, I really do. In fact I'd like to study it at university. Well, the classics anyway. Ancient history and its language are so fascinating. I'd like to have a proper go at Greek too. School won't let me study it but Mum helps me at home."

"Crusty subjects young lady, but I agree, fascinating. You don't fancy doing something a little more mundane then do you, like law or medicine?"

"Oh no, either of those subjects really would be boring. No, I've made up my mind. I want to be a Classics scholar. There's nothing else that interests me so much."

"Well, good for you. So it's Caesar's *Gallic Wars* for bedtime reading then. In the original Latin of course!"

"Of course."

For a while both of them lapped up the natural silence. Their eyes followed the waves as they sprinted along the deserted shoreline and stretched the sand dunes that prodded the sky with tips dulled by the greyness of winter. Seagulls raced with a few miserable clouds as they shrieked in defiance at a coldness they knew was here to stay. Father and daughter absorbed their own thoughts, comfortable and at ease with the peace of mutual discovery, while a solitary man traced unknown footprints in the sand. The man wore a hat and even at a distance he seemed self-contained and content. There was a dignity in his movements, a refinement that had been developed from birth. A brown waxed jacket and red scarf defied the cold as the man paused and bent from time to time to retrieve some rotting flotsam or even a conical shell capable of singing a romantic aria in times of maritime calm. There was also an inexplicable devoutness about him as he seemed determined to fill up an old, blue school duffle bag hanging from his shoulder. The man had no idea why he felt the need to scavenge, like those hell-bent on religion his actions were just an outrageous and irrational necessity. Now and again he would wave his arms at a neurotic Springer Spaniel who barked at his own tail as he tried to dodge the insolent waves that were trying to drown him. Unusually the crazy mutt had been shaved almost to the bone but seemed unaware of the heresy that had been committed upon his body. He yelped at the man's feet, ran around him, then bolted off to nowhere. Man and dog played with their lives and companionship, there was nothing serious in the air around them, it was as if they had both discovered all the answers and were satisfied with their own unique conclusions. Both Kristian and Angharad wondered what the lonely dog-owner was thinking about. He seemed so certain. So precise. They both wished their own lives could be so scheduled. So predictable.

The father's natural curiosity and thirst for learning had been passed on to the daughter – Myfanwy might have had something to say about this, however! Although fifteen years of estrange-ment had gone by, nothing could alter the blood that had been inherited by Angharad. There was a natural union between them both, a complete joining that no amount of time could ever spoil. Kristian and Angharad would always be father and daughter no matter what time and space threw at them.

"Does your leg hurt?" Angharad asked, "I notice you quite often rub it. You are doing it now."

"Oh, sometimes," Kristian smiled, "even though there is no leg below the knee. It's called 'phantom limb syndrome'. My brain likes to think that my left calf and foot are still where they should be. Stubborn devil, the brain."

"I have to go into hospital soon," Angharad said as her eyes darted away from the man and his dog and looked directly at Kristian. "It's not long now. A few weeks." Kristian looked up at his daughter and saw the fear in her bravery. He had seen that look many times in his life, he had seen it many times in his own eyes. "I worry about my legs. I know it's silly, but most boys love a good pair of long legs, don't they? Mum has great legs. Not too thin, not too fat and long . . . will you be coming to London with us? I'd like you to come . . . Dad."

Kristian took his daughter's hand in his and remembered again the chronic self-consciousness of chaotic and cruel teenage years. He remembered how an unannounced pimple could destroy his day. Apart from the uninvited pimples his adolescence had been reasonably smooth, but Lottie's . . .? God, he remembered all the slammed doors, the tantrums and the belligerent mood swings. Mind you, in his view, adulthood unfortunately didn't make a hell of a lot of difference where female kind was concerned.

"Of course I will be coming, Angharad. They'll have to manage here without me. I'll be there when you close your eyes and I'll be there when you open them. In fact you will probably be sick of the sight of my ugly chops!" Angharad smiled but the fear remained. "Don't you worry about anything now, Angharad. You mother and I will be with you every single step of the way. Before you know it you'll be out of that wheelchair and running along this beautiful beach under your own steam. Just think of that. Running around the dunes, running away from the waves and the wind. Keep these thoughts in your mind and you'll be fine. Damn, if I can still try to run now and again on one pin then you shouldn't have too much of a problem and at least you won't keep falling down on your backside either!"

They both laughed and this time Angharad's lips were a little more relaxed. "Come on, let's go back to the Cliffs, it's getting cold now and I don't want your mother playing hell with me for giving you a chill." He gave her a kiss on the cheek and added, "Be brave, my little Angharad, just be brave and I promise you that in a few years you'll have the best legs in Wales, you'll even have your mother seething with jealousy!" Kristian didn't say anything but he felt the surgeon's knife slicing his own body and for a few moments suffered as if Angharad's pain was his own.

As Kristian pushed his daughter back up a stony track, the sun started to creep around the horizon looking for somewhere to sleep while the dog owner leashed the dog and started to walk back to a life that only he and the dog knew about. The sinking sun looked, felt and was grateful for the long sleep that awaited it. It had seen enough of the world for one day.

CHAPTER 31

Three weeks later Kristian and Myfanwy were sitting in one of London's black cabs while it was tied up and knotted with all the other irritable vehicles that were trying to find a destination.

"Excuse me, Captain Treharne," – Myfanwy was having one of her manic episodes – "I didn't tell you to book us into the Savoy! The place costs a fortune!"

"Tough. I've booked it and that's where we're staying."

"And how am I supposed to pay my share for that then? We agreed joint operations where money was concerned. I won't be a kept woman!"

"I thought we agreed 'combined operations', there is a difference you know."

"You're splitting hairs now. You know exactly what I mean!"

"Oh for God's sake, stop moaning woman, the Savoy I've booked and the Savoy it is. I'm paying. Now belt up!"

"Don't you tell me to 'belt up'! Or call me 'woman' for that matter, you ignorant bastard!"

"Oh God, here we go again. Can't you exercise a little more imagination, woman . . .? You're starting to repeat yourself. Try something different, will you? 'Bastard' is becoming tiresome."

"Oh shut up, Kristian."

"And you keep telling me to 'shut up' too. I would have thought that by now even your comatose brain would have gathered that I never listen. In one ear and out the other. Now just be quiet and enjoy the luxury . . . So much for my romantic gesture by the way, typical."

"You, romantic? That's a laugh! First thing you'll do when we settle down in our room—"

"Suite." Kristian interrupted.

"Suite then, you snobby shit, anyway the first thing you'll do is christen the place with one of your bloody great farts! God help the neighbours is all I can say. God help them!"

"Very funny, Myfanwy. Well, at least I'm now a shit instead of a bastard, that's something I suppose. And where my 'condition' is concerned I will be exercising restraint, so don't worry. I keep telling you that I have a flatulent condition but you won't have it. I can't help it. I really can't. I eat too much fibre and that's all there is to it. Can you imagine what would happen if I kept all that wind inside me? Dear God, I'd raise the bloody Savoy to the ground! I don't break wind on purpose you know, I am a gentleman after all."

"Gentleman! You delude yourself, Captain Treharne. On the outside maybe, but let people see the real Kristian Treharne and wouldn't they just get a different impression. Gentleman – that really is a good one! Oh I forgot, you're also Mr Perfect, Mr Brain of the Universe and Mr Efficiency."

"You know, for a lady with a doctorate in philosophy you display a distinctly puerile form of abuse. I left the playground years ago, now will you please desist and stop going on about some of my less endearing personal habits. Which, I hasten to add, do at least have the virtue of being transparent and above board unlike your odious and sly expulsions of gas that sneak out of your arse in the middle of the night to ambush me with a stink that defies description. You think they just whisper onto my leg, well, let me tell you now, they don't, you filthy sod. Now for the last time, keep that manic gob of yours shut and let's try and enjoy a bit of decadent opulence, shall we? God knows the next few days are going to be hard enough. They're operating in two days time so let's try and stay calm . . ." – Kristian kissed Myfanwy which immediately took the wind out of her objectionable sails – "Look, I know you're beside yourself with worry. I am too, but we just have to ride this out. Everything will be fine Myfanwy. Now let's just stay calm. If we start to show too much anxiety it won't help Angharad. She's scared out of her wits as it is. She needs our strength right now. Not our weakness."

"Oh I know, I know," Myfanwy said quietly, "but I can't help it. She's my only child, Kristian, you must understand that."

"Mine too, but we still have to be strong for her sake." Kristian looked out of the cab window, "We're here. We haven't got long to unpack and freshen up. Angharad is expecting us back at the hospital in an hour or so, we will have to get a move on."

The taxi driver dropped them outside the Savoy and as he took the fare with a generous tip he said, "Tell you what guv, wish me and my missus were more like you and the lady. Bloody funny it was listenin' to you both. Love each other too, don't you, I can tell. Must do, to be that bloody 'onest 'bout things. Good on you! Oh and I hope everything goes ok with your daughter too. Got three of 'em myself, God 'elp me!"

CHAPTER 32

While Kristian and Myfanwy were going back to the hospital Justin Sewell was sitting behind his desk, his arms spread out before him as his eyes concentrated and seemed to blur with sheer pleasure.

"Is that all you have to say, 'It wasn't me'? Your whining doesn't impress one bit, Bethan. You're sacked, now get out of my office and don't try and come back here for a reference."

"But . . . but Mr Sewell . . . I didn't steal that money! I didn't!" Bethan sobbed.

"The evidence is irrefutable, Bethan. Now for the last time get out of my office and don't come near the Rose or the Cliffs again. You're extremely fortunate that I haven't called the police because, believe me, if it wasn't for our reputation that's exactly what I would be doing. Now go! Or do I call the police anyway and have you arrested?"

Bethan ran out of the office. She hadn't done anything dishonest. She hadn't stolen £500 out of the safe. How could Mr Sewell believe that she was capable of such a thing? The man wouldn't listen. He just wouldn't. Where was she going to find work again? What was she going to tell her parents? Bethan grabbed her things from behind the reception desk and ran out, tears rushed down her face as confusion and shame pushed her into a world that she knew nothing at all about. A dishonest world.

Bethan Jones had worked for the Treharnes since leaving school. She was now twenty-one and had been looking forward to promotion particularly as the Treharnes had now expanded into another hotel. There had even been some gossip about further expansion, that Justin Sewell was known to be pushing for a chain of hotels. The man was a creep and Bethan had never liked him. None of the staff liked him either and most of them couldn't understand what Miss Charlotte saw in him. Good looking he may be but looks weren't everything, were they? He never seemed to smile and all he ever did was sneer and treat everyone like dirt. If that's what London does for you then you can stick it.

What was she going to do? Her world had just fallen apart. How could Mr Sewell treat her like this? She had worked at the Cliffs for six years and had never even taken a day off sick. He had been so cold, so unkind. She had only been at the Rose for a few days to cover for one of the receptionists who had gone off sick and now look where she was.

Bethan caught a bus that would take her home to the Vicarage six miles away from the Cliffs. The grey, common land with its smatterings of unkempt sheep rushed passed the window and brought with it a sense of loss, a sense of hopelessness. Wind and rain kept tapping the bus with impatience, the bus had no right to be there, no right to disturb their misery. She jumped off the bus a couple of stops before her destination. She needed to talk to God. Not the God that her father preached about every Sunday but the God who laughed and always guided her in the right direction. Her God was a lively, happy soul who always spoke to her when called upon. He was the best of all Gods. Right now she didn't know what to do and the awful weather wasn't helping. The Gower could be a vicious brute when it wanted to be and cruel to those who would dare to take it for granted.

She pushed open the heavy oak doors of her father's church. It had been built in the 1850's as a bulwark against Nonconformist invasion. The Church of England ruled here, but Bethan's God was an insubordinate God and didn't really take much notice of sanctimonious pomp and ridiculous ceremony. She sat down in one of the pews, clasped her hands together and prayed.

After about half an hour of discourse with her Almighty she stood up and left the church. Her God, as expected, He never let her down, had given her the solution to her problems.

Paul Edwards. Or was it Paul Treharne now?

The following morning, Justin was again behind his desk. It was a powerful place to be. Control of the Rose was his. His impending marriage would seal his ambitions, first the Rose, then the Cliffs and then . . . who knows, the world was his oyster. He felt no regret at having to sack Bethan Jones. She was a thief and that's all there was to it. At least that had been the situation when he had sacked her. Unfortunately the brown envelope containing the £500 had turned up during the night. The night porter, Bert Powell, had discovered it while doing his usual security checks, he had noticed the edge of the envelope sticking out from behind the back panel of the safe. The damn thing had been in badly need of repair but Justin had been too busy to see to it. The discovery would make him look a complete fool in front of the staff and this was an intolerable prospect. He had given the porter a generous reward with the proviso that he keep his mouth shut. Just as he was about to finish his coffee and check the staff rotas there was a knock on his office door.

"Not now!" he shouted, "I'm busy. Go away!" In spite of his order the door burst open and Paul Edwards marched in.

"What the hell do you think you are doing, Justin, sacking Bethan Jones?"

Sewell remained calm. Paul Edwards was a fully paid-up member of the Treharnes now apparently, although he hadn't yet changed his name as far as he knew anyway. In spite of the fact that he considered Paul to be an inferior, he was young and owed his seniority to the greasy pole of nepotism, he looked at Paul and smiled.

"Sit down for a minute Paul." Paul remained standing. "I don't know what you've heard, but believe me I had no choice.

The reputation of the Rose and indeed the Cliffs was at stake. I had to replace the £500 out of my own pocket you know. Couldn't let on that one of the staff had swiped the money, could I? The money was in a brown envelope and had been put in the safe for safekeeping. The cash belonged to one of our regular guests, Mr O'Dowell, a surgeon. I believe the gentleman is known as 'O'Dowell the Bowel' by the staff on account of his specializing in stomach problems."

Sewell's face didn't even crease at the humour of the nickname; Welsh humour was utterly beyond him and always would be. "Anyway, by her own admission the money was placed in the safe by Bethan at 10.25 a.m. on the day Mr O'Dowell arrived. At 12.02 that same day Mr O'Dowell requested his property. It was not in the safe and the only person who had had access to it was Bethan. In fact she was the only person who had been anywhere near the safe for the whole of the two-odd hours. I checked. And before you say anything I was just as shocked as you are. I simply couldn't understand her stupidity. She wasn't even clever about it. It was almost as if she wanted to be found out. I felt awful about sacking her, Paul, but what else could I do? What with her father being a vicar and so on and the fact that she has been such a good employee for what . . . five or six years? It's a sad business and extremely regrettable, Paul. I'm as sorry as you are."

"And that's it, Justin?"

"I'm afraid so . . . er . . . I know that you and Bethan were . . . er . . . friends but I had no choice. I'm sure you understand. I have at least managed to keep the police out of things. Mr O'Dowell knows nothing about the theft. Bethan should be grateful for the fact I think." The two men looked at each other. The atmosphere in the room was hostile, fraught. For a moment it looked as if Paul might even hit Justin. He was a Treharne after all, in spite of his mild, unassuming manner. Instead he held Justin's innocent gaze for a few moments. He knew he had no argument.

"Make absolutely certain that nothing about this gets out, Justin, I mean it." Paul's voice allowed for no misunderstanding." My father and Lise are back next week. We will talk again then. Oh, and don't you forget either, Justin, that you are still only an employee like me." With that he walked out of the room.

Later that day Paul and Bethan were sitting down in a pub not far from the Cliffs. Paul hated seeing Bethan so upset. Even though they had never even kissed, a bond had developed between them. Paul would have liked things to have been more intimate but he was still reticent and shy where the opposite sex was concerned. Every time an opportunity arose to express his true feelings, courage would desert him and he would race back to the uncomplicated harmony of mutual friendship. Bethan was so lovely and her lips so kissable that sitting next to her was always torture. Did she feel the same way? That was the thing. And how was he to find out, which was even worse?

"You don't have to convince me, Bethan. I believe you. I know you wouldn't do such a thing. My father has never liked Justin and for all his faults I've heard he's a good judge of character. He has always reckoned that Justin is 'shifty'. Has told me enough times anyway. Now don't you worry about anything."

"But what am I going to do about a job? What am I going to tell my father. He's the local vicar for heaven's sake. My parents still think I am working at the Cliffs. And what will your dad and Lise think? Oh God, it doesn't bear thinking about!"

"I'll fix you up with a hotel in town," Paul said sympathetically, "I know most of the managers and I believe that I'm a damn sight more popular than Justin. He's not well liked you know. They'll believe me rather than him. As for the money, if you didn't take it, who did? What the hell is Justin up to? Why should he try and discredit you? It doesn't make sense. O'Dowell is certain that he saw you putting the money in the safe. Is it possible that you left the reception desk unattended at any time?"

"No, Paul. I'm sorry. I didn't go anywhere, not even to the toilet."

"In that case it's Justin's word against yours. I'll keep digging. In the meantime tell your parents you fancy a change and leave it at that. Don't worry about Griffith and Lise. I'll deal with them. I'll give them your side of the story if nothing else. One good thing, at least Justin didn't involve the police. We should be able to keep things fairly quiet, staff gossip notwithstanding."

"Oh God, I hadn't even thought of that . . . Look Paul, I know I can't come back and I don't expect you to try and make it otherwise but . . . you do believe me, don't you? I know I can't explain where the money went and I know that I was the only one on duty but you must believe me. You must. I can't prove my innocence, Paul, but I'm not a thief. I'm really not. I don't know what happened to the money. Someone has made a terrible mistake."

"Bethan, I know that. I know. Please stop trying to convince me, you don't have to." He looked into her eyes, big brown orbs that kept filling up with tears and just didn't know what to do. He wanted to hold her in his arms, to hug her, to kiss away her tears.

"Thank you, Paul. Thank you for believing me." She pecked him on the cheek and squeezed his hand affectionately. She always felt so safe with Paul. He would work something out.

CHAPTER 33

Kristian and Myfanwy had been told that the operation could take up to five hours, give or take one to two hours in recovery. There was nothing for them to do but wait. The doctors had assured them that Angharad was in no danger. There were always risks with any sort of surgical procedure but their daughter was a healthy young woman so they shouldn't worry. The medical staff would do their best.

Earlier, the consultant surgeon, a Mr D. Jagger F.R.C.S. Eng., had met with them and explained what was involved. The surgeon's glass eye peered at them, then jumped sideways and back again. The eye didn't inspire confidence, but the surgeon was apparently one of the best in his field so who were they to complain. As the middle-aged and obviously capable man talked to them, neither Kristian nor Myfanwy could help but be mesmerized by the jiving glass eye. Their eyes followed it, tried to pin it down and finally gave up. Neither of them had absorbed one solitary word of the surgeon's exposition on spinal surgery. Not only did the glass eye divert their attention but its reason for being there in the first place was just as compelling.

When the surgeon had finally finished, he walked off content with the fact that he had done his unstinting duty in allaying the over-anxious concerns of a couple of doting parents. Basically all parents were a pain in the arse, but such irritations went with the job. As a dedicated and extremely able surgeon he had learnt to live with it. His glass eye had too.

"Well," Kristian remarked as the surgeon's gowned back moved up the sterile corridor, "he'll be keeping a keen eye on Angharad, that's for sure."

"Oh God, Kristian," Myfanwy smirked, "Give it a rest will you? I'm beside myself with worry here and all you can do is crack stupid jokes."

"Sorry, bit inappropriate I suppose. I'm as nervous as hell too you know. The last meeting I had with a surgeon the bastard decided to shake my foot off instead of my hand. They give me the creeps."

"Oh shut up Kristian. Let's go and find somewhere to have a coffee."

"Good idea. Come on then, there's nothing more we can do here. I'll tell the nurse that they can find us in the coffee shop if they need to." Kristian took Myfanwy's hand and tried to hide the fear and worry that was tormenting him. His only child was on a slab and about to be mutilated. The thought made his stomach turn. He couldn't show Myfanwy though, she needed his strength, demanded it.

Three hours later Kristian and Myfanwy were still waiting for some news. They had been told time and time again that the surgery was normally straightforward and that there was nothing to worry about. That was all very well, but since when did any parent stop worrying when their child was undergoing major surgery? They had heard enough horror stories about botched operations, healthy people being left in comas never to wake up and brains being damaged beyond all repair due to a lack of oxygen. All these thoughts bombarded their minds as they waited and waited. All they could both do was hold each other's hands and plead for a door to open and for someone to tell them that everything was fine.

The frightening movement of hospital chaos continued to crash around them in spite of their rigid anxiety. Doctors and nurses rushed here and there intent on their own life-saving vocations. What did they care about death? They lived with it, slept with it and ate it. A young girl was being knifed and stitched up but they had other more important things to do – life saving didn't stop with one teenage girl.

Jagger stepped back and admired his handiwork. That's a neat bit of stitch work, he thought. If he was ever out of a job he could always become a seamstress, he decided. Yes, very professional indeed. In a few years time the girl wouldn't even be able to notice it or perhaps more to the point neither would any boyfriends if his own daughter was anything to go by. He sighed at the thought of his daughter, God the girl was giving both himself and wife sleepless nights. Drugs, abortions, you name it. And everyone thought doctors were above domestic traumas and the tragic foibles of everyday life – even above life itself. Their own fears and personal demons never seemed to figure in the eyes of the general public. Why should they? Doctors weren't human, were they? They didn't even crap and piss like everyone else either, did they? He sighed again, at least his job had more purpose than most. He did save and he did heal, regardless of his floundering home life.

"Right everyone, into the recovery room she goes. The tumour has been completely removed. Nothing more to be done. I'm nipping out for a smoke. I won't be long."

Angharad was wheeled into the recovery room. Medical staff clanked and clicked around the unconscious young woman while an experienced anaesthetist checked on her condition. He was about to turn away and prepare for the next operation when he noticed something was wrong. The patient's lips were going blue. He quickly checked Angharad's fingertips and toes. They were going the same colour. The oxygen should be making the patient go pink not blue! What the hell was going on? She wasn't getting enough oxygen and yet all the tubes were in the right place.

"Quick, sister. Find Mr Jagger, fast! Something's wrong. The patient is going to go into cardiac arrest any second! Quick! This is an emergency! We're going to lose her!"

Jagger arrived and took in the situation in seconds. "Give her more oxygen! Turn it up 100 per cent." Angharad turned even bluer. "There must be something wrong with the oxygen supply!"

He glared at the anaesthetist who could only mumble some non-sensical words and fumble around with rubber tubes, "Right, to hell with this—!" Jagger ignored the anaesthetist and wrenched all the tubes, pipes and masks from Angharad's face in order to let her breathe in normal air. The anaesthetist was horrified at having his medical prerogative so brutally overridden but within a few seconds he could see that Jagger's clinical acumen had been bang on as Angharad started to pink up and look reassuringly normal.

Jagger remained standing next to his patient, as he looked down on Angharad's face he said, "That was too damned close for comfort. By God, some heads are going to roll!" For a few moments there Jagger had feared he was going to lose the pretty young girl. A new life that hadn't even been run in yet. He was a father himself after all and at times an extremely anxious one, in spite of his impatience with other parents.

"What the fucking hell has gone on here?" he shouted. "Check the oxygen cylinders. Now! We could have killed her for Christ's sake!"

The theatre sister left the recovery room and returned a few minutes later. "Mr Jagger, it seems the porters have mixed up the oxygen and nitrus oxide cylinders behind the wall. The tubes were incorrectly attached."

"What? So we were feeding the patient nitrus oxide by mistake!" Jagger yelled. "Thank God I did what I did! This must never, ever happen again, sister! Is that understood?"

"Yes sir, I understand perfectly."

" Good," Jagger replied, "Now I had better go and have a word with the parents."

The sister was used to the temperamental Mr Jagger. In bed and out. Nevertheless, she would open an investigation and ensure that Jagger's order's were carried out to the letter. Nobody knew Jagger or his body better than she – not even his wife. As he started to calm down she conjured up the temerity to say, "Er . . . Mr Jagger, do you think it's a good idea to speak with the parents just now? They might receive the wrong impression. With respect sir, you are a little upset at the moment."

"What? Er . . . yes . . . you have a point there, sister." His anger was further calmed as writs for negligence flew around his brain. "Yes, quite sister . . . Right, all of you . . ." – he stared at all the medical staff in the recovery room – "not a word of this gets out, not one word . . . Do I make myself clear?" There were understanding nods from everyone in the room. "Good, because if it does we'll all be out of a job and I'm damned if I'm going to have my career ruined by some cretinous porters. Not a word, do you hear me?" He looked at the sister again," I'll go and see the parents in a few minutes."

Jagger viewed the parents through the window of the waiting room before going in to see them. My God, that was a close shave, he thought to himself before entering the room. He paused for a few moments to compose himself. He had yet to decide which was worse, sudden death or a hopeless crusade for survival. Comas were the worse. How the hell was one supposed to predict the unpredictable? Death, he knew, stubbornly trundled along the hospital corridors looking for likely recruitments on a daily basis, the younger the better. And it had nearly achieved its daily quota on his watch. He shivered for a moment, thought of his own children and then went into the waiting room. Thank God the parents didn't know how close they had been to sudden death. Or indeed, coma – their daughter had been close, so close. Had he not acted as quickly as he did then the lack of oxygen could have been devastating.

"Ah, Mrs Bowen and . . . er . . ." – he looked at his notes – "Mr Treharne. Well, you will be pleased to know that the operation was 100 per cent successful. Your daughter should make a full recovery." Relief poured out into the room.

"When will Angharad be able to walk again?" Myfanwy asked, trying to hide her shaking voice.

"Hard to say quite honestly, Mrs Bowen. She'll obviously have to undergo some intensive physiotherapy for a while, say a month or two, but quite frankly these matters are usually up to the individual. It depends how determined they are."

"That's something I know a little about, Mr Jagger," Kristian interrupted.

"Oh . . . how would that be?"

"My left leg is amputated below the knee."

"Ah, well then, you know what I am talking about."

"I have an idea."

"Well, as you know, full recovery in these matters can sometimes be hindered by the patients own mental state. Depression, feeling sorry for themselves etc. etc. My advice to you is to not let Angharad wallow in self-pity. It can happen. Particularly in the young. She's a lovely-looking girl, so there will be the psychological trauma. You must pull her out of it. Be harsh, even cruel if you have to. It's the only way, really . . . Now then, unless you have any more questions I'll be on my way."

"No, no, thank you Mr Jagger. You've been very kind. Thank you for everything," Myfanwy replied.

"Not at all, now then we'll be keeping Angharad in for a week or so, just to keep an eye on her, then she can go home. Well, goodbye now and good luck."

When the surgeon had gone Kristian hugged Myfanwy and kissed her, "I told you everything would be all right. Now, let's go and see this daughter of ours."

Little did they know.

CHAPTER 34

"I appreciate that it must be a bit of a shock, Mother, but I didn't want to spoil your honeymoon . . ." Kristian held the phone away from his ear while Myfanwy enjoyed his discomfort. He had just told his mother that she had a grandchild.

"Yes . . . I know that, Mother . . . but . . . I . . . Angharad." He put his hand over the phone, "Dear God, my mother is going berserk, Myfanwy."

"Serves you right. What else did you expect?"

"She wants to come up here straight away to meet her grand-daughter. She won't take no for an answer."

"Fine by me," Myfanwy replied. Kristian removed his hand from the phone.

"Ok Mother . . . yes that's fine. Myfanwy . . . yes . . . you met her a couple of times years ago, remember . . .? That's right . . . A character, yes . . . I'll explain everything when I see you . . . Ok, see you tomorrow then. Bye, bye." Kristian put the phone down.

"God, my mother can be hard work sometimes."

"How was she?"

"Angry at being left out."

"Understandable. She's coming here tomorrow is she?"

"With Griffith. Tomorrow afternoon."

"Well then, better get the best china out, hadn't we, and maybe I'll bake something special Your mother's not the only one who can cook." Kristian ignored the female rivalry.

They were sitting in Myfanwy's kitchen. The Aga oven was seeing to some Welsh cakes. Angharad's favourite.

"Where is Angharad?"

"Out with Dewi. At least he's pushing her around the farm. I made her wrap up and go outside with him. She's looking so pale and drawn, Kristian. What are we going to do with her? She is just refusing to make any serious effort to get back on her feet and out of that damned wheelchair. It can't go on like this."

"I know, I know," Kristian replied, he was as worried as Myfanwy.

Kristian and Myfanwy had brought Angharad back to the farmhouse in Mid Wales. It had been four weeks since the operation, but Angharad was making slow progress. She was refusing to adhere to the strict physiotherapy regime and seemed reluctant to exercise any sort of determination to overcome her illness. According to Jagger she should at least be walking a few steps on her own and unaided by now. They had checked with the hospital in London, Angharad had undergone some tests and the results were conclusive. There was nothing physically to stop Angharad walking again.

"What's the matter with her, Kristian? The doctors have told us there is no reason why she shouldn't be getting back to normal. She should be building up her leg muscles, exercising. God knows they've been damaged enough, but the longer she leaves it the more problems she'll have when she gets older. What the hell is the matter with the girl?"

"She's punishing you. Us."

"What?"

"She's punishing us. You, I suspect, more than me."

"What on earth are you talking about Kristian?"

"Sometimes you know, Mothers can be a little naive where their offspring are concerned. You don't walk back a few steps often enough. You don't look at your children with enough objectivity, particularly if there are things you don't particularly want to see. Unpleasant things. To be pretty basic about it, you are often 'blinded by love,' more so I think where an only child is concerned."

"And?" Myfanwy was prepared to listen, she had always respected Kristian's insights into the human condition. His perceptions were rarely far off the mark.

"Well, haven't you noticed how distant she is with you? She's the same way with me sometimes, but not as much."

"She's irritable sometimes I grant you, but wouldn't you be? She's a teenage girl too which doesn't help. She's frustrated and angry at not being able to walk properly – that's all."

"So why isn't she making an effort to do something about it then? Stop being so blind, will you Myfanwy? My God, you don't look further than the end of that lovely little nose of yours sometimes, do you?"

"Maybe, maybe. So what's the child expert's explanation then, Mr Know-all?"

"Now, now, no need for the sarcasm, Myfanwy. Are you going to listen or not?"

"I usually do – under duress though, I hasten to add."

"Right, well, Angharad is punishing you for depriving her of a father for all these years. Simple. She's upsetting you and making you worry on purpose. She's punishing you in the only way she knows how to. I might be a belated father but I know childish revenge when I see it. Children take a mother's love for granted and they will have no hesitation in using and abusing it. That's their power. From the cradle to the grave. Don't ever underestimate their capacity to thrust a knife in cold blood. They can be vicious brutes and quite ruthless when they want to be. And this is exactly what Angharad is up to. She ducks and dives with me, I'm not quite the enemy . . . at the moment. You now, that's a different story. You're too soft and she knows it. She's knows she can hurt you and that's the trouble. She's manipulating you like a good 'un, would that you could see it."

When Kristian had finished speaking the only noise in the kitchen was the mooing of a moody cow trying to attract attention. Myfanwy absorbed what Kristian had said and she didn't like it. She stood up and sighed.

"I have to admit that similar thoughts had crossed my mind but I've tried to ignore them, Kristian. I can't really blame her, can I? So what are we going to do about it then? I'm so worried."

"Come here," Kristian ordered as he held out his arms. Myfanwy sat on his lap and put her arms around his neck. "We sort her nonsense out, that's what we do, as suggested by the formidable Mr Jagger. Leave it to me, I have a feeling she'll think twice before starting to mess me about. Let the mothers be the softies and the fathers the hard bastards. We are not as emotional as you women. We're more detached. That's the way it's always been and that's the way it's going to be now."

"Don't be too hard on her, Kristian, I know what you can be like. You're not that callous I know, quite soft underneath the tough veteran exterior really, but when you put that face of yours on, then look out. You don't scare me but I've known plenty of people you do scare, so go easy please."

"As easy as I have to. Now leave our daughter to me. It's about time the little madam learnt to grow up and stop feeling sorry for herself."

The following morning Kristian took Angharad into Builth Wells. The small market town was in an area of Mid Wales renowned for its 'wells'. Back in the 1830's the Park Wells and Glanne Wells had become famous for their saline and sulphur. People flocked from all parts of England and Wales to indulge their medicinal delusions and vain hopes. The town had thrived and prospered as hoteliers and innkeepers exploited the thera-peutic journeys of those determined to believe. The inhabitants of Builth Wells were a shrewd lot. Even Edward 1's castle that stood above the town to glare at those who would venture across the Wye's only bridge had been plundered and raped to provide building materials for a population ravaged by fire back in 1690. Builth was a resourceful place and the railways of the 1860's had helped to encourage its quest for exclusiveness and wealth. These days the Royal Welsh Show had replaced 'taking the waters' but the profiteering went on just the same. A High Street encouraged the ambitions of voracious estate agents hell-bent on outdoing the ruthless greed of even Edward 1, while at the same time promoting the hypocrisy of a few beleaguered charity emporia. It also crammed in a sprinkling of easily forgotten shops, an occasional bank and of course the statutory pub or two. All these necessary commercial enterprises lingered patiently for tourists with easy wallets to come and fill their tills or buy a piece of bucolic paradise. Ancient commercial might still soldiered on even if the Waters had now dried up, their ghosts still wailed from time to time but these days no one took any notice.

Kristian parked the car in a car park that overlooked the river Wye. The morning was cold but sunshine managed to bring some relief from its painful bite. He pushed Angharad's wheel-chair along a path that ran parallel with the river. A lone fisher-man was trying to cast a fly across the frantic current of a river intent on its own journey and careless of any fish that had decided to join it. Kristian remembered other times with William. Times when his father had tolerated his clumsiness with the whip of a fly-fishing rod and the intricate knots used to attach the fly to a fly line. William had been patient, kind and yet he had been determined to teach. There were times when his voice changed. The tones more demanding and uncompromising. Kristian had known then that there was no room for mistake, no room for fault. As he pushed Angharad along the path he knew that it was now his turn to be the father. His turn to teach and his turn to change his tone of voice.

It was early so there were few people walking around. Stone houses, unable to laugh or smile, hung around not far from the river bank and made their own discreet comments as they watched the man and his wheelchair. They had seen it all before, or thought they had, but this was something different. New. There was no market today and no Royal Welsh Show so these new arrivals brought some excitement to their dour tedium. The people they protected had already gone back to sleep with bore-dom as their bedfellows.

They reached a secluded spot underneath an irritable oak tree that had recently been held to ransom by the greedy paws of conker-grabbing urchins intent on satisfying their destructive intent. Kristian stopped pushing and went to the front of the wheelchair to face Angharad. She had been quiet all morning, almost as if she had sensed that some kind of change was in the air. Kristian knelt down in front of her and placed his hands on the wheelchair's armrests. He looked into his daughter's eyes and saw both himself and Myfanwy. A formidable combination and one that his daughter was stubbornly refusing to acknowledge.

"Right, Angharad. You are now going to get out of that wheelchair and walk." His voice was firm, there was no room to manoeuvre. "No bleating now, no excuses. We don't leave here until you get that self-centred, self-piteous backside up and running. Well, maybe we can leave the running for now." Although his words were blunt and to the point, their tone was not unkind. Even so, Angharad knew that there was no room for negotiation. Her mother wasn't kneeling in front of her either. They were alone and she had no one to turn to.

"I can't," she replied, the defiance in her eyes was complete. Myfanwy stared back at him. Kristian had tamed her mother, he would now tame her daughter. He stayed where he was, his eyes never leaving hers. This was to be a fight to the death. Very well, so be it.

"You know, Angharad, many years ago I was struggling with some Latin homework. I asked my own father for some help. He knew the answers but he wasn't going to tell me. I remember that evening well. I was crying with frustration. Angry at myself for being so stupid, all I kept saying was 'I can't! I can't!' But do you think that my tears made any difference? Did they hell!

"All my father did was take a piece of paper out of my exercise book and the pen from my hand. He wrote 'I can't' in big bold print on the sheet of paper.

" 'What does that say, Kristian?' he asked.

" 'I can't,' I replied.

"He then crossed out the 'T' and said, 'Now, what does that say?'

" 'I can,' I answered.

"My father looked me in the eyes as he said, 'Well, there you have it. The solution to your difficulties, it's as simple as that, boy. Now get on with it and don't ever let me hear you say you "can't" again. There's no such word. You "can" and you will.' "

Angharad stared back at him. Defiance again. Silence.

"I see. Like that is it?" Kristian's voice hardened. Silence again. Kristian remained where he was. This time he raised his voice slightly, "You know something, Angharad, you're bloody lucky to have two legs to walk on. I wish I did. Now you listen to me, from this moment on you stop hurting your mother, you stop punishing her and you stop behaving like a spoilt little brat." Kristian's voice went up a few more octaves, his patience was falling apart, "She's been a fine mother to you and don't you damn well forget it! All right, so you've had a bit of surgery, a bit of inconvenience. So bloody what? And you want to be a Classical scholar? That's a good one. You can't even get your pathetic arse out of that damned wheelchair, so how the hell are you ever going to pass an exam? You've already got enough catching up to do as it is." Again there was no response from his daughter, she just stared back at him, she didn't even blink. "All right then, you stay in that wheelchair and be a cripple for the rest of your life, I'm sure that one day you'll find some man kind enough to take pity on you, he might even marry you, you never know your luck. You stay right where you are, Angharad, because I've had enough! You can stay here all bloody day for all I care, because I'm off! Wheel yourself over to one of the telephone boxes in the car park and ring your mother to come and get you. I'm finished with you, I've washed my hands of you!" Kristian stood up and started to walk back to the car. Not one word came from Angharad's mouth. In a funny kind of way he rather admired her resilience. She'd taken a blasting and hadn't fallen apart. She was his daughter then after all.

Kristian carried on walking for a minute or so before hearing a shout of "Daddy!" He turned around and started to walk back towards his daughter. He knew he had been cruel and desperately unkind, but he also knew that it had been the only way. He stood in front of his daughter for the second time that morning, but this time he didn't stand so close. Neither of them said a word as Angharad gripped the arms of the wheelchair and pushed herself up. Kristian took a few steps back.

"Come on Angharad, come on, you can do it," he urged. "Don't stop now." Anghared finally managed to stand up without any help. "Come on, Angharad. Walk to me. Walk to me. You can do it." Angharad grimaced but took a tentative step forward. Her legs nearly buckled but her eyes never left her father's. "Come to me, come on, come to me," Kristian urged as he held out his arms. A few more unsteady steps, then a few more until she finally fell into her father's waiting arms. He hugged his daughter tight, kissed her cheek and said, "There you are, my beautiful little flower, I told you it was as simple as crossing out a 'T'."

Later that day Griffith and Lise turned up at the farmhouse. Griffith was all bluster and tweed while Lise was her usual refined and elegant self. They both shook hands with Myfanwy who immediately noticed a certain nervous excitement in Lise's eyes as she asked to meet her granddaughter. Before doing so Myfanwy told Lise about all the problems her daughter had been experiencing. Myfanwy led Lise to the sitting room, this time there was no wheelchair standing next to the settee. She hadn't asked Kristian what had happened between him and Angharad that morning to effect this sudden change in her daughter's attitude toward the wheelchair. She wasn't so sure whether she wanted to know either, it was enough that her daughter was trying to be self-sufficient again. The shock of it all hadn't quite worn off yet. She introduced Lise to Angharad, who was sitting down reading a book on Greek mythology.

"So, you must be Angharad. That's a lovely name," Lise said as she sat down next to her granddaughter on the settee. The girl moved across to make room for Lise and said confidently," And you must be Grandma Lise. Daddy has told me all about you. You don't look anywhere near as severe as he makes out." Lise laughed, amused by Angharad's candour. It ran in the family.

"Well, you've certainly got the Treharne blood in you my girl. Frankness to the point of impertinence."

"Oh sorry, was I being rude again? Mum is always telling me off."

"No, Angharad, not quite rude, close though." Myfanwy was watching all this from the doorway. Kristian had taken Griffith straight into the bar, as far as he was concerned all these long lost reunions were best left to the women. The not so old and not so young had eyed each other up and down, inside out and backwards and forwards. They both saw something of themselves in the other. Beauty, fire, stubbornness and courage all clashed in the air between them but there was also an assumption of mutual and as yet undefined respect. Lise took Angharad's hand.

"How are you recovering from your ordeal?" Lise asked, her eyes saw the struggle and touched the pain. Her soft voice and the unfettered kindness in her eyes left Angharad in no doubt where Lise's unconditional love was concerned. She knew instinctively that she had a friend for life as well as a grandmother.

"Better now, thank you. It's a bit difficult having to learn to walk again, but I'm getting there."

"Good, that's the way. It won't be long before you'll be able to outrun that son of mine."

"Well that's not much competition, is it . . . Grandma? He's only got one leg after all!" Lise laughed again. The girl's boldness was refreshing, although by now she should be used to it, her own daughter was hardly short in coming forward, was she? "Oh, I'm sorry if I'm a bit slow with all this 'grandma' stuff but it's not so long ago that I discovered I had a father. It's all been a bit of a shock, really."

"And some father at that, Angharad. I fully understand how that son of mine can come as a 'bit of a shock'," Lise smiled. Myfanwy grinned too, impressed by Lise's refusal to see her only son as any kind of paragon of virtue like so many other mothers she had known. Lise had no illusions where Kristian was concerned – that was for sure. The two of them might just build up a solid friendship, and she had a distinct feeling that Lise would be an ally not an enemy. Mothers-in-law, or at the present time, putative mothers-in-law, didn't enjoy the most cooperative of reputations after all. For a few seconds the notion of being married to Kristian made her shudder. Good God, what had got into her even thinking about it! He was such a swine. Oh, and a bastard! In fact he had started signing his messages and cards to her as 'TB'. He even signed himself as 'TB' on the cards attached to bouquets of flowers that quite frequently arrived on her doorstep. She loved the flowers and they always made her heart miss a beat or two but somehow she always had trouble expressing her romantic inclinations. They were there, they always had been but it was the nature of their volatile relationship that stopped her from expressing the soppy side of her nature. Fortunately this wasn't true in the bedroom. There, when the lights were low and sex was answering all the questions she had no trouble being the sensitive and affectionate lover. Sex between the pair of them had always been wild, impulsive, inventive and downright filthy, so nothing had changed in that quarter. In spite of her incapacity to express any overt love they both knew it was there and that it rarely required any explanation. If she had been all lovey-dovey Kristian would probably have asked her to go and see a psychiatrist anyway!

Myfanwy left Angharad and Lise to it. They seemed to be enjoying themselves. Lise certainly had a way with teenagers. Myfanwy knew her daughter; usually Angharad was wary of strangers and could be unresponsive to the point of rudeness. Not this time. Lise seemed to be drawing her out without seeming to try too hard. She had to admit that Lise was a fine-looking woman too, groomed to perfection. She must pay a fortune for her clothes. Her skin was smooth and the holiday sun had accentuated her already bronzed Scandinavian skin. There was a lot more than the physical looks though. Myfanwy had noticed a subtle suffering in Lise's eyes. A resignation of sorts. A surrender even. Lise's real beauty lay in her face, a face which seemed to know many things, a face which had been tried and tested. The woman enjoyed a calmness that had been bought at a heavy price and yet there was no regret. No recrimination. There was only a magnificent acceptance.

Myfanwy knew Lise's story and wondered if she would ever have had the inner strength to overcome such terrible adversity.

As expected, Myfanwy found Kristian and Griffith in the home-made bar. They were talking and laughing.

"There you are," Myfanwy said, "Don't let Kristian get you drunk now, Griffith . . . you don't mind me calling you Griffth, do you?" Griffith leapt to his feet, ever the gentleman.

"Not at all, you delightful creature. I was just telling Kristian what a lucky chap he is. God knows what you see in him. Damn, if I was just a few years younger he wouldn't stand a chance! Now come and sit next to an old man and remind him of what he's missed in his sorry life!"

"Not much if I know you, Griffith," Kristian smiled, "you're still a lecherous old sod and now you're married to my mother!"

"Be silent young man and indulge an old man's fantasies."

Myfanwy sat next to Griffith. "Well, your mother and Angharad are getting along famously," she said. "She is a lovely woman you know."

"We know," both men answered at the same time.

"She, sorry Lise, can be imperious and extremely self-willed at times though I can assure you," Griffith added.

"Rather like Myfanwy then, Griffith. She needs a dose of taming from time to time."

"Taming! That will be the day. Don't listen to him, Griffith. He's talking nonsense as usual."

"Oh I don't know so much. There's definitely fire in your eyes, a bit of the brooding Celt too if I'm not mistaken. Still, provides some lively entertainment where bedroom antics are concerned, so far be it from me to criticize!"

"Oh God, Kristian," Myfanwy laughed, "have you been revealing all our personal secrets to this old rake of an uncle of yours?"

"Not at all, take no notice. Now shut up Griffith, or I'll be in for hell later on."

"Fair enough, my boy. Fair enough. Now, what's for lunch, I'm starving?"

CHAPTER 35

"You're very quiet, Lise."

"Thinking."

"Oh God, that's dangerous."

Griffith left Lise to her thoughts as he concentrated on applying his driving skills to the winding roads of Mid Wales. When she went into thinking mode she was best left alone, eventually she would come out of it and start acting like a normal human being again. When the Brecon Beacons were finally behind them and Swansea wasn't far off, Lise finally spoke.

"Kristian seems settled now, Griffith. Content. I never thought the day would come when he would actually become a 'family' man and a farmer at that. The boy never ceases to surprise me. He has a good woman there though, and a lovely daughter. I'm extremely pleased for them all. I really am."

"Good, I'm glad to hear it. Not a day too soon either, it has to be said. The boy was going downhill and that's a fact," Griffith replied.

"Yes. He was becoming more of a worry than usual. I hope they get married soon though. I don't like all this 'living together' thing. Shows a distinct lack of commitment as far as I am concerned. I really don't like it at all. And they have a daughter too."

"Steady on there, girl. Don't push them. They've been apart for a long time, no doubt they're still finding their feet. Give them time."

"Yes, I suppose you're right."

"I am, so stop worrying. They're two mature people and will make their own decisions when they are ready. Hell, Kristian has only just found out he's a father, that must have come as one hell of a shock. He's always been the consummate bachelor, after all."

"Well, you would know something about that wouldn't you, Griffith Treharne? Men, you're all the same."

"Not at all, we are just a bit forgetful from time to time."

"Forgetful! That's a good one!"

"Well, you know what I mean." Griffith was starting to laugh now and Lise was following suit.

"Anyway Griffith, we need to start making some serious decisions."

"Do we have to? You know what I'm like where 'decisions' are concerned and I don't like that look on your face either. It usually means there's money flying around your mind somewhere or other. I presume it's what all this 'thinking' has been about."

"Yes it has. Griffith whether we like it or not neither one of us is getting any younger. We can't run the Cliffs and the Rose forever."

"I didn't think we really 'ran' either of them anymore. What are we paying Justin and Paul for?"

"Oh, we still spend a lot of time looking after things and you know it. We still have our hands on the controls as it were. We still have the last word."

"So, what's your point? I don't have any trouble with handing over more responsibility to others. We have another trip planned in a couple of months time so full-blown retirement is fine by me. Will it be fine with you though, Lise? That's the thing."

"I think so."

" 'Thinking' isn't good enough, my girl. You've really got to say goodbye to having anything to do with the business if you want to do it properly. Retire, that is."

"Not necessarily. We could form a limited company. You and I could have executive positions on a board of directors. We would retain some say in the business. You know how our accountants and solicitors have been nagging us to go for incorporation. Perhaps now is the time, besides there are other considerations."

"Oh, and what would they be?"

"Something close to your heart, Griffith."

"Well . . .?"

"Tax."

"Tax! Tax! Don't mention that obscene word to me!"

"Well, there is Capital Transfer Tax you know and believe me our liabilities will be huge if we don't start listening to the people who know about these things."

"Capital Transfer Tax? Death duties in other words, the scourge of the privileged few! Which Bolshevik bastard thought that one up! Bloody socialists and their malevolent distribution of wealth principles! Hang 'em all I say! Hang the bloody lot of them!"

"Now calm down, Griffith, will you please? I have it all worked out."

"I bet you have! Do I have a say in all this then? It's my money too, you know."

"Now, now Griffith, don't be petulant." Lise leaned across her seat and gave him a kiss on the cheek. She knew exactly how to handle her husband.

"What do you have in mind then?" Griffith asked more calmly. A kiss always did the trick.

"We form a limited company, we can call it the Celtic Group of Hotels or something. Never mind the details for now, we can do all that with the lawyers and accountants. We can make our three children the principle shareholders – equal distribution of course – and as I have already said, we can retain non executive positions. We at least maintain some say in what goes on. Having said that, I don't think the children would ever go against our wishes on anything. The point is, that provided we both survive seven years then the Chancellor gets nothing."

"That's all very well, Lise, but what about my ticker?"

"There are ways to distribute the tax burden between husband and wife. Besides you're as strong as an ox, you'll last another seven years if only to annoy me!"

"Well, isn't that gratifying to know."

"I could die before you you know, Griffith." Suddenly the reality of what they were discussing made Griffith's stomach turn. He had never been one to worry about money nor had he been one to ever worry about death, his temperamental heart notwithstanding. He was finding the whole conversation extremely disturbing, worse of all was the thought of Lise dying before him. That, he knew, he just couldn't bear thinking about.

"All right, all right Lise, I'll leave it all to you, you know how I hate dealing with detail. There is one thing though."

"Oh, and what might that be?"

"Justin Sewell."

"Oh no! You aren't going start on Justin again, are you?"

"Look Lise, I'm not worried about the children and that includes Paul. Technically of course they could throw us out of the business, but I don't believe any of them are remotely capable of anything like that. They are all responsible adults and capable. Kristian has obviously decided to be a farmer and good luck to him. As long as he's happy, who cares? Lottie, well she's determined to become the next Lord Chancellor and seems to be as disinterested in the business as Kristian. So that leaves Justin and Paul to run things. I have every confidence in Paul, but Justin will effectively have control of Lottie's shares – she's still young, Lise, impressionable, whether you like it or not. And there's a devious streak in the bugger, I don't care what you say. There's something not right there. I saw it when we interviewed him and to date I've seen nothing to change my mind. He gave poor Bethan the boot without so much as a 'by your leave'. I still don't believe that the girl stole that money. The man is shifty . . . and ruthless. I said it then and I'm saying it now. He could cause a great deal of trouble. Put Lottie's shares in trust or something."

"That wouldn't be fair, Griffith, and you know it. We have always treated Lottie and Kristian equally. We will also treat Paul equally. If we tried to do what you suggest then I know

Lottie would feel humiliated and demeaned, rightly so too. She is a grown-up woman now you know, and a barrister at that. She's nobody's fool. We can't exclude her. Apart from anything else, I don't agree with you where Justin is concerned. The man does a grand job, at least I've never had cause for complaint. He and Lottie love each other and will no doubt be getting married soon. I have never seen anything 'shifty' in him as you put it. Lottie isn't that stupid, you know."

"Love is always stupid, Lise."

"Oh, stop being so cynical will you, Griffith?"

"There is another point."

"Go on."

"We will be signing away all our worldly possessions you know, and that really would upset me if Justin Sewell ever got his hands on my money."

"That's nonsense, Griffith, and you know it. There's still Kristian and Paul to keep their eyes on things. Anyway, we have plenty of money to see us to the end of our days, hotels or not. God forbid, but if things did go seriously wrong we still have ample capital to protect us. Apart from all the financial side of things, Griffith, who on earth is going to keep things going when we are dead and gone? How would you feel if some big London conglomerate got their hands on all our hard work. And your father's? At least like this everything stays in the family, one way or another anyway. There will be more grandchildren too I hope, so maybe some of them will be more enthusiastic about the hotel business that Kristian and Lottie. Now, Griffith Treharne, stop being so negative. Think of all the time we will have together on our own. Think of the peace and quiet and all that sun!" Griffith looked into Lise's eyes and knew there was no point in any further argument besides he loved her too much.

"Very well. You win as usual. Just tell me where to sign."

CHAPTER 36

As Griffith and Lise were driving home Justin was sipping a mineral water in his hotel room. He had come to London to see an old friend, at least that's what he had told Lottie. She had left London the weekend before to return to Wales where she was to pursue her legal career. A few discreet telephone calls had secured a junior tenancy in some Swansea chambers. That was the rich for you, he thought, everything fell into their laps. He had had to work hard and all hours to get where he was. Nobody had given him a thing. A bitter smile twisted his lips for a brief moment. How the wheel turns full circle, he thought. He was confident that one day the Treharne 'Empire' would be his, it would take time he knew but he was a patient man. Lottie adored him and was so wrapped up in the law that he was sure she would eventually relinquish any of her personal responsibility for the hotels to him. There were other problems of course, namely the rest of the family. How could he buy all the others out? How could he achieve full ownership of the business? Kristian and Paul could be bought off he was certain. As for Lise and Griffith, well, age would see to them. Natural selection. Lottie would comply with his wishes if he requested a large loan from her he was sure; she could certainly afford it, even he had been surprised at how much she was worth when she had finally told him. She was a naive fool in lots of ways, like the rest of them. He would keep up the pretence of doting husband for as long as he had to, it was, after all, a small price to pay.

He looked around his indifferent hotel room. He had to admit that the Treharnes had style, if nothing else. The room he now occupied was cold to the eye, featureless. There was no colour, shape or form. Lonely people passed through it on a regular basis and it rarely bothered to try and cheer them up. They were never there long enough to try and be truly comfortable anyway. He sipped his mineral water and continued to scheme and plan. So far the Treharnes had taken him in like one of the family – that was a good one, 'one of the family', it almost made him laugh with joy for once. He wanted to keep it that way though. Caution was the order of the day. Thus his trip to London 'to see an old friend'. As far as Lottie was concerned he was staying at the house in Chelsea, the hotel room was a temporary measure only. There were too many eyes at the Treharne's London residence.

A knock on the door disturbed his thoughts. He put his drink down and got up to answer it. There would be no surprises. It was always the same although he might choose a different colour from time to time. He opened the door and saw a familiar face. "Come in," Justin said with a hint of excitement in his voice. The teenager did as he was told. He was slim, smooth-skinned and deliberately attractive, just how Justin liked them. The boy – Justin never bothered to find out their names – crossed between male and female, his gender uncertain and bland. That was the sexual thrill, Justin could be having sex with a man or a woman. The conundrum was exquisite.

"Undress then," Justin ordered, "we can have a shower together first."

The young male prostitute started to undress and hoped that on this occasion the sex wouldn't be too painful.

A week later Justin was sitting down having dinner with Lottie, Lise and Griffith. He hated these weekly social events that Lise had forced on them since Lottie had come back home. He was always his usual charming self, his ambitions demanded it, but underneath his forced smiles and amiable manner he seethed. Griffith annoyed him with his bumptious humour and Lise irritated him with her superior airs. Few people would ever have accused Lise of being superior, but nevertheless that's how he saw her and wanted to see her. At the moment Lise was gushing over Lottie's ring.

"Let me have another look, Lottie. It really is beautiful. I can't stop looking at it. It's so different. Where on earth did you get it, Justin?"

"In London, after a great deal of rummaging around in Hatton Garden." Justin smiled and all the women fell for it.

"Well, it was worth the effort Justin, believe me," Lise replied.

Griffith looked on, as bored as Justin with Lise's insistence that they all meet up for dinner at least once a week. Paul, the crafty sod, had managed to arrange his rota in a way that prevented him from attending. Every time they were supposed to meet up Paul was working. It was all rubbish of course, the boy disliked Justin as much as Griffith did. Apparently there had been a falling out over the Bethan girl. It had been a sorry business all round but they had been left with no choice. Griffith groaned inside as Lise took her daughter's hand and enthused over the bloody engagement ring. He couldn't help but take another casual look if only to be polite. It was a beauty, no doubt about it. There was even something familiar about it. He had wanted to buy a similar ring for Lise but had been unable to find exactly what he wanted. Trust Justin Sewell to beat him to it. The man really was a smug bastard.

"Well Mum," Charlotte piped up, "we do have something to tell you as we are on the subject of engagement rings. Justin and I have decided to get married next August, if that's ok with you. We've found a house in Caswell Bay. It's a real gem. It overlooks the bay."

"August is fine. And the house. How lovely all this is! It's November now so that gives us plenty of time. Wonderful! An August wedding. I'm so pleased for you both, I really am!" While Lise got all excited Griffith groaned again. Oh God, he thought, here we go, women and weddings. That's all he was going to hear about for the next nine months or so. Justin sat back in his chair and looked at Griffith with a self-satisfied sneer. Only Griffith would have recognized it. He had seen it before but he had no idea where or how, and for a split second Griffith felt an inexplicable fear as Justin's eyes met his. The man was revealing something of himself that only Griffith could know. He was challenging Griffith, pushing him into territory that was both violent and insidious. For a moment Griffith was speechless as his throat dried up and his tongue refused to respond. Words failed him as he confronted and held the look in Justin's eyes in spite of his fear. Then in that one moment there was an instant and mutual recognition that they were now both at war. Nothing was said. They both knew and both welcomed it.

Lise would neither listen nor hear and Griffith knew it. He looked at the love that sat at the table and feared for a family that had already suffered enough.

PART III

August 1985

CHAPTER 37

Charlotte opened the envelope that Lise had just given her. She read the contents and sat down.

"Oh Mum! For once I am speechless . . . I really am. I don't know what to say."

"You don't have to say anything Lottie. It's your wedding present from Griffith and me. We both hope you will be happy." Charlotte stood up as soon as she had partially recovered and hugged her mother.

"You have given me one-third ownership of the business, Mum. Are you sure about this? I mean I've never shown much interest, have I? And you know how important my career is."

"Well, you will have Justin to help you, won't you? Griffith and I had already thought about that."

"It will certainly make Justin happy, Mum. Oh, I still don't know what to say!" Charlotte hugged and kissed her mother again. As she held her she said, "You know Mum, I'm so grateful for everything you have done for me over the years. I know I haven't always been the easiest of daughters but I appreciate how hard you have worked to educate me and to make sure I have never gone without. Thank you Mum, thank you for everything. I mean it." Tears started to fall from each of the women's eyes as they held each other.

"Now," Lise said as she stood back from her daughter and wiped her eyes, "we are both getting sentimental and silly. It's your wedding tomorrow, my girl, and there's still lots to do. So let's not be maudlin. Come on, let's go and have another look at that dress of yours. It might just need a few final adjustments." Lise took Charlotte's hand and started to walk to the study door.

"Oh, just one thing, Mum. That was very fair of you and Griffith to split the business three ways between me, Kristian and Paul. Paul will be particularly delighted. I still can't get over that rascal of a husband of yours. Fancy keeping Paul a secret for all those years! Anyway, to be fair to Paul he has far more interest in the hotels than either me or Kristian and he has worked incredibly hard over the past couple of years. I still can't help wondering though what's got into you. I never thought for one moment you would ever give up running the business. You have always lived for it, particularly the Cliffs."

"Well, Griffith and I both need to take things more slowly now. Neither one of us is as young as we used to be. We aren't giving up totally you know. Both of us will still be keeping a careful eye on things, you obviously haven't read the small print, Lottie. You a lawyer too – tut, tut! Apart from anything else we are not really giving up anything. All our hard work is being passed on to our three children. The Treharnes will go on and so will their hotels. That will be the best gift you can ever give to me, Griffith and your father William, so don't you ever forget it, my girl. You must always keep the hotels in the family. Promise?

"I promise."

"Good, now let's go and try that wedding dress on again. Everything must be just right."

It was yet another day of 'I do's' for the Treharnes of Ragged Cliffs. Thatcher's 'free market' was nowhere to be seen. Brash, kaleidoscopic waistcoats had been banned along with outrageous and uncouth pink limousines, by order of Lise and 'old', dignified money. Outside the church, policemen kept the crowds at bay while showers of confetti leapt from happy hands intent on forgetting for just one day. The Treharnes and a solitary Sewell stood on the steps of the church while a photographer flashed images of romantic euphoria and awkward faces waiting for the shout of starters' orders at the bar. This was Wales after all and every wedding was piss-up time, although the same could be said for funerals – when it came to an excuse for overindulgence the Welsh were none to fussy. Even heart disease was given a reprieve for the day as Griffith had kept telling his lady wife. Will Jenkins turned up, flat cap, roll-up attached to his lower lip and crumpled morning suit sticking to his hobnailed boots. This was his third Treharne wedding. Three of his own engagements, three weddings and he still remained a confirmed bachelor. Never mind, he thought, as he puffed on his yellow dog-end, he had his roses and they were far less troublesome than women. That Charlotte was a real gem though, if he had been any younger he might even have tried for a fourth engagement! They weren't marriages after all so where was the harm.

Dai the Death had replaced his fleet of black hearses for grey wedding cars with a touch of white ribbon. He had been ordered to keep everything understated and refined. No Tizer bottles, no Heinz Baked Bean tins and certainly no gaudy ribbons. This was a Treharne wedding not a frantic and vulgar carnival. Charlotte stood next to her man while the people gawped and envied. The handsome couple were the thing of fairy tales, their looks, intelligence and their wealth taking the onlookers on a journey to paradise, if only for a few moments. As they climbed into the wedding car to take them back to the Cliffs Charlotte threw her bouquet into the air but was unable to see who had caught it. She held on to her man and loved him like never before. He was hers now come what may and she was his. She would always be his no matter what.

Ben Yehuda Street, the Park Lane of Tel Aviv, was quiet. It was early evening. The Golan watched over the people as Israeli fighter jets made never-ending sorties across their heights. The country was at peace for now, albeit that a Jaffa orange was four times more expensive that one being bought from a stall in Swansea Market even though it had travelled hundreds of miles from its place of birth. Proud Israelis didn't mind their rocketing inflation as long as it kept the peace and the fighter jets flying.

Justin and Charlotte were sitting down at a pavement café drinking some expensive coffee. There were plenty of darker, cheaper cafes down the side streets but they had experienced enough excitement for one day. Charlotte had chosen Israel as their honeymoon destination. She had been a kibbutznik there a few years before. An idealistic law student with six months to spare and an intention to see at least some of the world, she had worked on a kibbutz cutting down bunches of bananas and avoiding the fat, overfed rats that sometimes jumped out of them. Up at 4 a.m., it had been hard work with only one day off a week, from dusk on Friday to dusk on Saturday. The kibbutz she worked on came to a stop on the Shabat. Then the volunteers could get drunk on Arak, the milk of lions', and smoke themselves half to death on cheap 'Nobbler' cigarettes. Money was always in short supply but no one really needed it. There was always plenty of food in the communal dining room. Food, a bed and a better understanding of the Balfour Declaration and Yom Kippur were the wages and no one complained. As she sipped her coffee she remembered a young German boy and their journeys to other parts of Israel. Jerusalem, Haifa and the elite holiday resort at Elat all passed through her mind. For a moment she blushed at the recollection of sex on the Shabat and their laughter at the heresy. They had meant no harm. She remembered the Kalashnikovs and M16s that never slept and eyelids that never closed as they wandered around the kibbutz, she remembered the love that the people had for their country, both Israeli and Arab. She remembered their kindness. The violence of nationalism and religion trapped her mind for a few moments. The wailing at bricks belonging to ancient legend, the place where Messengers rode up to the Cosmos in order to chat with prophets as they fought for ascendance over a father's desire to kill his own son turned her memories into a sadness for mankind that she knew could never be resolved.

"What are you thinking about, Lottie? You're miles away."

"What? Oh sorry. I was just thinking about the time I lived here on a kibbutz. It was an experience. I have so many memories." Charlotte knew it would be impossible trying to make Justin understand her thoughts. For him everything was blacker than black, whiter than white.

"Well, I hope they are not as expensive as this coffee. Dear God, have you seen the price?"

"Oh stop fussing, Justin. We're on our honeymoon."

"Aren't we just! I nearly had my toe bitten off by a bloody great crab earlier on, so some honeymoon!" Charlotte started to laugh again as she recalled the look on her husband's face as a huge crab had jumped out of the water where he had been cooling off his tired feet. They had been sitting on some rocks next to the Sea of Galilee. Justin had been dangling his feet in the water when an enormous crab had tried to take his foot off. Charlotte had never seen him move so fast. She had warned him, she knew all about the crabs but he had taken no notice. He rarely took any notice of anything she said. This time he had done so at his peril and paid the price. She had done nothing but laugh and this had made him even angrier.

"It's not that funny, Lottie! I could have lost my big toe you know. Then you would be in trouble. Who would run the hotels then?"

"Oh, the loss of a big toe wouldn't stop you, Justin, of that I am certain. Now stop being such a sissy!"

"Talking of the hotels, that was very good of your mother and Griffith to give you all those shares, wasn't it?"

"Yes, not that I want to have much to do with them. We've already agreed that you take full responsibility. You love the hotel business."

"Yes I do but . . ."

"But what?"

"Well, even though you are my wife I still feel a bit like a kept man. It doesn't sit easily with me that I'm almost working for you."

"Don't be silly, Justin, it isn't like that at all. You earn a good salary, you pay your way. You don't get any charity from me."

"That's not the point, Lottie," Justin said quietly, "the fact that I have no vested interest in the business makes me feel like an ordinary employee, a second-class citizen if you like." Justin lowered his head and played with his fingers. His voice was almost apologetic as he continued. "It also tends to undermine my authority at least where the staff are concerned. I can almost hear them whispering 'It's Miss Charlotte who pays the piper and Mr Sewell just jumps to her tune'. It is a little humiliating you know, Lottie . . . You see the fact that I don't have any real ownership of the business, at least in the legal sense, also tends to take away any incentive to make sure that it continues to grow and succeed . . . Can you understand . . .? Oh I'm sorry, Lottie, I'm probably just being silly, like you say." He looked down at his shoes again, his voice had been humble almost sad. Charlotte looked at her husband and couldn't help but understand. She had her pride too and knew how painful it could be if it was hurt. To hell with it being destructive and the harbinger of a fall.

"Look I do understand, Justin. I really do. There is something I have been thinking about. Something that might help your fragile male pride."

"It's not fragile, Lottie, just . . . well, sensitive." Justin gave her one of his rare and sincere smiles. As usual it made her feel all sexy and soppy.

"Well, how about if I give you a limited power of attorney over my shares . . .?"

"But . . . I can't . . . well, it wouldn't be right . . ."

"Don't be stupid Justin. Your reticence is very commendable and all that but you're always banging on about not having enough control over the way the business is going. You don't stop going on about expansion, change and so on. And I have to say you're quite right about most things. I have every confidence in you and no doubt you will make a great success of the business. At least this way you may be able to increase profits and buy your own way in. You won't be answerable to me either for any decisions you make. The power of attorney gives you full legal ownership to do what you like with my shares. It will be limited to my shares by the way, so don't go getting the wrong idea where the rest of my money is concerned, Mr Sewell."

Charlotte teased, she didn't really care much about money, as far as she was concerned everything she had was Justin's and vice versa. Yet even though they were married, she was still a lawyer.

"I don't know, Lottie. What will your family think?"

"What can they say? Mum can't take the shares back. She has given me full legal ownership of my share. One-third. Paul and Kristian have the other two-thirds. Look Justin, I can't be bothered with all this hotel business thing. You love it, I don't. The law, now that's something different. Kristian doesn't care much for the business either, he's more interested in tractors and cow dung. As for Paul, well, he's conscientious and I know he too loves the business. Mum and Griffith are virtually retired from it all and believe me if Mum felt you were some kind of threat or likely to do something stupid she wouldn't have given me the shares in the first place. I know my mother. No doubt she and Griffith knew exactly what they were doing when they handed everything over to the three of us. They knew where Kristian and I stood, so that left you and Paul. Paul is Griffith's son and you are my husband. Everything is kept in the family which is just what Mum has always wanted. So stop worrying, will you? Mum and Griffith will be fine. If anything they will be quite happy to know that the business is in safe hands. If you ask me, Mum has known all along who would really be running the hotels anyway. You and Paul. Why do you think they handed over all the shares the way they did? Shrewd lady my mum, always ahead of the game. Should have been a bloody lawyer!" Charlotte laughed and Justin breathed in a deep sigh of relief as he laughed with her. This time there wasn't so much sincerity in his mirth.

CHAPTER 38

Bert Powell sat in his local pub and stared at the froth on the top of his beer. He was fifty next week and felt it. His short, grey curly hair stuck to a head that had been banged about on numerous occasions although it wasn't quite as squashed as his nose. That had almost disappeared altogether. The tie that never left his neck was stained, his shirt collar worn and threadbare. Most of his clothes had given up and most suffered a form of shock every time they were ever pulled out of his one, battered and small wardrobe. As usual he thought back to his army days. Life had been good then. As an RSM he had been a leader of men. He had been respected and feared. When he barked men jumped. He had done numerous tours in Northern Ireland and had done his bit in the Falklands. The army had been his life, the grub had always been good, not to mention the dentists and docs. As an infantryman he had never had to worry much about the more obvious things in life, the necessary things. Twenty-two years he had given to Queen and Country, and since leaving the kindly arms of Her Majesty life had never been the same. Civvy Street was a cruel place, a place of responsibility and decision. Neither of which had come easily to Bert. These days he was able to rest his hands on his guts, he had lost all his teeth, he refused to accept his liver's flag of surrender and his lungs rarely felt the sweet touch of fresh air. All in all he was a magnificent wreck, one that would have made even Turner shake with excitement. As he reached for the beer his hand trembled slightly as he wondered where the money was going to come from for the next pint. There had to be a next pint, it was the only thing that would stop the shakes. He cast his bleary and worn-out eyes around the bar and saw an old friend walk in.

Deliverance. He sighed with relief, the problem of his next pint had been solved. He would tap his pal for a few quid until his army pension arrived the following morning. The friend would weigh over, everyone knew that Bert always paid his debts. Even the bookie allowed him tick. The bookie. Jesus, the bastard had caused him more trouble than the drink and Civvy Street put together. The trouble was he just couldn't resist the gee-gees or for that matter the *Racing Post*. Fags and booze were all very well, he may have been a drunk and a heavy smoker but neither ever stopped him functioning in a reasonably normal way. He never fell about and he never slurred his words. He got by, at least in his own modest way. But the horses, that was a different matter. The damned animals had cost him the nice cosy number up at the Rose and his self-respect. Neither the booze nor the fags had ever demanded such a heavy price.

Bert thought about the Rose. His integrity. Captain Treharne had trusted him. Old comrades in arms had been his saviour. He had fallen on hard times and the Captain had given him a chance where most employers would have shown him the door. He had never served under Treharne but he had heard about him. An outstanding officer apparently and not one to be fooled with. As he sipped his beer he started to despise himself again. The horses. They had taken everything, even his self-respect. Bert considered himself to be a man of honour, an honest man – until, that is, gambling had taken over his life. So far he had managed to avoid out-and-out thieving. Even so, he had allowed himself to be bought, he had sold his honour for a few lousy quid which had been lost on the track anyway. He had also let down the Captain. He took a long sip of beer, but guilt took the enjoyment away. There was that poor receptionist. She had been kicked out of her job because of his lies. How could he have done such a thing? It was over a year now since that nasty incident with the doctor's money. That bloody Sewell had found out about his weakness and had exploited it, the bastard. Bills had been mounting up and his bookie was getting impatient. Sewell, the sly sod, had kept him on for another few months until giving him the push – arriving a few minutes late on two occasions had been enough. Jesus, it wouldn't have been so bad if he had been discovered pissed on the job, that he could have understood. God knows he had helped himself to the optics behind one of the bars often enough. He had left gracefully, after all he was conditioned to punctuality and should have known better; in the past men's lives had depended on it. In spite of this brave acceptance Bert still felt guilty. He had lied and a young girl's reputation had been ruined. He remembered the girl. Always smiling, always polite. She didn't deserve to be a casualty of his gambling extremes. Her face had been bothering him for months, her innocence continued to trouble him. He had no right to mess up another person's life even if his own was a load of crap. He finished his pint and growled at the remaining froth. Things had gone on long enough. In his time he had been a courageous man, now it was time to resurrect some of his old self. It was time to fight back. Why should the booze and the racetrack have everything? Sewell could do nothing to him now, but he could do something to Sewell. He could also pull back some self-respect from the finishing line, or at least he could try. The Captain was the man he needed to talk to. One soldier to another. The Captain would understand.

Bert grabbed his empty glass, stood up and walked up to his friend. Decisions always required some alcoholic fortitude.

"Mornin' Jim. Need to tap you for a few quid till tomorrow. Throat's a bit dry."

"Bloody 'ell, Bert," his friend replied with a hint of annoyance in his voice, "that's the second time this week! You think I'm made of bloody money or what?"

"Oh stop moaning, will you? Come on now, twenty quid until tomorrow. You know you'll get the money." Jim knew he would have his money back as promised, even so his friend could be a bloody nuisance. He had only come in for a quiet pint, his missus was giving him a headache again, the nagging bitch. "Oh and by the way," Bert added, "like the 'aircut, barber's done a good dyeing job too . . . twat! An old sod with jet-black hair, you dull bugger!"

"Piss off, Bert! Here we are, you old bastard." Jim handed over twenty pounds. "Now fuck off and let me have some peace and quiet. That bitch of a missus of mine is off again. Never bloody stops I can tell you. Fucking woman should have been strangled at birth!"

"Ta, Jim, you're a real pal. See you tomorrow."

Bert ordered another pint with a whisky chaser and went back to his table. Now, how the hell was he going to pin down Treharne? The last he had heard the man had buggered off to Mid Wales or something.

Bert stood on a small platform and watched the arse end of the train disappear around another mountain. It had been one hell of a journey, slow and lonely. He dropped his bag to the ground and dug inside his coat. He found the silver hip flask and took a sip. Not too much, but enough to keep him going and enough to keep the October chill out of his bones. He remained standing and looked at his surroundings. A tiny village station, some dead flowers and isolation. As a professional drunk he was used to isolation, used to detachment. There were no fellow passengers anywhere to be seen. In fact he had been the only passenger on the train for most of the journey. He lit up a cigarette and took another swig from the hip flask. It couldn't really do any more harm. For a moment he wondered what the hell he was doing here. Instinctively his eyes looked for any dangling signs declaring the sale of alcoholic beverage. There weren't any. Not at the station anyway. Briefly he longed for the safety of a smoke-filled room lit up by shining optics and the hazy grins of other drinkers trying to bring some sense to their lives. It was all futile of course and he knew it, even so the booze gave him purpose, a reason to carry on. He reached into his trouser pocket and pulled out a piece of paper. Fragments of tobacco floated to the ground along with a beer-bottle top. Christ, he wondered, when was the last time his trousers had been washed? There was a time when he had been the most immaculate NCO in the regiment. He remembered standing proud and tall in his dress uniform and the women who adored, their eyes undressing him and creating their own depraved fantasies. He had obliged many of them too in the days when he had been clean, handsome and an RSM. He dropped the cigarette to the ground and allowed the alcohol therapy to prevail. He would find a pub somewhere if it killed him. He needed a bed for the night anyway, there were no more trains that day. He picked up his bag and passed through a creaky gate, the same gate that had announced Kristian's arrival in this forgotten part of Wales.

The Llewelyn Hotel with its dusty windows beckoned as Bert turned a corner. Captain Treharne lived not far from here he had been told. He still had friends at his previous place of work. He walked through the door, saw the bar with its tower of coins and decided that this would be an excellent place to spend the night. The Captain could hang on until the morning. He sat down on a bar stool and waited. Five minutes passed and still no one appeared. He saw the brass bell, assumed it was for service and gave it a shake, at the same time an untidy St Bernard lying in front of the log fire let rip a powerful fart, so powerful in fact that it would have shamed a furious thunderclap about to announce the arrival of a roof-bending typhoon. Bert jumped and nearly fell off his stool, instinctively wanting to dive for cover as the noise was more terrifying than any IRA sniper's bullet. The stench that followed was more lethal too, it even began to make his nose pop out!

"Jesus Christ!" he exclaimed when he had come to his senses. "Bugger me, dog, that was better than one of my best after a month on the piss!"

The following morning, having eaten a breakfast fit for a king Bert set off in search of the good Captain. Dai Twice had given him directions, so finding the Captain shouldn't be too much of a problem. Eventually he arrived at the farm-come-pub. He saw the Captain and a raven-haired woman talking in the yard. This must be the girl that everyone had been talking about at the Rose. No wonder, she was a real beauty. He walked up to them.

"Good God, Bert Powell! What are you doing here?" Kristian exclaimed.

"Er . . . 'ello Captain, 'ello . . . er . . . I'm sorry I don't know your name."

"Myfanwy . . . Bert."

"Myfanwy it is then." Bert stood in front of them looking awkward and shy.

Kristian had given up trying to make Bert Powell call him by his proper name a long time ago. The army did other odd things apart from fighting.

"What can I do for you, Bert?" Kristian asked. "Must be serious for you to turn up here? How the hell did you find me?" Myfanwy stood by and watched.

"A friend at the Rose – 'ope you don't mind. It is important though. Important to me anyway. I wanted a word, Captain, confidential-like." Myfanwy took the hint.

"Right," she said, "Come on inside, Bert. It's cold out here. I'll make us all a cup of tea . . ." As she looked at the man's eyes, she also noticed a slight tremble in his hand and voice. They were all familiar, she saw them everyday. "Perhaps something a little stronger on this cold morning, Bert? Brandy ok?"

"That will be fine, miss, very kind of you."

"Come on then. I'll get you a drink and leave you and Kristian alone. Oh, I don't like all this silly military stuff by the way. 'Captain' my backside!" Myfanwy led them to the sitting room, poured Bert a brandy and left the bottle next to his glass. She knew he wouldn't take advantage, he was too much of a pro.

"I'll bring you some tea in a minute, Kristian." Myfanwy disappeared leaving the two men alone.

"Now Bert, sit down and tell me what all this about. You're like a cat on a hot tin roof. What's up?"

When Bert had finished his confession Kristian said, "Well, thank you for telling me Bert and for coming to me. You haven't told anybody else, have you?"

"No. No one. I don't feel good about any of this, Captain, I really don't. It's been on my mind for a long time. I'm sorry, I really am. It's just that the bills were coming in faster than I could pay them and well . . . the bookies were giving me a hard time. You know what's it's like, Civvy Street. It's 'ard Captain, it's 'ard." Kristian looked at the ex soldier. He knew all about the destructive nature of a civilian life. He didn't judge. He didn't condemn.

"Yes, yes I know, Bert. The booze won't help though, believe me I know. Try and do something about it will you? And the gambling. You're a bloody mess, man."

"Yeah Captain. I know you're right but thing is it's all I've got left. All I 'ave."

"Well, you haven't lost everything Bert, have you? You're here. You haven't lost all your self-respect. Your honesty. Get a grip man, will you? You were a fine soldier, you know."

"I'll try," Bert replied as he downed a large gulp of brandy. Kristian knew it was hopeless. Bert was one of many the world over. Ex soldiers who had lost their mother and didn't know where to go. Kristian had found Myfanwy and Angharad, he'd been lucky. "Will there be any police involved Captain? I've never been in trouble with the law . . . well, only the odd bar room brawl anyway."

"No. Don't worry about that. No police. I'll deal with it my own way. One thing, Bert."

"What's that?"

"You mustn't tell anyone else about all this, is that clear?"

"Of course."

"No one, Bert. I mean it."

"Don't worry Captain. You can trust me."

"I damn well hope so, Bert, because if one word comes back to me I'll find you and you'll have a damn sight more than a bar room brawl to worry about, I can tell you. Don't let my peg leg fool you either."

"Oh I won't, Captain. I won't. Message received loud and clear Captain." Bert knew all about Captain Treharne and one thing you didn't do was mess 'im about. One pin or not.

"Good. Right, how did you get here? I didn't see any car."

"Train."

"Ok, well you come back to Swansea with me then. I'll just go and have a word with Myfanwy. I need to see to all this straightaway. Oh and Bert, thank you again for telling me." Kristian stood up and shook Bert's hand. They looked in each other's eyes and Bert realized that it had been a long time since he had seen the coldness in a combat officer's eyes. Particularly an SBS officer.

CHAPTER 39

Justin and Kristian were sitting in Justin's office in the Rose. There was no character in the room, no personality. It was a utilitarian wilderness, cold and functional, just the way Justin liked it. His desk was free of any clutter, there wasn't a pen or even a paper clip out of place.

"Justin . . ." Kristian said calmly, his voice was friendly, unassuming, "could you tell me exactly what happened over that business with Bethan Jones . . .? She was a receptionist here a while back."

Justin was sitting behind his desk. He looked at Kristian with a confused expression. "Bethan Jones? Er . . . let me think. Forgive me, but so many staff come and go, Kristian, as you well know. That's the hotel business for you."

"Not really, Justin, I'm not a great enthusiast where this game is concerned."

Justin continued to think and concentrate. "Bethan Jones," he said out loud, "now let me think . . . ah yes, it's coming back to me now. She was a receptionist here about a year ago. Maybe more. Good worker if I remember correctly. Now then . . . yes, it's all coming back to me. It was a sorry business. Caught with her hand in the till. Very embarrassing for all concerned. I had to dish out £500 myself to keep the matter under wraps as it were. Didn't want the reputation of the business damaged did we?"

"You were reimbursed eventually though, Justin, no doubt."

"Oh yes. There were no problems there."

"Good. I'm glad to hear it," Kristian replied.

"Look Kristian, what's all this about? It was a long time ago."

"I appreciate that but I met her father a few days ago. You know he's a local vicar. He's still very upset about it all, Paul was too at the time. The lad had a soft spot for her if I remember correctly. Was convinced of the girl's innocence. Totally out of character and so on."

"You seem to remember an awful lot, Kristian, for someone who was sowing his wild oats in Mid Wales at the time." Justin smiled, but a sharp knife was cutting his voice. He was on his guard. Kristian didn't react to the covert spite. He was far too calm and calculating.

"Yes I was, Justin. You're quite right. But things get back as you know. My mother and Griffith weren't too happy about it all either, and my mother does confide in me as I'm sure you'll appreciate."

"Oh quite so, Kristian, but why are you dragging all this up?"

"As I have already said, the girl's father still has doubts. Understandably so, I think. He wants me to look into things again. To make sure that his daughter wasn't wrongly accused, God forbid. So can you at least go over things for me again so that I can satisfy the man." Justin remained cool and unperturbed. He reiterated the story with just the right amount of sympathy and understanding. When he had finished Kristian put his hands on the desk and leaned forward slightly. He said quietly, "You are absolutely certain of all this, Justin, are you? I mean you investigated fully before reaching any conclusions?"

"Oh yes. Most definitely. Beyond reasonable doubt as they say. I can assure you that it wasn't easy sacking the girl. As I have already said she was a good worker. Had been with us for quite a few years. Never missed a day off sick and she had certainly never given cause for anyone to question her honesty. The whole business was really quite shocking. I was as surprised as everybody else, believe me."

"I don't." Kristian's voice hardened.

"I beg your pardon, Kristian?"

"You heard. I don't believe you. You're lying."

"What! How dare you! Are you suggesting I made all this up?"

"I'm not suggesting anything, Justin. I'm telling you. You're a lying bastard and that's all there is to it." Kristian's voice remained quiet but his words left no doubt. "You nigh on ruined a young girl's life all because of your pride. You couldn't bear to lose face, could you? You cheap little shit. The night porter found the £500 tucked at the back of the safe, didn't he? No one had stolen it, least of all Bethan Jones. Before you try and lie your way out of this, I've spoken with Bert Powell. You even managed to get him out of the way too. What kind of man are you?"

Justin remained calm too. His voice didn't even tremble. "A man who is looking after your best interests Kristian and that of your family, so I can do without your petty histrionics. Someone has to use some business acumen around here, someone has to make sure the business continues to grow and prosper and that someone sure as hell isn't you, or for that matter your sister. You're too busy playing Farmer Giles and Lottie is too busy trying to become the next Lord Chancellor. As for your mother and Griffith, right now they are somewhere in India no doubt gorging themselves on curry and chapattis!" Justin started to raise his voice, "God, you make me sick! You come into my office – my office, I stress, because in case you don't know I have power of attorney over your sister's shares in the company – and start playing the great moralist! Christ, so what if the stupid little slut got the boot. Your stepfather probably breathed a sigh of relief too, no doubt she was yet another of his conquests—"

That was as far as Kristian allowed Justin to go. He reached across the desk and grabbed Justin by the throat. "Now listen to me, you lying, conniving bastard! I've tried to keep this between the two of us. I don't want to upset my sister by letting on what a sly, contemptuous little worm you are." Kristian's grip tightened and Justin started to choke. "You ever try and pull a stroke like this again and I swear to God I will chew you up and spit you out. If you ever compromise my family's integrity or our reputation again, then pity help you. The same goes for Lottie. You ever hurt her then I will kill you and believe me I don't make idle threats." Justin was starting to go blue. "Do you hear me? Do you?" Kristian loosened his grip. "As for the power of attorney that can soon be changed – and don't you forget it!"

"Yes . . . yes . . . you madman . . . yes!" Justin just about managed to splutter. Kristian pushed him back in his chair.

"Good. I will be re-employing Bethan at the Cliffs. Paul will be a better boss, I think."

"You can't—!" Justin was about to object when Kristian grabbed him by the throat again.

"I can't what, Justin?" He gave one last squeeze, almost lifting Justin out of his chair, then threw him back down. "Don't ever, ever bother me again, you disgusting little turd. And consider yourself extremely fortunate that for the moment this little altercation will be kept between you and me. For my sister's sake and the family's. Luckily for you." With that Kristian walked out, leaving behind a man who would never rest until vengeance was his and his alone. His Lord would have nothing to do with it.

Later that day Justin drove to a car park in Caswell Bay. He needed some time to think. That business over Bethan Jones had been a close shave. As for his brother-in-law, well, he was an animal, no two ways about it. Justin rubbed his throat for a few moments, it still hurt. The bastard. Typical soldier. All brawn and no brain. Mind you, he had known one or two in less stressful times, they could be quite inventive when they wanted to be. At least the young squaddie variety could, especially if they were a bit hard up. He had never screwed one of the officer class though, more's the pity perhaps. He looked out of the car windscreen and could just make out the red-tiled roof of his home. Lottie's money had bought it, in fact his whole position relied on the generosity of his wife. He hated being the underdog, loathed it, but it would have to do for now. He would soon have his independence, he just had to be patient. Thank God that fool of a brother had kept his mouth shut. Things could have been awkward. If their positions had been reversed he would have blown the whistle without a second thought, but then sibling love, loyalty, was beyond him. Most things where love was concerned were beyond him, in fact. He felt for Lottie, even cared for her a little, but that was about it. Anything more would have left him vulnerable, open to attack and that wouldn't do at all. As long as Lottie believed in his love, that was all that mattered. He stretched his neck up to the rear-view mirror. No marks, at least nothing that couldn't be explained by an overtight shirt collar. Kristian had known what he was doing. Somehow he had managed to inflict agony without any obvious signs of the assault being left behind. The man was a trained killer, so no doubt he was an expert in the art of inflicting pain. Justin sat back in the car seat and shrugged. The business with Kristian had been unfortunate but that was all. He would get over it. At least his overall plan hadn't been jeopardized. He still ran the Rose and he was still in a position to push for some new hotels. He was sure he could convince the others to follow his lead. He would invest Lottie's money wisely, the returns would be his and so would his independence. His business empire would grow and in time he would own the Treharnes instead of the other way around. Then they could all rot in hell. For a moment his lips turned into a bitter smile while anger made him clench his fists. For all his calmness he knew that Kristian could not be allowed to treat him like a dog. The man needed taming, even if he was never fully aware of it, and Justin Sewell had just the whip. Charlotte Treharne. The idiot was so besotted with him that he could do what he liked to her, up and coming Lord Chancellor or not.

Apart from Kristian there was the whole Treharne clan. The lot of them were in desperate need of being brought to book.

Justin smiled at the mirror and yet his eyes contained only poison . . . in time, in time. He had already waited for most of his life, a few more years wouldn't make any difference.

Justin was sitting in the conservatory when Charlotte arrived home. Moonlight shone through the glass ceiling but was unable to penetrate the darkness in Justin's mind. Huge, exotic plants competed with the shadows and tried to bring some comfort to the room. There was a coldness in the room, a rawness that went beyond the stark frost that was beginning to ride the lawns outside. Charlotte's arrival had already been announced by the crackling gravel on the forecourt. For a moment he wondered at her honesty, her openness. She couldn't even hide her arrival home. The woman was so transparent, there was never anything unknown about her. Although it was late he knew that she couldn't embark upon some torrid affair if she tried. Deceit just didn't enter her world of right and wrong. It was no wonder that she was rapidly becoming one of the most able defence barristers in her field. He sighed. She was just like all the other Treharnes, a wilder streak than most of them perhaps, but even that was being cowed by her ambitions to excel in her chosen profession. Integrity, substance and an almost obsessive desire to always do what was right came first in their lexicon of human propriety. For Justin these noble principles were as nauseating as unconditional love, whatever the hell that was anyway. Charlotte had been so easy to seduce, so easy to fool. The naivety of the Treharnes would be their downfall, their nemesis. Justin sneered at the moonlight – fools, the lot of them. He heard the front door open and close, forced a smile upon his lips and went to meet his beautiful, intelligent young wife. Charlotte was standing in the hallway, black suit, black coat and crimson hat. As usual the hat brought an air of mischief into the house. Some of the old Lottie still struggled to keep up.

"Hello, darling," Justin said as he put his arms around her and kissed her on the cheek. Charlotte returned his kiss.

"What a lovely surprise! I thought you were going to stay overnight at the Rose, you know to make sure the night staff aren't up to any skulduggery. Sitting in the dark again, were you? Don't tell me. You were thinking. Thinking about me I hope!"

"What else, Lottie? Now come on, take your coat off and relax. I'll get you a glass of wine and you can tell me about all the villains that you've managed to get off the hook today while I finish off the supper."

"Ooh, supper too! I am being spoilt! Pour the wine then while I go and take a shower and slip into something more comfortable." Her smile told Justin all he needed to know. Advocacy sometimes had a strange effect on his wife's libido, something to do with the adrenalin flow apparently.

"Food first I think, Lottie. Now go on and don't have too many filthy thoughts while you're in the shower – well not too filthy anyway!"

"God, do you know, Justin, I still get horny just looking at you! Terrible isn't it? Control yourself, Charlotte Sewell! Control yourself!" With that she kissed him again and ran up the stairs.

Justin watched her perfect body leap up the stairs. The tight black skirt accentuated the roundness of her buttocks as they tempted and flaunted. For the briefest of moments he thought that in another time, another place he might truly have loved. It was not to be.

Later that night Charlotte undressed slowly. Justin was standing by the four-poster bed, naked and erect. He absorbed her full, tight breasts. The nipples that were already taught and groaning for attention. Her body flowed and lifted. Tempted and almost threatened desire. Her hips and buttocks lifted in harmony as she removed her knickers and stood before him naked.

"God, I've been thinking about sex all day, darling." Charlotte said as she touched her lips with one of her delicate fingers. She stood in front of him and fondled. "God, you're so hard. So sexy," she whispered as she kissed him. They remained standing for a while as their tongues searched and caressed. When some minutes had passed, Charlotte moved her lips from Justin's and lightly bit his neck, his ears. She ran her tongue across his shoulders as she licked and nibbled. Her teeth gently stroked his nipples while her fingers continued to play. Up and down. Justin started to moan as she teased and touched. She sank to her knees and whispered, "You're so big. So strong. I love you. God, how I love you." As she used her tongue and throat Justin reached down and played with her nipples. He squeezed and pinched. Charlotte moaned and urged him on. "I can't wait any longer darling, I really can't." She stood up, still stroking him. "Now, please now," she begged. "From behind, from behind." Justin lay her on the bed, face down. He entered her slowly, deliberately. He played with her while his fingers reached under her and touched. Moved upwards and downwards. Charlotte started to lose herself. "Harder my darling! Please harder! Don't stop! Please don't stop!" Justin did as he was told. He pushed with greater speed. His thrusts became more rapid, more brutal. Charlotte started to grip his buttocks, her nails digging and pulling. "Faster! Faster! Don't stop! Don't stop! – Oh God don't stop!" He stopped for a moment. Paused. Moonlight stretched their bodies into one another. He pushed himself up on his elbows as an uncontrollable urge to hurt and inflict pain overtook his sexual ardour. Suddenly the day's events with Kristian, the years of rage and mental agony took over. Possessed. He looked down at the white innocence beneath him and wanted to destroy. He clenched his teeth as years of cruelty and rejection forced his mind to bleed and lash out. He withdrew from Charlotte and tore into her other orifice. There was no feeling now, no desire. Hurt was the only word flying through his mind.

"Ahhhh! – God . . .! What are you . . . ahhhhh . . . no Justin . . .! No!" Charlotte screamed as she tried to move her body away from him. It was hopeless, Justin was far too strong.

He ripped into her again, there was no mercy. He was tearing her apart. "Jesus . . . ahhhh . . .! Oh Christ Justin! . . . Stop . . . stop . . .! Please stop . . .! Ahhhh . . . you're hurting me . . . oh . . . oh . . . please!" She tried to reach up and pull his hair but his hands quickly restrained her, her wrists were roughly pinned to the mattress. She was powerless to stop the abuse. "You've always liked it rough Lottie . . . haven't you!" Justin snarled as he continued to invade her body. "Haven't you Lottie . . . Answer me! Haven't you! Rough and hard, that's what you like . . . like most women! You're all sluts, all whores!" He didn't stop. Even Charlotte's whimpers went unnoticed by his desire to hurt, to exact a terrible revenge. Eventually he stopped. He finally heard the sobs of Charlotte, not that this meant anything. He had heard the sobs of young boys many times and they hadn't meant anything either. He lay on his back and stroked Charlotte's buttocks with his fingers as he said, "Goodnight, Lottie. I enjoyed that."

Sunlight tried to touch and heal Charlotte as she lay on top of the bed, naked and alone. She was curled up, her two hands resting on her groin. Although her eyes were closed she wasn't sleeping. That would have been too much of a release. Justin had gone to work without saying a word, he had left her in bed devastated by confusion and horror. 'What had happened?' she kept asking herself over and over again. 'How had it happened? Had she made him do it? Had she urged him on?' She opened her eyes and felt the pain – the physical and mental pain, the tearing of her body, her mind. She remembered an incident in the Crown Court only the day before. An application to imprison a husband had been made to the judge. The man had breached a non-molestation order, part of an injunction that had banned him from going anywhere near a three-mile radius of the former matrimonial home. The man had ignored the order. His wife had stood in the dock. A small woman. Her jaw had been wired together, some of her teeth were missing and one of her eyes was closed from bruising. The judge had asked her if she wanted her husband, her attacker, to be sent to prison. Through the agony of her injuries she had managed to say an unequivocal 'No'. Charlotte had looked on in disbelief. Other counsel had looked, had sighed in dismay. They had seen it all before a hundred times. The judge could only do so much. There was no law against love. Now as Charlotte lay in her own violence, her own degradation, she began to understand the woman. She began to understand why.

She left the bed and went to the shower. Perhaps she could wash away the illusion. Perhaps she had encouraged Justin after all. He couldn't have meant to hurt her, could he? He loved her far too much. Perhaps he just got carried away? No, he couldn't have meant it. Justin was always so calm, so in control. She had never been given even the remotest reason to fear any violence or loss of control. For a split second she remembered that look in his eyes when they had been staying in her mother's London house. A look that she had not encountered since. It must have been an aberration, a moment of silly anger, that was all.

As the hot water soothed her aching muscles Charlotte convinced herself that their love was everything and that things had just got out of hand. She would speak to Justin later and tell him that he must never treat her body like that again. She had said "No!" after all, had screamed "No!" He had obviously placed his own sexual interpretation on her objections, albeit that it was the wrong one. As she soaped her body and came to terms with what had happened her lawyer's mind didn't quite give in. Neither did her inherent strength. Both twitched quietly in her psyche but refused to do any more, she wouldn't let them. Her love for Justin was far more potent than the law or her, now subdued, strength.

Charlotte spent the rest of the day trying to understand what had happened the night before. Her body still ached and her mind still fought. Conclusions clashed with doubts and both resisted the unthinkable. Thank God she had not been booked in for any court appearances, her clients would have been badly let down. She spent the day trying to research the case law on a point of evidence for a case that she was soon about to try or at least a case on which she was to be the junior. The law reports refused to respond to her uncommitted fingers, and in the end she decided to nip out to Joe's Ice Cream Parlour for an ice cream. A Knickerbocker Glory in fact. As she walked to the Parlour she was grateful for the sea air that attempted to clear her mind. She breathed in as deeply as possible in an attempt to help the air along its way. Questions and answers still tried to flatten her but she wouldn't give in. Love. Love with all its impossible rules and regulations. It was worse than the bloody law. She found a seat in a quiet corner of the Parlour, an ice-cream emporium renowned throughout Swansea for the finest Italian ice cream in the world. It was 3.30 on a weekday afternoon, there were no school holidays so she was actually able to order her fruity excess without having to queue or be pushed by exasperated parents. The creamy creation eventually arrived and Charlotte gorged. She dug a long spoon into a man-made mountain of tinned fruit, ice cream made for the Gods and wafers that cracked and ranted at the wanton destruction of their artistic splendour. It didn't take her long to destroy the moment of obscene decadence, a gentle belch into a paper napkin finished off her self-abuse as she sat back and started to feel decidedly better. Damn, the Knickerbocker was better than sex in some ways – and not so bloody messy! For the first time that day she managed to smile at her own irony. Oh Justin, she thought, why do you have to be such a complicated bastard? Why do you have hide who you really are? Why is your love so hard? Once again the answers flew out of the Parlour and danced with the winds that blew grains of sand around on the scruffy beaches that taunted Swansea Bay.

"I honestly thought you were liking it, Lottie . . . I'm so sorry. I really am. I had no idea. You know what you're like for experimenting. I mean, we have tried a few pretty unusual things, haven't we?"

"That's not the point, Justin. If we weren't husband and wife what you did to me was rape, rape of the most degrading kind. I told you to stop, begged even and you still carried on." So far Charlotte's voice had been measured. Balanced. Suddenly the day's pain started to erupt. "You were like some bloody animal for God's sake! What the hell had got into you? Why for fuck's sake? Why?" She was shouting now, her control demolished by the pain of her body. "Why, Justin? Aren't I good enough in bed for you? Don't I satisfy you enough? Is it me?" Tears started to stream down her eyes, her body shook with the violence of the night before and her own hurt.

They were sitting down in their drawing room. Charlotte had determined to confront her husband and at least try to understand. She had also determined to keep things calm, although that had become impossible. She ached far too much. Her Treharne temper was starting to overwhelm. It didn't often explode, but when it did look out.

"Look, Lottie . . ." Justin said quietly, he knew the signs and knew when to placate, ". . . you know I would never do anything to hurt you. I love you for heaven's sake. I suppose I just didn't think. I got carried away with the moment. You're so sexy you know, you're enough to drive any man insane. I didn't really know what I was doing . . . I really didn't. I am sorry. So very sorry. You must believe me. I promise you it won't happen again. Ever." Charlotte looked at her husband. The contrition in his green eyes struck, and challenged as it pleaded. The voice had been humble, touching even. His sincerity swept all before it. How could she resist or disbelieve. How could she not love?

"Right, that's all very well, Justin, but it must never happen again!" her voice was still boiling, still loud. "Never! Do you hear me! When I say 'No' I mean 'No'. Understand?" She added more quietly, "You hurt me, Justin, I mean really hurt me. You degraded me and treated me like some Soho tart. If you ever do anything like that to me again then it's over. Over Justin, and I damn well mean it!" Her voice had now turned into court-room mode, it was more deadly, there was no room for negotiation, no pleading. Justin had heard the voice many times and knew when to keep quiet, his wife was so easy to manipulate. That was love for you, the nectar of fools and Lottie's cup was full to the brim. Justin allowed the silence between them to confirm his wife's words. Now was not the time for mitigation or empty words of denial. He looked into Charlotte's eyes and went over to her. He took her hand and kissed it.

"I didn't realize, my darling. I really didn't realize. Please forgive me. How could I hurt the most precious thing in life to me? I love you too much, I really do. I am so very sorry. I can't say anymore. There are no excuses I know that and I am not trying to make any. My behaviour last night was unforgivable, I know. It won't happen again . . . I promise . . . Now can we put this behind us, please? We love each other far too much, Lottie. Let's not spoil it." He kissed her gently on the lips. Charlotte looked into his eyes, her heart floundered as it always did, her anger softened as it always did. Her fear turned into classic female neuroses as it always did. She took his hand, felt the skin she adored and said, "Never again, Justin. Never again." She kissed him and knew that everything had been a huge mistake and that their love would continue to grow and deepen.

CHAPTER 40

"It's good to have you back, Bethan," Paul beamed. "It really is." They were standing in old William Treharne's study. He reluctantly handed Bethan a bouquet of flowers, he had never bought a girl flowers before. Going into the florists alone had demanded an exercise of will. He hadn't known what to buy or what to do. The young girl behind the counter hadn't helped either. He could see that she had noticed the colour of his face, his stuttering inadequacy. She had smiled and bloomed along with the rest of the floral displays in the shop. "Are they for a girlfriend?" she had asked. "Well . . . er . . . no, not really," he had replied. "A girl though, a friend . . . I think." The shop assistant's eyes had twinkled at him, "How lovely, what a lucky 'friend' she is! I have just the thing." She had gone off into a back room and returned ten minutes later with a floral work of art. Lilies, carnations, freesias, roses, chrysanthemums and smatterings of gypsophila had been crafted into a gift of beauty, a gift fit for Bethan.

"Oh, Paul . . . I've never been given flowers before!" Bethan enthused, "they're beautiful!" She put the bouquet up to her nose and sniffed in a way that only a young woman can. At that moment she was the only girl in the world. The only human being that mattered. Paul looked on and tried to hide his relief. The girl in the shop had known what she was doing after all.

"And what's this? A card too!" Bethan opened the small envelope and removed the card. It read 'Welcome back, Bethan. From Paul.' There were no crosses next to his name but Bethan knew they were on his lips. She sniffed at the flowers again and looked at Paul. "Thank you, Paul. Thank you so much." She stood on tip toe and kissed him. She held his lips for a few moments, their eyes met and both young people knew that this small kiss would never be forgotten. Paul at last took the initiative and held Bethan's hand, "Come on, let's go for a walk. It's a bit cold but never mind. Actually, this time of year is great for sketching. There's something more beautiful about nature when she's wild and undressed. I still go out on the cliffs to sketch when ever I get the chance . . . it hasn't been the same without you though, Bethan." They looked into each other's eyes again. The moment held them and finally finished off their 'friendship'.

As they walked along a shoreline that was grey with misery and cold Paul said, "You know Bethan, I always believed you. I never doubted you. I tried asking questions after you left but no one knew anything. I even spoke with Bert Powell but he was adamant. Funny how the money turned up after all this time. Had gone through some crack in the safe or something. Good job Justin had decided to have it repaired, had been like that for years apparently. In fact he insisted that you come and work at the Cliffs instead of the Rose. Perhaps he fancies himself as a bit of a matchmaker or something . . . no, on second thoughts I can't quite see that. Doesn't seem the romantic type."

"You're right there, Paul. He was a pig to me you know. Wouldn't even listen to anything I had to say about it all. I was so hurt. And my father wasn't too happy either. In the end I had to tell him the truth. The bugger's got God on his side after all!" They both laughed as they continued to hold hands and experience the first twitches of stomach-wrenching magic that love can bring. They were young and helpless. All that mattered were the fingers that intertwined and touched and the closeness of each other. The rawness and terror that flashed from cliff face to cliff face, the bitter cold that swarmed across the sea and sand, left them alone. For a good while they walked without words, they were two young people content with a future and content with themselves. They needed nothing but each others' hearts. Paul was the first to break their silence.

"I have missed you you know, Bethan."

"Same for me." Her grip tightened around his hand. "I've missed you too . . . That hotel in town wasn't the same either. Oh, I'm sorry Paul I don't mean to sound ungrateful. I know you got me in there and thank you for that, but it wasn't the same. Things move more slowly out here and there aren't so many townies. Some of them can be rough buggers you know. I always felt a bit frightened if I had to go home after a late shift and the buses are awful from town to the Gower. Quite often I stayed with one of the other girls rather than try and brave the late-night buses. Swansea on a Friday or Saturday night is terrible. Everyone's drunk and fighting."

"Well, never mind, you're back home now. Home for good, I hope."

"I hope so too, Paul . . . home with you."

CHAPTER 41

A month later the Treharnes and the Sewells were sitting down in the Treharne study. "It's the only half decent hotel in town and within spitting distance of the station. It's been allowed to go to hell because the owner has lost his marbles and the manager has been able to do what he likes. There's been no strong management there for years. The whole place needs total refurbishment and a great deal of money, but nevertheless we would be insane not to buy it and get it back on its feet. It's a goldmine, believe me." Justin looked around the room. Lottie already knew about this venture and his enthusiasm, she was behind him. Paul and Kristian sat in their chairs absorbing the paperwork in front of them. Lise and Griffith had also been called in for the meeting as a matter of courtesy. And that's all it was as far as Justin was concerned, courtesy.

"The company would be extremely foolish to let this opportunity pass it by," Justin persisted. "We should expand, the company is cash rich and our potential investment funds are sitting idle doing nothing. Now is the time."

"Why, Justin? Why must we 'expand'?" He knew it. Bloody Lise Treharne. He hadn't wanted that damn woman anywhere near this meeting but Lottie had been adamant. Lise was the only real threat to his ambitions. She had more business acumen than the rest of them put together. She was a shrewd bitch whether he liked it or not.

"As I have just said, Lise, each year the company is building up a substantial cash surplus. There are also the tax implications. At present we have two extremely successful hotels, however they serve a different market from the one we could expect from an establishment in the town centre. We deal mainly with patrons who have time on their hands, who want to sit back, enjoy the sea air and be pampered. Holiday-makers if you like. A town centre hotel will provide top-class amenities for business executives and their corporations. We can provide excellent conference facilities for example. The property I have in mind here is big enough. It will manage 150 rooms if my plans are approved. There will be no other hotel like it in this part of the world. The stock market is booming, investment is bullish. Now is the time, Lise. Now is the time."

"Well, I can see you have done your homework but I'm still not convinced, Justin. I'll ask you again, why must we expand? The family does very nicely out of the present situation. We may well be building up high amounts of capital, but so what? That's money in the bank, isn't it? Better than owing the banks surely? They come to us cap in hand, not the other way around. Your plans look fine on paper but the fact is that the company will need to borrow. Borrowing means providing security. That security will be the Cliffs and the Rose. If the economy slips and inflation rockets, interest rates will rocket with them. We could lose everything."

"The company could lose everything, Lise." Justin was quick to remind Lise that she was no longer the boss. For the first time Lise felt a moment of disquiet where her son-in-law was concerned.

"The company then, Justin. Still, whilst I appreciate that neither Griffith nor I have any executive powers here we are free to voice our opinions and my considered opinion is that this proposed expansion is both unwise and ill-conceived. I read the *Financial Times* too, Justin, and in my view our markets have been opened up far too quickly. I believe we are witnessing an investment bubble. It cannot go on. I trust my instincts, Justin, and with the greatest of respect I have been in business a little longer than yourself – indeed, were it not for me your plans wouldn't even be on William's desk in the first place. No, I must advise all shareholders to desist. Now is not the time." Lise stood up, she had said all she needed to say and the expression on her face left no one in any doubt as to her decision. She was still the boss, non-executive or not. "Come on, Griffith, let's go and have some tea, I believe Balzac has something special for us." Griffith did as he was told. It wouldn't be the same however when it came to the amount of cake he ate. His loyalty only went so far.

As the study door closed Justin seethed. He knew he couldn't beat Lise. Not where Paul and that bastard of a son of hers were concerned. Kristian broke the silence, "Well, sorry about this, Justin, but I go with the old girl. Always had a good head for business has Ma. Me now, I'm bloody hopeless. Anyway good to see you all but I have to be off. Cows to milk!"

"Pardon?" Lottie said.

"You heard, Bigjugs, cows to milk."

"Really, I have a feeling that it won't be cows udders you'll be milking somehow."

"Now, now Bigjugs. Don't be prurient." Kristian bent down and gave his sister a kiss. "Don't forget you're coming up to the farm next week. We'll be expecting you and Justin and Bethan too, Paul."

"We'll be there."

"Good. Well, I'm off. See you."

As Kristian said his goodbyes and closed the study door Justin continued to rage. He didn't need to ask Paul what he thought. The moron would follow the pack. He always did. He kept his anger and frustration to himself. He was an expert at doing this after all. Instead he stood up and faced his wife. "Ah well, Lottie it was worth a try. Maybe next year, ay?" he smiled. Lottie took his hand, "Don't be too disappointed, Justin. Mum did have a point you must admit. I was backing you anyway. As you say, maybe next year." She kissed him on the cheek. "Come on let's go home, it's getting late and I've got a big case on tomorrow." Justin took his wife's hand, no hard feelings and no bitter disappointment. Besides, he had a back-up plan.

PART IV

March 1986

CHAPTER 42

Philip Rose sat in the meeting room and begged for the silence to never end. His mind raged with uncertainty. For the briefest of moments one certainty did manage to break through his turmoil. God was not about to make him speak though, His spirit had deserted him and rightly so. Philip Rose no longer deserved God's grace or his charity. His eyes looked at the other Quakers. They were peaceful and content with their silence, their religion. He thought of all the charities he was a director of – Barnardo's, to name but one. Little, helpless children. Deprived and lost. His own children, secure and happy. His wife, a lovely undemanding woman. A woman who had never stopped loving him. What was he to do? What could he do? A secret party in London over a year ago. Young boys and a chance meeting with a young fellow from Swansea. Nothing had happened between them. Both men had been there for other attractions, younger attractions. Rose cursed himself, his uncontrollable desires. His secret insanity and hidden dreams. That afternoon the young man from Swansea had entered his life again. Justin Sewell had turned up at the bank and requested a huge loan. Security was provided but nowhere near enough to satisfy Head Office. Rose had been unable to refuse, Sewell had made the consequences of any such refusal quite clear. The bank manager, his charitable works, his respectability, his reputation and his family were all damned. Philip Rose sat still and knew that there was no way out. Sewell's evil green eyes contained no mercy, no doubt. If he didn't comply details of the London party would be sent to the *News of the World*. Sewell had gambled on his own exposure being secondary. He had been right.

Later that same day Charlotte and Justin were each sipping a glass of wine in their sitting room. This, like the rest of the house, was all Charlotte. There was nothing silly about the décor and furnishings, but even so any onlooker would have had no trouble recognizing that a woman's hand had been at work. Colours and furniture were restrained, modern and direct. None of the rooms screamed or shouted for attention. Everything was subtle and intelligent, warm and friendly. There was no chaos, no clutter. Every room enjoyed space, air and sunlight. Comfort and well-being mingled with the determination of modern art, straight lines and subdued strength. The house defined its real owner, Charlotte Treharne.

Charlotte was the first to speak, "You might have consulted me, Justin."

"Why? You gave me a power of attorney over your shares and all I have done is exercise that power. Everything is perfectly legal and above board."

"You've signed the loan agreements then?"

"I have."

"Using my shares—"

"Our shares, Lottie," Justin interrupted, "remember we are husband and wife as you keep reminding me. Community of property and so on."

"Using 'our' shares then as security."

"Yes. Oh and the house."

"What!"

"You heard. The house had to be put up as well. Buying hotels is an expensive business even if they are run down." Justin was not in the mood for his wife's questioning. In fact he wasn't in the mood for her at all.

"I didn't sign anything!" Charlotte protested.

"No, sorry about that. I had to forge your signature, I'm afraid. I knew you wouldn't mind. To use one of your quaint legal expressions, 'time was of the essence' as it were.

"Are you serious?"

"Very." Justin didn't even raise an eyebrow. He was used to Lottie's outbursts. She would simmer down in a few minutes. He would just have to humour her for a while.

"You forged my signature! Sign away my shares without even consulting me! And sit there as if nothing as happened. You . . . you arrogant bastard! Who the hell do you think you are? I thought you had given up on that hotel in town. Had seen some sense!"

"Don't get so worked up, Lottie. None of your worldly goods are at risk so stop being so neurotic, will you? I have every confidence that our investment will be trebled within five years, so it's not going to be a problem."

"Dear God, Justin. I'll give you that, you've got some nerve." Justin stood up and filled Charlottes glass up with more wine. It usually did the trick. Not this time. Something inside Charlotte collapsed. The breakdown was sudden and came without warning. Her will overwhelmed, her love snapped. Before Justin had reached for the bottle she stood up and slapped him hard across the face. The force sent him back a step or two. For a moment there was total silence. His green eyes seemed to change colour as murder and hatred tore into Charlotte and ripped her to pieces. She had seen that look before, only this time there was a terrible difference as she saw a madness erupt. A dark madness. Before she could move, before she had time for any fear he hit her. The impact sent her flying back into the chair. He hit her again. And again.

"You bitch!" Justin screamed. "You Treharne bitch!" he screamed again as he dragged her up from the chair and punched her hard in the stomach. She fell back in the chair, winded and struggling for breath. Justin stood before her, his face had changed. It wasn't the face she had come to love. It was the face of a man she had never seen or known. An ugly man, a brutal creation thrown together by some unholy Trinity. "Don't you ever hit me again, you Treharne slut!" he continued to scream. "Not ever! Do you hear me? You ever hit me again and

I'll kill you! Understand? . . . Understand?" He turned around and walked out of the sitting room, slamming the door with such violence that the whole house seemed to shake.

After a few minutes the shock of what had happened started to wear off as her breath gradually returned to normal. Charlotte stayed where she was. Fear kept her in the chair. She thought she had heard Justin's car drive off but she couldn't be sure. Her mind was confused, her thinking chaotic. Her fingers touched her lips. Blood. She had never tasted her own blood before. One of her front teeth had also been loosened. Her stomach turned as nausea attacked and her love rebelled. This time she knew she had done nothing wrong. This time there was no doubt.

Later that night Philip Rose sat in his study at home and read for the umpteenth time the paperwork in front of him. Sewell's paperwork. All that was left for the loan to go through was his own signature. He had made sure that everything was in order for Head Office. He had exaggerated and lied. He stopped reading and looked around the familiar room. He placed his fountain pen back down on the desk without signing. He had made up his mind. Instead he took some writing paper out of a drawer along with a large brown envelope. For the next hour he wrote. When he had finished writing he placed the letter together with the papers on his desk in the envelope and stood up. There was no rush to catch the post. The letter with its enclosures would go early the following morning. He left the front door open and walked to the post box. A few minutes later he returned. No one had noticed his absence, it was late. His dear wife would already be fast asleep as would his two young children. The house was quiet, nothing moved, nothing ticked or scratched. It was an old house with old noises but tonight it had decided to go to sleep along with everyone else. The bank manager walked up the familiar stairs. He kissed both his children goodnight. They didn't feel his lips but they knew he was there. He was their father. He walked into his own bedroom and looked at his wife. Her face hadn't aged and her heart still loved as did his. He sat on a chair and continued to look at her. His mind ignored the truth and delight of memory. The past was to be his epitaph, his only hope. The future called but he was unable to greet it. He saw himself in his wife's closed eyelids, the peace and the unknown. His heart broke with remorse and love. There was nothing else it could do. Instead of undressing he went back downstairs and into the garage. A few minutes later with a rope tied around his neck, he kicked away the chair he was standing on and died of unbearable shame.

He had left no suicide note on his desk.

CHAPTER 43

Two days later Lise and Griffith were sitting down in their apartment at the Cliffs. They were having breakfast, Lise eating her usual piece of toast, slightly burnt and Griffith tucking into his bacon and eggs. Well, one egg which had been poached and two slices of grilled bacon. There wasn't a drop of fat anywhere near his plate, neither was there a dollop of butter anywhere near his toast. Low-fat spread was the order of the day and he had given up trying to corrupt Balzac, Lise's might was greater than his where the staff were concerned. When they had finished eating Lise began her ritual of reading the *Financial Times* word for word while Griffith contented himself with the fascistic bile of the *Daily Mail*. Both were quite happy in their own news-bound worlds when a knock at the door announced the arrival of their post. As usual Griffith went to the door to collect the mail from one of the staff, God forbid that Lise would get off her arse while embroiled with the scrupulous overseeing of their mutual fortunes. He put the correspondence on the breakfast table, sat back down and continued to annoy himself with the 'Quick' crossword. His wife was adept at crossword puzzles, particularly *The Times* but he never asked her for help and by God, even these quickies needed a helping hand now and again. Griffith would hold on to his chauvinistic pride to the end, and to hell with all feminists! Men ruled the world and that was that. Lise humoured him.

At last Lise put down the pink pages of the *Financial Times*. There was a look of concern on her face. Judging by the fact that there were still a few pages of the newspaper to go Griffith knew instantly that something was up. His wife always finished her morning ritual.

"Lottie was supposed to have come with me to Cardiff yesterday to do some shopping. She rang me to say she wasn't well. Cold or something. She didn't sound too well on the telephone I must admit. Even so—"

"Even so what, Lise? I know that expression of yours, something is worrying you."

"Oh I don't know. I offered to go around to the house to see her, but she was adamant that I stay away. She didn't want me catching any unpleasant bugs."

"Seems perfectly reasonable to me. Very reasonable in fact. You catch something, it usually means that I'm next in line."

"Yes, I agree. But Lottie seemed almost worried that I should call there. Her voice seemed strained. I can't describe it but I know my daughter. Something is wrong. She always was a hopeless liar. She was hiding something, I'm sure of it. She just didn't sound her usual self, cold or no cold." Griffith was used to Lise's constant concerns where her children were concerned and this occasion was no different. She was always fussing about something or other.

"Lise, my darling, you worry too much. Lottie is a big girl now. I have no doubt that if something serious was wrong you would be the first to know. Now stop worrying and finish reading your paper. Give Lottie a ring later to check that she's all right."

"Yes. Yes, maybe you're right, Griffith. I know I do tend to be over-protective of the children."

"Adults, Lise. Adults."

"Oh all right – adults then. I know they're both grown up now with their own lives to lead, but I'm still their mother and I'll fuss if I want to, Mr Griffith Treharne."

"Please yourself, Lise. Now stop your wittering and try to work out how you are going to take over ICI."

"Very funny."

"Yes, I thought so too."

Lise eventually finished her newspaper and began working her way through the mail. Griffith was sitting down on one of the settees still struggling with his 'Quickie' crossword. She came to a large brown envelope and immediately noticed the hand-written address. It wasn't a hand that she recognized. She opened the envelope with her silver letter-opener and read. For the third time in her life Lise's world disintegrated.

Griffith was used to Lise moving around. He was used to her sound. Suddenly an unusual silence stopped him reading. He looked up from his book. Lise was still sitting at the breakfast table. Her hands were resting on top of a bundle of papers. She was still. So still.

"Lise? What's the matter?" Griffith went to her immediately. Something had happened. The mail. Bad news. Lise's face had drained of any colour. She looked at Griffith, her eyes implored, begged. She started to speak but no words came from her tongue. She coughed and seemed to tighten her body as she searched for strength.

"Griffth, do you remember that article in the *Evening Post* last night? The bank manager who had committed suicide. Philip Rose. We had met him a few times. He often came to the Cliffs with his wife and children."

"Yes. I remember. Sad business. Awful for the family. Two young children too. Why?"

"You had better read these." Lise handed Griffith the letter and all the documents.

He sat down and read. "Oh, dear God! Dear God . . .! I . . . what . . .? Jesus Christ!"

"Justin had also tried to mortgage the Rose as well as Ragged Cliffs, Griffith. He forged the signatures of both Kristian and Paul."

"Yes . . . I can see. The bastard! The total bastard! And a queer at that! Christ, I'll kill him! I'll kill the bastard! Jesus Christ, Lise, he tried to blackmail that poor bugger Rose. The man hung himself. Justin killed the poor sod! He may have liked men, but so what? No one deserves to die the way he did!"

"I know, Griffith. I know," Lise said quietly. She was holding on with all her strength. All her fortitude. She wanted to scream. To shout. She too wanted to hurt and destroy. "Calm down now, Griffith, will you? We must stay calm. We must. We have a crisis and it must be dealt with." Suddenly Lottie entered her mind. Lottie. Her only daughter. Her whole body went cold and her hands started to shake. "Oh my God Griffith, Lottie! She's in that house alone. I told you there was something wrong. She must know about some of this. Not all perhaps, oh God I hope not all! For her sake not all. Oh dear God what are we going to do, Griffith? What are we going to do? We can't stay here. We must go to Charlotte, now! We must. I knew something was wrong, I knew it. Come on Griffith! Get the car out. Quickly! We mustn't waste a second. God knows what he's done to the girl!" Before they reached the door Lise suddenly pulled Griffith back by his arm, "Wait, wait Griffith. I must call Kristian." Griffith looked into Lise's eyes and for the second time in his life he saw the dark blue pupils turn into tiny shards of ice. Her family had been hurt. Her love had been damaged.

"Is that wise, Lise?" he asked, already knowing the answer.

"We need him, Griffith . . . Now go and get the car, I'll meet you in the forecourt."

Lise found Charlotte curled up in bed. She had used her own key to open the front door, determined to discover exactly what was wrong. On this occasion good manners were ignored as was her daughter's right to privacy. Someone was trying to harm the people she loved, there were no rights, only her own. Justin was nowhere to be seen, he was probably at the Rose unaware that his nefarious schemes were no longer secret. Lise hadn't thought about the man or what to do about him. Right now all that mattered was her daughter. Lise had left Griffith downstairs, her instincts had told her that he was best kept out of the way until she had spoken with her daughter. She knew that they would need to be alone.

"Lottie? Why are you still in bed at this time of the day? Why are the curtains still drawn?" Lise asked as she sat down on the bed next to her daughter. Her voice was gentle, coaxing even. Her hand went to her daughter's head and stroked her hair. Lottie was a little girl again. A young, untried innocent. "What's the matter, my darling? What's the matter?" Lise felt the sobs as her daughter sat up and put her arms around her.

"Oh Mum, oh Mum," she cried, "Oh Mum . . . I've . . . I've married a monster. He hit me Mum . . . punched me . . . Oh Mum, I don't know what to do, I just don't know what to do . . . I loved him so much . . . so much . . ." Lise let her daughter sob her lovely, beautiful eyes out. She held her tight. Tighter than she had ever held her before. Her hands pulled her daughter's face away from her shoulder. She saw the cuts, the dried blood, the swollen eyes. Her heart broke with an anguish that she had known and held once before in her life. She felt every blow, she felt every sneer of violence. She took her daughter's agony and made it her own.

"Oh Lottie, oh Lottie . . . we must get you to a hospital, now—"

"No Mum!" Charlotte almost shouted, "No. No hospitals. No police! This can't get out. It can't. I feel so ashamed. Take me home and get our own doctor. Bill will know what to do. I don't think I'm badly hurt. No bones broken anyway, although my ribs are a bit sore when I move."

"All right, all right Lottie . . . whatever you say." Now was not the time to argue with her daughter. "I'll help you get dressed and we'll take you home. Griffith is downstairs waiting. I'll just go and have a quick word. Now don't try and get out of bed until I get back." Lise touched the tears that still ran down her daughter's cheeks and pulled her to her again. "My darling Lottie . . . don't worry now. Don't worry. We will sort all this out one way or another. We'll get you home. You'll be safe. I promise you that Justin will never hurt you again, I promise you . . ."

It was late afternoon. Charlotte was asleep in her old bed, heavily sedated and the cuts and bruises attended to. A few stitches had been sown into the cuts but hopefully there would be no permanent record of Justin's calling cards. The family doctor and friend had thoroughly examined the child and listened to her words, he had brought her into the world, he had done his best but had been unable to guarantee the healing of Charlotte's betrayed mind. This, he had advised, could be healed only by time and even then there was uncertainty as to its effectiveness. There was never a prognosis for rape.

There was a stupefied silence in the room. One minute it was bright, the next, faded and worn. No one seemed to know what to say. Would their words provoke or would they help? Kristian was standing and staring out of the French windows while Griffith and Lise sat next to each other and waited. Neither knew exactly what they were waiting for. At last Kristian turned around, "Well, the man must be confronted. There's no other way." His voice was firm and yet anger didn't taint his words. There was determination without hostility. "I'll go and see him and sort this out. Obviously he must leave this family, he must leave the business."

"Yes but there is Lot—" Lise started to say but was unable to get any further.

"No 'buts', Mum. The time for indecision has passed," Kristian interrupted, his voice remaining steady, collected. "The man has hurt Lottie, that's all I need to know. I will sort this mess out once and for all. The police can't deal with this. It's a family matter. Now, no arguments, please." With that he walked out of the sitting room. As he did so Griffith stood up and said, "Wait for me! I'm not being left here to pickle!" Then he turned around to Lise, hating his desertion of the desperate love in her eyes. "I'm sorry, Lise, but I must. Kristian is right." He followed her son without turning back.

For the first time in many years Lise knew that matters were now totally out her hands. There was nothing she could do. Nothing at all.

As Griffith's red Jaguar pulled into the drive of the Rose both men saw Justin Sewell placing a suitcase in the boot of his car which was parked outside the main entrance to the hotel. He read the newspapers too. He turned at the noise of gravel against tyre. He knew there could only be one driver of the brash and raw Jaguar. He didn't stop long to look. He closed the boot of his car quickly and jumped into the drivers seat. There was a passenger next to Griffith and he didn't need to exercise much imagination as to whom this passenger was. He drove off at speed. Griffith changed gear and followed, his driving skills coming into their own. Justin could only take one exit from the hotel grounds and this led nowhere. The man was trapped.

Justin looked in his rear view mirror and slowed down, he knew too that there was no way out. He could only drive along a small lane that led to one of the highlights of the Gower Peninsula: a panoramic cliff top view that distinguished Wales from the rest of the world and ensured its immortality. A view that forced past and present to clash and fight to the death. As he drove there was no fear in his hands or eyes. He had mastered this frailty of the human condition many years before. He had always survived and he would survive now. He was stronger and more deadly that his pursuers. Eventually he came to a stop, left his car and walked to a popular spot for those who were foolish and stupid enough to cherish nature. He waited. He knew that Kristian and Griffith wouldn't be long. The narrow lane wouldn't hold them for ever even if they had slowed down to follow him. There was no need to rush. Within a minute or two Griffith's red Jaguar parked next to his car. Both men got out and walked toward him. Justin held his ground and faced them. His green eyes seemed to change into another more intense shade. Kristian was the first to speak.

"I warned you, Justin, I warned you," his voice remaining calm even elusive as resignation seemed to fend off anger. His little sister had been attacked, mutilated. The attempted fraud was a trifle.

"No one 'warns' me, Kristian Treharne!" Justin sneered. "No one, do you hear? And certainly not you or any your pathetic family! You warned me once before, remember? Where did that get you, eh? Remember? The warning is all mine, Kristian Treharne, all mine you bastard!" Kristian heard the hatred and saw it in Justin's face. It was the face of the fanatic, of unbridled madness in its purest and most deadly form. Poison oozed through the man's words, the destruction in his eyes was complete. For a moment Kristian froze as a compassionate streak of understanding halted his step. Griffith started to move forward but Kristian held him back. He knew danger. He knew its warnings.

"Why, Justin? Why?" Kristian almost pleaded. "You could have had everything. A beautiful wife. Children. Security. Why, for the love of God?"

"Why?" Justin screamed. "Why? You fool! You Treharnes, you're so fucking smug! So content with your wealth, your precious schools and upbringing! I wanted to bring you all down. To destroy you all!" For a moment Justin's voice quietened, he looked at Kristian and Griffith and for a brief second there was agony in his eyes, an ancient humanity and pain. "You see, I am one of you. Yes, a pure-blood Treharne."

He looked at Griffith. "I am Megan Treharne's son. Your only sister's child. While you all wallowed in money and privilege I was shunted from one filthy, squalid home to another. I know that my mother never wanted to give me up, but what else could she do? My father – the bastard! – screwed her at one of those posh socialite parties then, just like her family, disappeared and didn't give a damn, while my grandfather, the rotten sod, had cut her off. He gave all his money to that bitch Lise Jacobson and you Kristian, her bastard son!" Justin started to scream again, the insanity was back. There was no holding him. "And what did you all do? You killed her! All of you killed her! My mother. She died in the fire that tried to bring her happiness. I found out! I found out! None of you can hide from her only son! I'm a resourceful man, it didn't take me long. I worked hard for this day. I haven't succeeded quite yet. I've only managed to destroy one of you. Lottie for my mother. Fair exchange I say. One daughter for another!" There was a terrible silence for a moment as violence and madness tried to strangle and kill the air. No one moved as both Kristian and Griffith recognized that the man standing before them had inherited the same tragic insanity that had killed his mother. Before either man could speak Justin's voice became slower more precise as he drew out a revolver from underneath his overcoat.

"Do you recognize this?" he asked. "Do you? I found it in the cellar at the Cliffs. It needed some cleaning up, it's perfectly functional now though, I assure you. I knew who it had once belonged to. My mother had made sure that I knew. She left me her whole story. Solicitors tracked me down after her death. The story of her life was her gift to me. My inheritance. It was all she had left. You stole what was rightfully hers and mine, all of you! You left us with nothing. Nothing!" Griffith and Kristian both knew the revolver intimately. It had been William Treharne's. The old service Webley revolver was held by a steady hand. Neither Griffith nor Kristian moved. Justin started to move back a few paces, as if taking aim. A sheer drop stood waiting a few feet behind him. The cliff face leered and spat at the waves that sucked at its feet oblivious to the fight for life that was taking place above it. "Did you recognize the engagement ring I gave Lottie, Griffith?" Justin snarled. "You should do. It was my mother's, Megan Treharne's, your sister, you murderous bastard." Griffith had known he had seen the ring somewhere before but had been too stupid to remember where. He cursed with shame. The barrel of the revolver passed from one man to the other. It stopped moving for a moment and pointed to a space between

Griffith and Kristian. This one moment was enough. Kristian lunged at Justin, the revolver went off and Griffith fell to the ground without making a sound. Kristian was neither the strongest nor the fastest of the two men, he was older and limited by his amputation. But he knew more about unarmed combat. Much more. They wrestled with each other as Kristian tried to free the revolver from Justin's hand. They fought and tried to kill. Kristian managed to wrench back Justin's wrist and snap it, the gun fell away as Justin howled in agony even so the pain seemed to spur him on. He wanted to murder, to hurt, like his mother before him he wanted revenge. The two men rolled on top of one another, each man trying to gain a deadly grip. After a few seconds Kristian who was lying underneath Justin managed to use his legs to catapult Justin away from him. There was a scream and silence.

The waves below the cliff face didn't even murmur as they claimed yet another human trespasser. Some seemed to stop and pray for a moment or two but that was all. They didn't really care.

CHAPTER 44

Two days had passed since the sea of the Gower Peninsula had declared its rights on human kind. Nature had raised its flag of omnipotence and mocked the stupidity of humanity. It always won. Always.

Lise sat next to her husband who lay in a hospital bed trying not to show the pain that ripped through his shoulder. He had been lucky. Again. The bullet had passed through the ample flesh that cushioned his shoulder. Treacle pudding and custard had its uses after all.

"I knew, Lise," Griffith winced, "I damn well knew. Once, when we were having a family meal together, I saw Megan in the man's eyes, his face. He scared the hell out of me but I didn't say anything, for Lottie's sake I suppose. He looked at me so intensely, I saw the madness. Megan's madness. I bloody well knew, Lise. I didn't do anything. And Lottie's ring. I knew I had seen it before. Christ, if only I had thought a bit more then all this could have been avoided." Lise leaned over the bed and used her fingers to brush away the white hair that always kept falling into Griffith's eyes whenever he was lying down.

"You're being stupid now, Griffith. You listen to me. There was nothing you could do. Nothing at all. How could you have proved your doubts for heaven's sake? I won't listen to any more of this talk. All you have to do now is get well. I mean it."

Griffith looked at Lise and wondered for the millionth time what he would ever do without her. He looked into the blue eyes and the ache in his shoulder started to recede. He held her hand. "My lovely Lise. I love you so much, you know."

Lise gripped his hand tightly.

"I know, my darling. I know. I love you too, believe me. You give me more strength that you can ever know." She continued to stroke his forehead as she tried to come to terms with another tragedy. Another death. Griffith would see her through.

"Now then, Lise. Just for you to know, when I get out of this hellhole you can tell that imbecile Balzac to serve me with bacon, eggs, fried bread, cockles and laverbread, oh and some baked beans, every morning for a week and no bloody arguments about it. Do I make myself clear?"

"You do, Griffith Treharne. You do. Now rest. I'll be here when you wake up."

At last a smile touched Lise's lips. Her recovery would be slow, it always was, but it would be certain.

"Your fingerprints are all over the revolver, Captain Treharne. Would you explain to me one more time please how they got there?"

"Oh God, Inspector, for the last time, I fought with Sewell. He was pointing the damn thing directly at myself and Griffith, Mr Treharne. In my opinion he was about to try and kill us both. I can't say there was much time for social niceties or calm negotiation. I saw a chance and I took it . . . although I have to be honest here. Sewell paused for the briefest of moments. He didn't lower the gun but he seemed to point the barrel away from us, at least he pointed it between us if you can understand that. For a moment I thought . . . well, I just thought. I don't suppose anyone will ever know what was going through the man's mind. The way he was ranting and raving left me in no doubt that he was capable of shooting us both. No doubt at all. As I have already said I grappled with him. Tried to disarm him. We struggled, I think I may even have broken his wrist. Anyway, I managed to get the gun out of his hand and away from us. We continued to fight. The man was as strong as an ox, believe me. Fit. Well, I knew I was in trouble, I only have one leg after all, but years of training came to my rescue. That was my only advantage. I managed to throw him off me. Unfortunately this effort sent him over the cliff edge. I can assure you it wasn't intentional. It really wasn't. At that point all I knew was that the gun had gone off. I had no idea that Mr Treharne had been hit. I heard a scream and that was it. Of course my fingerprints were all over the revolver, I was trying to get the damn thing off him. I'm sure that by now your ballistics experts have already established the discharge of one bullet, not to mention of course that Mr Treharne was shot in the shoulder. Good God man, how much evidence do you need? Sewell's death was a tragic accident. You have been made fully aware of all the circumstances, the history, that led up to these terrible events. What more do you want?"

The Inspector, a balding man with little character apart from an ill-fitting suit, grunted at the uniformed policeman standing by the door to the study. This time William Treharne's ghost had decided to come out of hiding and smile at the irony of it all. "Yes, Captain, your recollection of events certainly tie in with the statement made to us by Mr Treharne. The body of Mr Sewell has yet to be recovered by the way," the Inspector grunted again, "so until his remains are in our possession there is little evidence to contradict your version of events. A sad business I must say. Very sad . . . Well, I think that will be all for now, Captain. You're not planning on leaving the country in the near future are you?"

"No, Inspector. Unless you call Mid Wales another country."

"Very amusing, Captain Treharne. We will be in touch, the case isn't quite concluded yet you understand. There are still some further enquiries we have to make and the sea out there usually reveals its secrets eventually. It's the Gulf Stream you know. Throws things back at us from time to time." Kristian ignored the cryptic threat. "We have your contact numbers?"

"You do, Inspector."

"Good. Then that's all for now. We will be in touch." The Inspector walked out of the study with the uniformed officer trailing behind him. Dear God, Kristian thought, the daft bugger had been reading too much Agatha Christie. 'The Gulf Stream? We will be in touch!' Who did the idiot think he was? He had certainly never been near one of Poirot's tailor's that was for certain. Kristian sat down. He was glad to be alone. There hadn't been much time for him to properly absorb things over the past two days. He lit a cigarette and enjoyed the smoky comfort zone. He always thought better when his lungs were filled with carbon monoxide.

Violent death. He thought he had seen the last of such things. He had killed before but in a different way. Then there had been wars, sovereignty. Kristian's life for somebody else's. The choice had always been easy. He had not known the victim of his knife or his bullet. Now, as he explored the events that had caught up with him, he wasn't so sure. Had he ever been sure? Did knowledge of his victim make any difference? Did it even matter? He had killed again. There was nothing to hide behind. Self-defence? Self-preservation? These were straightforward concepts, like sovereignty and unquestioning loyalty. He knew he could not, nor should he, escape the consequences of his actions. Revenge. Kristian had learnt that it served no one. He had not wanted Sewell's death. He had wanted him away from the family, away from Lottie but not his death. For a brief moment on the cliff top he had understood the hatred, the desire to seek a balance to the injustice of Sewell's life. The man had despised for far too long, if only he could have accepted and come to the family with clean hands. If only. How many times in his life had Kristian said these words? How many times had he listened to their futility, their easy tune? Smoke billowed around his guilt and tried to placate as it poured from his nostrils and mouth. His breath caught the joy of unhindered nicotine abuse. He had killed again what harm could a cigarette do?

There was a knock on the door and his wandering mind came back to the present. Lottie walked in before he could reply. He stood up and went to her. He put his arms around her and held her tight.

"Time, Lottie, time. Don't fight the grief. Let it come and go, which it will do for a good while yet. You will heal Lottie. You will heal. You're a Treharne and don't you ever forget it." Kristian felt his sister's tears soak into his shirt. There was nothing he could do apart from hold her and feel her pain. "I'm here, Lottie. I'm here," was all he could say.

EPILOGUE

A year had passed since Justin Sewell's revenge and tragedy. The sea hadn't loosened its grip on his body. The Cliffs and the Rose continued to prosper under the careful and steady management of Paul Edmunds. These days Griffith and Lise were rarely seen at either establishment, having bought a luxury apartment overlooking Langland Bay which they only used for one or two of the summer months. The rest of the year they travelled far and wide, Lise had learned to laugh again and Griffith was back to a low-fat diet. They continued to love and tolerate one another. Their exotic nights together were still lively, even if Lise continued to boss. Griffith always gave in at the right time, he knew his Lise.

Charlotte had started to accept the odd brief again. Occasionally her sense of humour would overwhelm her grief, her confusion and her shock. The fun inside Lottie would never go away, it was in her forever – no matter what. Time, as her brother had promised, was starting to heal. The hour glass turned slowly but it was turning.

Myfanwy was sitting on top of a sand dune watching her daughter and Kristian walk along the seashore. They often came back to the Cliffs at weekends, there was more life for Angharad. More boys. Myfanwy looked at her battle-scarred veteran. The warmth and passion inside the cantankerous old bastard who was now truly her man held out their hands and tightened around her heart. She had never stopped loving him. In all the years that had gone by her daily thoughts had been flavoured by Kristian's touch. A touch that was sometimes angry, sometimes gentle. Each and every day he had lingered somewhere deep inside her.

She watched as her daughter suddenly shouted 'Ziggy!' and ran after a Springer Spaniel. A man wearing a hat looked on and enjoyed.

Kristian had been right. Angharad was now able to run along the beach under her own steam.

THE END